TAKESHI KAIKO belongs to the generation of writers who grew up amid the horrors of the Second World War and reached intellectual maturity just as Japan entered its post-war boom. Born in 1930, in the east-coast city of Osaka, he graduated from the law school of Osaka City University.

He married a poet, Yoko Maki, in 1953, and moved to Tokyo. It was there, while working as a copywriter, that he published his first short stories, 'Panic' and 'The Naked King', which was awarded the coveted Akutagawa Prize in 1957. Several novels later, Kaiko was sent by a Japanese newspaper to cover the Eichmann trial in Israel. In 1964 he was sent as a special correspondent to Vietnam, where he was briefly detained by the Viet Cong. *Into a Black Sun* first appeared four years later and was awarded the Mainichi Cultural Prize. In 1981 Kaiko was awarded the Kikuchi Kan Prize for fifteen years of outstanding journalism.

'One of the best works of fiction, or fact, that I've read about Vietnam. It revived more of that experience than I ever realized memory had retained.'   BRUCE DUNNING
CBS News Vietnam Correspondent, 1970–73

'Every writer, every soldier, had his own private Vietnam. This is the most original account that I have read.'   MURRAY SAYLE
Sunday Times Vietnam Correspondent, 1965–75

Takeshi Kaiko

Into a Black Sun

Translated by
Cecilia Segawa Seigle

FONTANA/Collins
In association with Kodansha International Ltd

First published in Great Britain by Fontana Paperbacks
in association with Kodansha International Ltd 1990

Copyright © Kodansha International Ltd 1980

Printed and bound in Great Britain by
William Collins, Sons & Co. Ltd, Glasgow

CONDITIONS OF SALE

This book is sold subject to the condition
that it shall not, by way of trade or otherwise,
be lent, re-sold, hired out or otherwise circulated
without the publisher's prior consent in any form of
binding or cover other than that in which it is
published and without a similar condition
including this condition being imposed
on the subsequent purchaser

We see now through a mirror
in an obscure manner,
but then face to face.
Now I know in part, but then
I shall know even as I have been known.

I Corinthians 13:12

1964

I

I was reading in bed toward evening when Captain Wain came into the hut, naked. He took a whiskey bottle from under his cot and waved it gently at me in the setting sun. It was the only real 'sippin'' bourbon, he said: Jack Daniel's. I put down my book and followed him out.

About ten yards from our quarters was a hut nick-named the 'Waldorf-Astoria'. It was where the men played ping-pong and wrote letters. The hut was like a furnace, stifling heat shut in all the long afternoon hours. No one was there, but the reek of sweat and cheap cigars hovered thickly in the air.

The captain scowled and waved his hand about. 'Smells like sheep,' he said.

There was a makeshift bar in one corner. The captain put two glasses on the cracked plywood counter and poured out careful measures of whiskey. 'Now, then,' he said, rubbing his hands. 'Yes. . . .' I echoed. The fresh scent of soap and hot water moved about him; he had just taken a shower, and the thick mat of golden hair on his chest glistened.

'Scotch has a metallic smell, but bourbon smells like wine, that's what we say. Especially this stuff. It's superb, isn't it? You sip, savor it, then swallow it down.'

I raised my glass, lingering over the taste.

It was light and straightforward, but had a ripeness to it and the aroma of dry hay that all corn whiskey has.

Evening came to the windows.

Beyond the windows on one side were trenches and minefields; farther off were groves of rubber trees, a highway, and rice fields that had been harvested. On the other side there were rice paddies, a copse, a gentle slope, and then a great wall of jungle stretching over the horizon. The long fingers of the evening sun were partially hidden behind the blue-gray treetops. There were no peasants, or children, or water buffalo about. A wide, whispering dusk had begun to unfold. The entire sky was fire and blood: purple, gold, vermilion, ultramarine, the complete spectrum crying out in its last surge of the day. There were moments when, with the echoing boom of a great bronze gong, it seemed the hut might ignite and go up in crackling flames.

The captain swiveled his strong face toward me and murmured:

'It's quiet.'

I put down my glass. 'It's a beautiful country.'

I felt as if we were standing, sipping whiskey, in the core of a ruby. As the sun sank, the lurid glow shifted swiftly from brilliance to flamboyance to radiance, and when it finally slipped down over our shoulders, the night began to seep out from the corners of the hut like thin water, submerging everything below the windows. A glint of light lay melting lazily at the bottom of my glass and drowsy saffron lit the shoulders of the bottle. I thought of To-nga. Saffron would be gleaming on her neck, too, as she hurried toward the square along the iron fence of the Botanical Garden back in Saigon. I felt my throat suddenly and painfully contract.

Wiping sweat from his chin, the captain said:

'It's going to be a fifty percent alert.'

'It was the same last night, wasn't it?'

'Yes. Several VC companies are supposed to be on

the move tonight. We don't know whether they'll go south or west. If they move southeast, they'll come here.'

'What time?'

'If it's us, the first wave will be around one or two. The second, four or five. I hear they're telling the peasants they'll do something big before the New Year. They're saying they'll ride through our gates in buses and smash us.'

'But can they?'

'It's happened before. They'll take guns, ammunition, uniforms, helmets, anything. Some bases even lost typewriters and steel cabinets.'

'I've heard about penicillin and malaria pills – we know they need medicine; but that's the first I've heard about typewriters.'

'Oh, yes. Anything they want. It's almost like we're supplying them. But here we're OK. It's a stronghold. Only, we can't let our guard down. They have to stick to their promises too, you see, otherwise they'd lose the peasants' trust. They're clever, careful, and brave. The Commies fight bloody wars, but they fight impressively.'

'You respect them, don't you?'

'Sometimes.'

The captain spoke softly and smiled. He paused to swill the liquor around in his mouth. Darkness gradually stole up his arm, which lay on the counter like a heavy wrench. The pageant of pure light and color was over and the tropical night prevailed.

Somewhere a telephone rang, sounding like nutshells knocking together, and Corporal Haines opened the door and summoned the captain. Wain filled my glass, generously this time, and pushed the bottle over.

'Help yourself.'

'Thanks, Captain.'

'You're not a guest, you're my friend. Make yourself at home. Ask for anything you want. *Compris?*'

'*Compris!*'

The captain left the hut with a smile. His face was craggy, but with his eyes narrowed in a smile there was a childish look to it. I was only a Japanese journalist moving slowly through Vietnam, but on my first day there he'd taken me to his own hut and, without my asking, given me shirts, towels, pants, and even the rubber slippers that he was wearing. I had quickly declined them, but he'd said it was OK, that there were no strings attached, and had pulled another pair of rubber slippers from under someone else's cot and gone off cheerfully wearing those.

I had promised to play chess that evening with Lieutenant Binh. Welcoming me into his murky quarters, lit only by a small lamp, he treated me to dinner and beer. Then we turned to a rickety table and started to play. I lost eight out of ten games; charitably, he let me win twice. From time to time his old orderly, the tanned and wizened Trinh, brought tea in an earthenware pot, looked at my move, and chuckled, covering his mouth with one hand.

Dinner had been broiled catfish, crisp-fried bean curd, and vermicelli with minced herbs. The beer was lukewarm 'La Rue' with a strong tang of zinc from the mess tins we used for glasses. Binh drank ten bottles of it every day. While we played, he kept a Colt on one side of the table, periodically slipping it back into its holster and taking it out again. I asked what it was for. He said that one of his men had gone into town a day ago and hadn't returned; as soon as he showed up, Binh would chew him out, but in case that didn't do the trick, he was prepared to shoot the soldier in the hand.

'Why his hand?'

'So he won't be able to gamble.'

'But he won't be able to fire a rifle, either!'

'His left hand,' Binh said simply; 'one or two fingers on his left hand,' and moved his chessman.

Coming to his hut from the 'Waldorf-Astoria' was like falling through a manhole. It was abject; a pigsty rather than a barracks. It had brick walls but no door, and though the frames were in place there were no windowpanes. The entrance had no threshold and the floor was neither wood nor concrete; the bare earth had merely been trampled hard. The walls were marked with bullet holes made by soldiers killing time, and the only furniture was a lame table. Whether in hammocks or on shutter boards, the soldiers slept in total darkness. And though they had only just interrupted a nap before dinner, they were already back in bed, their breathing and light snoring rising like smoke from various points in the dark.

A single red pinprick glowing like a firefly in the dark was an incense stick that was kept burning in an empty corned-beef or coconut can placed in a cardboard altar on the wall. Buddhist soldiers had bought the altar and incense with the pittance that was their pay. Catholic troops had pasted a picture of the Virgin Mary on the wall and hung a metal-plated cross from it. The Buddha and Mary could almost have been calendar pictures lifted from some old country inn. The two figures were transfixed in the dim lamplight, one in meditation, with eyes closed and legs crossed, and the other staring, eternal tears resting under round eyes.

Lt. Binh moved his hands swiftly and said, 'Check!'

I looked at the board in dismay and groaned, '*Troi-oi!*'

The chess played in Vietnam is the Chinese version. The pieces are discs inscribed with the Chinese characters for 'soldier' and 'cannon'. The rules are much simpler than those of Japanese chess, more like the Western game in which captured pieces can't be used against one's opponent; the enemy can't change his colors, and once captured he's dead.

I thought about Japanese chess as I made a move. I wondered who could have devised the Japanese rule, so subtle and vigorous, that turns an enemy into an instant ally, where a piece captured from an opponent can be dropped straight back into the enemy base, a private being promoted to a general. What war experiences in Japanese history could have inspired this stroke of genius?

Binh murmured a song as he fingered his pieces.

> Loo, loo, loo,
> Sleep, sleep, sleep,
> Mummy's got to go to market. . . .

Nonchalantly, he picked up a piece, peered into my eyes feigning hesitation, then slyly slipped it onto a square. I began to sweat. Binh smiled, gloating, and slapped at a mosquito.

> Sleep, sleep, sleep,
> If you don't go to sleep,
> Mummy will be home late,
> Loo, loo, loo. . . .

When Binh first taught me how to play, my acquaintance with the complexity of Japanese chess unfortunately made me look down on it. In fact, I still had a tendency to sneer at it somewhere in my mind; yet, no matter how often we played the game, I almost always lost. Even with the simplest of rules, this chess had its own range and depth, its own unique gambits. With no knowledge of them, I recklessly challenged Binh with a game of different rules, and naturally got slaughtered every time: sieges were broken; lines of retreat were blocked; broadsides were smashed; and last-ditch schemes of ambush were immediately seen through. Invariably I fell into a sort of sweaty stupor.

Binh whispered lazily, '*Troi . . . o . . . i!*'

It was hot.

I felt as if I was soaking in a hot porridge that rose to my hips, my chin, and past my forehead. The chessmen, the mess tins, everything sweated and festered, decomposing. Alcohol oozed from my pores and sweat trickled down my belly. My mind, my words, and all that was concrete and tangible about me evaporated, leaving one gigantic, eyeless, earless invertebrate that, squirming, expanded to fill the room, crawl on the walls, and reach out to the night sky. The suffocating heat rustled its myriad feet, roamed around the windows, soiled everything it touched with clammy prints. I was just a heavy sponge propped, leaking, against the wall. The whiskey and the beer, too, were heavy. I couldn't lift a finger, just gazed at the grimy chess pieces. I thought of the cluster of leprous beggars in the park at festival time. The heat of this country had the same effect as 'wet' leprosy, which gradually erodes one's flesh. I wished I were still with To-nga in the corner of her garage apartment. Splashing water from the large earthen jar, we'd have washed each other, laughing softly, clapping our hands. The jar breathed through its unglazed, dew-drenched skin. Even in the tropics, the water is cool at midnight. Shivers running up our spines. . . . Trembling, on all fours, like dogs. . . .

★

'Have you had your furlough, Lieutenant?' I asked Binh.

'No, not yet.'

'When will you get it?'

'Who knows!'

Binh muttered lazily and stared into the lamplight. A bedbug was crawling past the pistol; a house lizard appeared, gulped it down, and vanished.

Binh's large, moist eyes still gazed at the light. His sideburns were long, his lips thick, and his eyebrows dark and bushy. A faraway look lay on his sweaty, twenty-eight-year-old face.

In a Delta town, his twenty-four-year-old wife was expecting a baby within a month. And here he was, stuck in an outpost in this dangerous D-Zone jungle, not knowing when he'd get any leave. A few days after I first met him, at the end of a rambling chat, I heard him mumble a couple of times, 'One day, I'll die.' Was it only because the water here was so foul that he got through ten bottles of 'La Rue' in that mess tin of his?

'Let's play again tomorrow,' I said.

'Yes, tomorrow, again.'

'I'll be a bit better tomorrow.'

'All right. Come any time.'

Binh shook my hand with the wise smile of a weary man. His dry, bony hand had a surprisingly firm grip.

When I returned to my hut and its fluorescent light, the two-blade fan was turning slowly on the ceiling. The men had gone to see a movie in another hut but no one was around. I showered, rolled into bed, and began reading Mark Twain again. After a while, Wain came in carrying an AR-15 and began to write up his daily report. Day or night, he never forgot his rifle; he even took it to the command post, less than a hundred yards away. In the evening, he wore a white band on his arm or somewhere on his fatigues in case we were overrun during the night; he said there was no other way of distinguishing friend and foe in this inky darkness.

Even in the hut's pallid light, the captain's powerful build stood out – the back arched gracefully and the muscles jostling beneath his immaculate white T-shirt. And yet this fortress of a body was as much a prey to a bullet scarcely three-eighths of an inch in diameter as the meager flesh of his miniature orderly. It was hard to believe, but it was a fact.

I'd developed a gravedigger's eyes lately. I used to feel awed whenever I saw some brawny American coming toward me, breasting a wave of slow air; but now the awe was gone. Once the vitality, whether yellow or white, has drained out through a hole only slightly larger than the diameter of a fountain pen, what remains is little more than a collapsed bag, a jellyfish washed ashore. The captain's intestines, too, were kept from spilling only by a fragile membrane over a trellis of bones. Looking at him I thought of the thousands of hamburgers, tens of thousands of Cokes, that had been consumed to form this body; it intrigued me to imagine how far they would stretch put end to end.

Gray hairs shone like needles at the captain's temples. Amid short, coarse, chestnut hair, white shoots had sprouted all over.

'Captain!'

'Yes?'

'You're going gray!'

He didn't answer.

'You didn't have any two months ago.'

Wain put down his report and lit a cigarette. He narrowed his eyes, following a wisp of smoke from his cigarette, then said:

'Last week, I was sniped at five times when I was on jeep patrol. They say Charlie's offering the peasants around here two thousand piastres for my head. That's a lot of money for the locals. Even five hundred is something.' The captain raised his hand and said 'Pow! Pow!' pointing a finger like a pistol.

I calculated quickly. 'In the black market, five hundred is a little over four dollars.'

'I wouldn't know.'

'Two thousand Ps is a bit more than sixteen dollars.'

'Maybe. I've never had anything to do with the black market.'

'How are they going to get you?'

'With a machete,' he shrugged, 'like cutting a melon, in the middle of the night.'

'A melon? . . .'

He whacked his neck with his hand. 'Kheee!' he went. It was common enough, he said. A machete is heavy, sharp, and cuts well. The captain frowned and spat out his habitual 'Shit!' A scowl darkened his face, but there was a fierce pride in his eyes.

'You didn't have any gray hair two months ago,' I repeated.

'Is that so?'

'In the suburbs of Fai Fo. You were supervising the "Magic Fish Water" operation at that pond, remember? You had no gray hair then.'

'Fai Fo. . . .' he mumbled wistfully. 'Ah, yes, the "Magic Fish Water".' Wain burst out laughing and his shoulders shook. He glanced at me and laughed again, as though he couldn't repress it. 'Shit!' he yelped, and slapped his knee.

I had run into him two months earlier on the outskirts of Fai Fo, a river port near Danang called Huian by the Chinese. It's a small country town, but it contains the ruins of a community of Japanese converts to Christianity who, persecuted by the Shogun's government in the early seventeenth century, escaped to this distant refuge and grew flowers for a living. I was traveling north, following the rain clouds. Having seen Cape Ca Mau, which marks the southern limit of this country, I was planning to reach the northern boundary at the 17th Parallel. In this way, provided they didn't step on any mines, my shoes would eventually have scuffed at least the margins of this country.

The dry season had reached the Delta then, but the rainy season lingered in the central region, and a drizzling *crachin*, as it was called, drenched everything. Wherever I went, the towns were sealed off with barbed wire at six in the evening, and on the highways the traffic died out quietly in the dusk. The day I left Fai Fo, however, was unusually clear. The tropical sun beat down indiscriminately, and the walls, the roads, the noodle vendors' stalls all steamed. The bus had left the town and run along the highway for a few minutes when it suddenly stopped and the driver and all the passengers scampered off in a cloud of dust. I followed them and came to a pond surrounded by pine groves at the foot of a gentle hill. A flock of peasants and townspeople stood around the pond, their palms together in prayer. An ARVN platoon had heavy machine guns leveled at the pond. Presently, an American officer who looked like the captain of a football team sauntered onto the scene. It was Captain Wain.

Suddenly, several soldiers threw hand grenades into the pond and fell flat on the grass. Explosions ripped the air, and jets of red muddy water shot toward the sky, showering the spectators' heads. The crowd screamed and scattered. But people soon started drifting back, watching anxiously to see if the soldiers would repeat their attack. Prayers were resumed, and some of them ladled water over the children's heads. Others carried some of the water away with them. They seemed to do this with inordinate reverence, careful not to spill a drop.

I approached Captain Wain, showed him my press credentials, and asked him what it was all about. The captain's face was rugged, but his eyes and voice were gentle, immediately likable. His forehead was burned a vivid red and I thought suddenly of a cross section of rare Chateaubriand. Vietnamese soldiers were all bones and tendons and probably salty, but he was tender, fleshy, juicy. I thought of meat rubbed with garlic, with a lot of watercress.

'This is "Magic Fish Water",' he answered.

'What?'

'This fucking water contains a magic fish. We're in the middle of a strategic operation. We're trying to pacify this pond, with grenades and machine guns.'

'I don't understand.'

'Nobody does.' The captain smiled generously and began to explain.

That night, I stayed at an inn about four towns north and heard the same story from the Chinese innkeeper. He knew all about the pond. The notes I took from their separate accounts were as follows. It resembled the story of Lourdes and its miracles. A rumor had started at some unknown point in the past that a magic fish lived in this pond. A woodcutter's mute child was cured after drinking the pond water. A man dying from TB recovered completely. A soldier who had been paralyzed from bullet wounds suddenly stood and began to walk. People from all over South Vietnam began to come and take the water: peasants, merchants, soldiers, officers, Chinese tradesmen — a variety of citizens poured in. The wife of a Chinese millionaire from Cholon came in a Cadillac, accompanied by a jeep trailing an Army water truck, and they pumped out gallon after gallon of the miraculous water. A crowd had surrounded the Cadillac, demanding that she return the stuff. Caught in the angry press of people, the Chinese woman scattered hundred-piastre notes and narrowly escaped. Hearing this story, more peasants arrived from neighboring villages. The Ministry of Culture and the Department of Psychological Warfare in Saigon, fearing an epidemic of superstition, ordered division headquarters to take some action. The fish was to be caught or killed, then displayed in the city square to put an end to the excitement.

Troops were dispatched. First, they planted dynamite on the bottom of the pond, but the explosions only brought up harmless catfish and carp. Then they dragged the water with a net and the soldiers felt some large creature struggling in it, but when the net was hauled in, they found it empty. An L-19 went on a reconnaissance flight. Aerial photography revealed nothing, but a picture sneaked by a Vietnamese copilot with his own camera clearly showed a giant shadow. As a result, the copilot swore off meat and fish, kept away from women, determined to purify himself. Copies of the picture he had taken were sold on the black market for a hundred and fifty piastres and the police were making ineffectual attempts to halt their sale.

Originally, the magic fish had appeared in a pond in a northern province. Only recently, it had turned up in water about forty-seven miles east of the pond; it had also appeared about twenty-five miles south. It stayed no more than ten to fifteen days at any given place. The creature was apparently distressed by the war that was everywhere.

'Just now, we chucked in a few grenades,' the captain said. 'Next, we'll sweep the pond with machine guns. If that doesn't do the trick, we'll call in a gunship tomorrow and loose off some rockets. That's all we can do.'

I was dumbfounded.

'The only other option is a missile,' he told me.

I looked into the captain's blue-gray eyes, but there was no sign of madness. Neither was there any cynicism or scorn; apparently, he was just following orders.

In the shade of a pine tree, I spotted a yellow-robed monk praying. He was covered with sweat and dirt, and was obviously a mendicant. Most middle-aged monks here had some knowledge of Chinese Buddhist literature and were capable of communicating in written Chinese. I had often stoppped at temples and conducted written dialogues with the priests. My Chinese is neither literary nor conversational, just a random arrangement of characters, but somehow no priest had ever failed to understand my atrocious sentences; they always came up with answers.

I took out a notebook from my Japan Air Lines bag and wrote 'Reverend Master' in it. I followed this archaic salutation with a string of characters and stuck the notebook and a fountain pen under the nose of the meditating man. The monk was surprised by the sudden appearance of a notebook, but he pondered my question and slowly wrote down his response. His sentences were far better than mine, correct and refined, and his handwriting was superb. Our dialogue went roughly as follows:

'Reverend Master, I am a Japanese journalist-novelist passing through this community. When I arrived here I saw this commotion. What is it all about? Please enlighten me. It seems like sheer superstition to me.'

'It involves the water of a sacred fish. It isn't a question of superstition, despite all the disturbance. It is holy water, and the people believe that it has some miraculous curative powers. The name of the fish is "Eminent Zen Master Immortal Fish Bodhisattva Dragon King".'

'Has the water been medicinal for a very long time?'

'No. It's not just legend or local custom. Nobody announced that it was curative. The water suddenly became medicinal.'

'Is there really a sacred fish in there? What do you think? I'd appreciate a frank opinion.'

'The people say a holy fish lives there.'

'But you, Reverend Master, don't believe this?'

'I haven't said so.'

'I can't help thinking that it's all mumbo-jumbo, that there's nothing in the pond. The government is trying to calm people down, but their methods are completely wrong.'

'The important thing is whether the water works or not. If it has the effect of soothing people's minds, that's enough. You're right in saying that the government is wrong. But have you spoken to these people directly?'

'No, only you and an American officer. I can't speak Vietnamese, so I just look at their eyes and faces. I've traveled a lot and often communicated with people in this way, though English or French speakers have sometimes helped me.'

'That's good.'

The incandescent sun blazed down on that wild land; the scorched earth radiated heat, the grass withered. The monk and I were soaked with sweat, and sweat had smudged my notebook yellow. The monk's shaven head had been stained a sooty black by the sun on his days on the road, and his hands and legs had shriveled into creaky sticks; yet his eyes were deeply serene. Calmly he put his hands together and began to chant, slowly, *'Nam-mo a-di-da phat.'* This I understood:

21

Save us, O merciful Lord Buddha. His eyes half closed, the monk continued to whisper, sounds trickling from his lips like water from a faucet.

Suddenly, a memory flashed in the blazing sun, a memory of my mother, who had been addicted to a form of table-turning called 'Kokkuri' about twenty years earlier. There were supposed to be many ways of invoking the spirits of 'Kokkuri'. My mother's method was to write out the fifty-letter syllabary chart on an old newspaper, hunch over it with a chopstick, and wait for the stick to poke automatically at the letters spelling out the message. While B-29s rained oil-and-sulphur incendiary bombs and 'Molotov Bread Baskets' all about them, Japanese women would be busy seeking 'Kokkuri's' forecast for tomorrow. When would the divine wind blow? Where could they buy potatoes? Would there be air raids in the next place they were evacuated to? Everything was asked of 'Kokkuri'. Since 'Kokkuri' only worked if one's mind was completely empty of thought, my mother would concentrate, holding her breath, and a performance always left her exhausted. A high-school boy in despair, I used to tear up the newspaper chart and throw it away whenever I found it.

Once, my mother confronted me, glaring. 'I know you don't like what I'm doing, but what else *can* I do? Who else is going to help us? If you don't like "Kokkuri", then get out and find some potatoes! If you can't even do that, just leave me alone! Go on, then, tell me where you're going to get some potatoes!'

Her little eyes were glittering, ignorant, mean, obsessive, and I couldn't look her in the face. I was only an anemic fourteen-year-old schoolboy. Having lost Father early on, we eked out a living day by day, exchanging Mother's meager wardrobe for potatoes. I was furious, but had to hold my tongue. Later, I chased my mother into a corner of the veranda and left her sobbing there for hours.

I looked at the people jostling, bunched together by the pond: the poor – young and old, men and women all skinny and angular, prostrating themselves on the grass, praying fervently. They had only one doctor to perhaps a hundred thousand, and no one knew when bombs or napalm would fall on them. Time and again I'd sat at a bus window and seen peasant women wailing '*Troi-oi! Troi-oi!*' as they led their children away by the hand, not even turning back for a last look at their burning village. I could see so many in that crowd by the pond who were like my mother twenty years ago. Yes, how alike they were! The odor of perspiration, the brilliance of the sun. Everything reminded me of that summer, that year in Japan.

I wrote in my notebook: 'I'm deeply grateful and moved. I have learned a great deal.'

The monk bowed, his palms together. I put away my notebook and also bowed, in the same fashion, then walked back across the grass and red earth and talked briefly to Captain Wain.

'You know, that magic fish flies,' he said.

'What does it look like?'

'Some say it's a yard long; others, fifteen feet. It flies around visiting different ponds in this province. It lives in one pond for ten, fifteen days, then moves on to another.'

'What color is it?'

'They say the back's black and the belly's yellow.'

'Then it's an Indo-Chinese carp.'

'Is that right?'

'Has anyone really seen it?'

'Everybody has. It's only me that hasn't. The strange

23

thing is that whenever I turn up, the fish disappears. It's really weird. The Cong's cadres even brainwash fish.'

Sodden up to the armpits of his jungle fatigues, Wain shrugged and laughed cheerfully. Just then, three heavy machine guns opened up with an ear-splitting roar. Flat on the grass, the gunners mowed the pond, sweeping their guns to left and right. Spray rose and the red water surged and rippled. Screaming and yelling, the people ran, stumbling. After a while a Vietnamese officer wandered over. His uniform was crisp, without a single wrinkle, and his boots gleamed. When he spoke, his English had a thick French accent. The captain sprang to his feet and listened politely before replying, 'Yes, sir. OK, sir.'

'We shot machine guns. Nothing come up. This is all for today. Trucks come soon. Don't know when. We rest until trucks come, Capitaine Wain.'

'Fine, sir.'

'Time for siesta, Capitaine Wain.'

'Yes, sir.'

'Sleep well.'

'Same to you, sir.'

The officer strolled back to his troops, who were talking excitedly. He dismissed them and then walked with casual dignity to the foot of a pine tree, lay down, and closed his eyes.

Back in our hut, I asked, 'What happened to that area afterward?'

'The VC.' The captain sighed as he smoked.

Here in this outpost he had none of the innocent cheerfulness of that morning when he'd gazed around, amused, sitting in that wild grassland. Now, etching a dim shadow under the fluorescent light, his large frame, especially his shoulders and the back of his head, seemed to exude a sour smell, the smell of loneliness. Violence, aimless and forlorn, sometimes welled up in his crude rock sculpture of a face.

'The Cong gained control because the ARVN shot the village god. Their cadres told the villagers that the ARVN and the Yanks were to blame, so they all went over to the VC. That village was completely neutral before the operation, and here they are suddenly fixing booby traps and punji sticks. Vietnamese peasants are intelligent, tough, and patient, but religion's another matter. We shouldn't be doing what the peasants don't want us to do.'

'The peasants have nothing,' I said.

'I know.'

'They don't even have floors in their houses.'

'I know.'

'They have a lot of babies, but they get sick and die. No doctors. The doctors are in Saigon or in the Army. Even without the war, the Viets die at an average age of thirty-four, or less. If they get sick, all they can do is drink pond water.'

The captain hung his head and muttered, 'Number ten!'

The profile of the man as he sat on his bed was mournful. I even wondered for a moment if he was praying. All I had done was recite my routine lines, as I had done any number of times in the past. But there is an allegory: that a stone thrown by a playing child can be fatal to a frog. And his profile reminded me of this.

He raised his face after a few minutes and spoke slowly.

'Our civil action teams,' he started. A gleam came into his eye and he seemed a bit more relaxed. 'Those teams give the villagers pigs, they give them medicine,

25

too. They dig wells. Not in my territory but in others there are some "ugly Americans". The "ugly Americans" there work with the peasants, sleep with them. They work hard. Even Charlie won't cut melons in their villages because it would make the peasants mad. We hear good rumors.'

'You mean the USOM?'

'The USOM is part of it.'

'I've heard that if the Americans give the government in Saigon ten pigs,' I said, 'by the time the aid gets to a village, there's only one pig left. In the same way, rice disappears, blankets and tractors vanish. Recently there was a flood in a village and some blankets were sent out. They showed up at the thieves' market in Danang the next day. The word is that USOM is short for "You Spend Our Money", right? The Buddhist monks say there are too many rats in this country.'

'Yes, I hear those rumors, too,' Wain nodded. 'The government's rotten to the core; not only the Commies say it, everyone does. So we should shake hands with the peasants, with each one of them. My country spends stupendous amounts of dollars here every day. We should spend it on pigs and medicine and deliver them ourselves to each village. We should never leave it up to those Saigon bastards – or the Commies, either.'

'But can you do that?'

'Why not?'

'Washington and Saigon are friends. If you did it your way, Saigon would raise hell. They'd say the US should give aid, not interfere.'

'The bastards do nothing for the peasants. What claim do they have on us?'

'Yes, but what did you do for them with your "Magic Fish Water" operation?'

Suddenly, the captain flung his cigarette on the

floor. 'Saigon isn't Vietnam!' he spat out in a low, fierce voice. Sincere and utterly serious, a great rage born of frustrated good will flared up in his blue-gray eyes. He had vast reserves of conviction and incorruptibility, crippled by a lack of power and a sense of futility. I sensed a humiliated farmer in him. He was a professional soldier from Minnesota now wearing coarse olive-drab jungle fatigues; but wasn't he still a farmer underneath?

'There are only two kinds of people in Saigon. There's no in-between. Only haves and have-nots. Do you understand?' he asked.

'Means rich and poor, doesn't it?'

'Yes. People who have a lot and others who don't have a thing. The haves get richer and richer the longer the war goes on. And the have-nots get poorer by the day. No, the have-nots don't even have proper floors to walk on, so they can't get any worse off; but the haves just rake it in. I don't want to criticize our allies, but the generals just take it in turns to line their pockets. When one team's pockets are full, they set up a coup and give the others a swing. That's what I've heard, though I haven't any proof.'

'Some monk said that the only thing the peasants have to lose is the hair on their heads. That puts them in a strong position, doesn't it?'

'Definitely. The VC are the same. They've got hair on their heads but no shoes on their feet, except some have Ho Chi Minh sandals. They run barefoot over minefields in their suicide attacks. They don't even have lives to lose.' He looked at his watch and stood up. 'It's ten o'clock.'

It was time for lights-out. He walked to the corner and flipped the switch and sudden darkness engulfed us. Wain took his automatic and left the hut without a word. He was like a large ship gliding on dark water.

Just then, three clangs rang out in the east. They were banging on a shell cartridge to let the others know that they were still awake. The northern trench responded, as did the western. The sounds traveled like giant birds through the night. The darkness swayed and swung back to my forehead. I lit a cigarette.

My ears began to buzz.

Footsteps on dead leaves.

The sound of breaking twigs.

Hushed voices calling to one another.

2

Jones, the KP from Montana, took me on one of his ice-buying expeditions. With hunched shoulders his small body swam in a large uniform, and he had a rodent's sharp face. He was good at horseshoes, but his cooking was plain lousy; and he was usually very quiet, perhaps because he stuttered. For dinner, he'd bring in a T-bone steak scorched to solid leather, stealthily put the plate down on the table, then dash back to the kitchen.

Around nine, I finished my apple juice, corn flakes, bacon and eggs and was ambling out of the mess when I saw Jones hurrying into a jeep, a carbine in his hand.

'Where're you going?'

'To pick up ice.'

'With a carbine?'

'Sure.'

Another soldier was already in the jeep, wearing a helmet, a submachine gun resting on his lap.

'Take me with you,' I said.

'Get in.'

Jones drove the jeep out through the gate. A national highway ran alongside the outpost. A gentle slope descended to a town five hundred yards away – or rather a village, for before you could count a general store, a noodle shop, and a few other stores, you were already beyond it. On the road we passed some ARVN idling the morning hours away, munching sugarcane and eating fried noodles. Jones stopped the jeep at the edge of the community and approached a thatched house, still holding his carbine. I started to get out, but a large hand on my shoulder held me back.

'You stay here.'

The guy with the submachine gun glared at me from under his helmet. His finger was on the trigger.

'Keep your head down.'

I was confused.

'Head down!' he repeated.

I crouched and watched Jones calling outside the house. He had his finger on the trigger of the carbine. A man peeped from the doorway and smiled.

'How you, soldier?' he said and disappeared.

The man immediately emerged with a large block of ice held in an iron ice claw. Jones handed him a crumpled bill and took the ice with his left hand. Holding the carbine in his right, keeping his eyes on the man, he stepped slowly backwards. The man leaned against the door and with calm black eyes gazed at Jones. Jones climbed in hastily as soon as he had dumped the ice in the jeep, then backed up with a terrible screech, made a wide U-turn, and drove straight back to the camp. The bodyguard took off his helmet and put down his submachine gun only after the jeep had passed through the gate.

I went into the kitchen building and helped. Cracking ice, Jones told me that the iceman smelled suspicious. A truck from a Saigon ice company delivered ice early in the morning to various villages along the highway, so Jones made a trip every morning. Recently, he was sniped at on his errand. He wasn't hit, but a bullet grazed his bodyguard's cheek. The iceman had run into the house when the shot rang out, but the fact that otherwise he hadn't appeared particularly concerned made it seem likely that he'd had prior knowledge of the sniping. Where the shots came from, though, was a complete mystery. Troops were called in and the area was thoroughly searched, but there wasn't a scrap of evidence. Only a child was seen wallowing in some mud with a pig.

'You buy ice from the enemy?' I asked. Jones snorted and said that it wasn't only ice. He eyed the oranges, cabbages, bananas, and papayas all around him and said that they bought everything from the VC. Piled up in heaps, they were proof of some heavy trading. Impassively, Jones said that the local peasants brought them to the post early in the morning. In this area, ninety percent of the villages were Viet Cong and we were buying fruit and vegetables from them.

'It's always been like this around here,' Jones said casually as he put the ice in a bucket and carried it out of the kitchen. I followed him and watched him empty the thing into the Coca-Cola icebox in the 'Waldorf-Astoria'.

I hunched over the bar and said aloud, 'It's for cooling Coke!!'

Jones gave me a quizzical look and went out.

A bird's-eye view of the outpost would have suggested a pinhead pressed into the shore of a large sea of foliage. But after taking leave of Jones, I made a survey of the base and realized that there were as many as twelve M-24 tanks, seven 105-mm and 155-mm howitzers, and several companies of infantry and Special Forces. There were plenty of firearms, from pistols to 81-mm trench mortars, new and old. Mounds of unused ammunition lay rusting at the bottom of trenches. The 105s and 155s snarled away morning and night, and there were some nights when as many as a hundred and thirty shells were fired for no obvious purpose. The camp was undoubtedly 'a stronghold' and 'armed to the teeth', as Captain

Wain said. But Jones had to go to buy ice, armed, only five hundred yards from the front gate. And they could smash thatched huts eight miles away, but couldn't nab a sniper under their own noses.

On the day I had first landed here, I was taken by Captain Wain to meet Colonel Kiem, the Vietnamese commander. The colonel treated me to a beer and told me that he was neither Buddhist nor Catholic, but Confucian. His Confucian kingdom was vast, embracing a wife and nine children in Saigon and a concubine and six children in Dalat; in addition, a young woman made a nightly appearance in his room here, a *dea ex machina*. It was common knowledge. As soon as the sun went down, the colonel would change into blue striped pajamas and prepare for sex. Early one morning, the enemy flung a mortar shell into this Confucian's palace. When I stuck my head in, two carpenters from the village were working at repairing the roof. Kiem led me away, a beer bottle in his hand, and whispered that the carpenters were Viet Cong.

I gawked and the colonel nodded.

'We got them from Viet Cong village. So they know my room and sometime they shell me again. I'll trick them. I'll put an iron sheet over the ceiling and pile sandbags!' He laughed loudly.

Every three or four days, a barber from the village visited our fortress. I had a haircut once. The barber would turn up with an old bag containing a hand mirror, scissors, and a razor. He hung the mirror on the trunk of a flamboyant tree, sat a Vietnamese or American officer in a chair, and began snipping away under the blue sky. He was a gentle, humble man who hardly ever spoke. His job done, he bowed politely and reverently picked his modest charge out of his customer's palm. But, according to Wain, the man was a veteran Viet Cong courier. As he was cutting hair, he'd surreptitiously glance around to see how many tanks were where, how many guns were facing what direction that week, then pass it on to the cadre back in his village. The night attacks were planned on the basis of his information, said Wain.

Moreover, the captain swore that a substantial percentage of the Vietnamese soldiers at this post were Viet Cong. No one knew if they became VC by coercion or voluntarily, but the work of a *binh van* was unmistakable. The *binh van* were operational units whose aim was the defection of government soldiers; groups focusing on intellectuals were called *tri van*. A *binh van* cell had burrowed deep into this camp, remained well hidden, and an uprising or a massive breakout could have occurred at any time. Impoverished Vietnamese soldiers had no qualms about selling bullets, drugs, even guns to the VC, said Wain. His words were endorsed by the fact that a triple barbed-wire fence separated the Americans' quarters, where I lived, from the Vietnamese quarters. If not for fear of uprisings, why should allied troops be segregated by barbed wire? Why should Wain always carry an automatic when he was walking around?

We were thirty-two miles northeast of Saigon. The jungle stretching beyond the minefields was an enemy sanctuary; the area was known as 'Maquis D', 'Iron Triangle', or 'D-Zone'. This jungle, together with the Plain of Reeds toward the Cambodian border called 'C-Zone' and the U-Minh forest near Ca Mau, were the three famous strongholds that were 'theirs'. It was thought that their headquarters, training grounds, rest homes, hospitals, and arsenals were all hidden in these areas, and tunnels crisscrossed them four or five yards deep – subterranean passages that, according to Wain, extended three to four hundred miles. I had also been told that the network of creeks in the Mekong Delta covered a total of two thousand five hundred miles. In small boats, the Viet Cong slipped in and out as freely as they liked. The entire country, as small as a dime compared to the United States, was a haven for guerrillas, with their great mobility, and Vietnam for them was tens of times larger than its actual size – perhaps a hundred times larger.

On the Long March, the Chinese Red Army covered over six thousand miles, and at the end of it built a base in Yenan. Our revolutionaries had their Yenan only thirty miles from the capital; the adversaries could almost see each other's faces, and it had been the same since the onset of the war six years ago. Small reconnaissance platoons, sapper teams, and special task forces constantly infiltrated the D-Zone; firefights broke out on highways and in nearby rice fields and villages all the time. But, according to Wain, the government forces had never once, in six years, attempted a large-scale cleanup of the sanctuaries. The VC, in the meantime, had steadily infiltrated south and west, attacking for thirty minutes here, then fighting for two hours elsewhere, and quickly withdrawing. The scale of their activities was gradually mounting, deepening; their lightning speed and savage daring were hard to match. The long wall visible from our windows might be deathly still in the evening, but a step farther out and the sea of foliage could be bursting with men and arms.

This outpost was trying to stop a flood with a sieve.

They crossed the rice fields, ducked through the night. The jungle was no longer a Sherwood Forest, but the wood that Macbeth beheld: it moved, flowed, laid siege. The airport, the police station, the embassies, hotels, bars, restaurants – they attacked any target at will and with impunity. The Vietnamese police were always slow to arrive on the scene. Occasionally a terrorist was spotted running away through the crowd, but when the police gave chase, they had to run a gauntlet of shrill abuse from sugarcane vendors and women selling cooked gizzards. A month ago, a forty-four-pound time bomb was discovered in the ceiling of the US Command Headquarters, which had been considered absolutely secure, the most tightly guarded place in Saigon. Non-Americans weren't admitted, yet someone had crept in undetected to do a job that required a good deal of time. At Bien Hoa Air Base, about forty bombers were shattered in fifteen minutes by an irruption of eighty-seven mortar shells. The airfield was also 'secure', and the surrounding mines were supposed to blow up even prowling rats; yet they smashed those monolithic machines as if they'd been marshmallows and retreated cleanly back into the jungle with no visible casualties. Four or five thatched cottages stood like earth tumors on a lonely hill near the airfield, and the mortar shelling had undoubtedly come from there, after a month or two of preparation. But when the military police stepped in to investigate, they only made the peasants gape and weep like water bugs, and moan that they'd gone to bed early that night because the owls were hooting ominously.

During the day, the life here was like camping and I thoroughly enjoyed it. I ate a lot, took long siestas, read Mark Twain, and worked hard at Chinese chess. A rumor had it that the guys up in the hills were eating monkeys, but here we got T-bone steaks, kidneys, wieners, unlimited quantities of fruit juice, McCormick pepper, Heinz ketchup; we seemed to have everything. Jones gave us knives, forks, and paper napkins, and we even had movies every night. A chopper brought in a new reel every morning, guarded by two gunners. I'd seen movies here that I missed in Tokyo: *West Side Story* and *Lolita*, among others. After a sweaty siesta, I just threw a bath towel over my shoulders and headed for the showers. A gigantic hot water tank, heated by gas, supplied any amount of water at any temperature. I was always intrigued by all the modern conveniences in this hinterland. I could turn the cock to four different settings: hot, medium, lukewarm, and cold, and the response was always dead accurate. Late at night I went and sat in the latrine and listened to the sharp cries of the lizards. Water was drawn from a well dug under the minefield and, pumped around the clock by a heavy-oil generator, it responded to a pull of the chain with the same flushing noise as at the best hotel in Tokyo. I daydreamed about the route that the generators, pumps, and flush toilets must have traveled to reach this base. I could picture a long convoy of Army trucks, guarded by tanks and armored personnel carriers, moving along Route 13 – the one that had been mined to hell many times over. The highway had been famous since the days of the French Army and nicknamed 'Bloody 13'. Lives may have been flushed down in ambush because of a toilet bowl.

The GIs used to unroll blankets over the trench mounds, smear suntan lotion over their bodies, and sunbathe in their shorts. Some stretched out in the sun on the cistern next to the latrine. The ARVN dozed like cattle in their barns, lost to the world. They were all so addicted to sleep that, playing volleyball, they looked like sleepwalkers jumping up and down.

That afternoon, I saw a group of soldiers clambering onto three trucks bound for Route 13. I went back to the hut and told Haines about it, but he laughed and said no, it wasn't an operation.

'What is it, then?'

'They've gone to build a house for Colonel Kiem's woman. He's using his troops to get it built in town. It's been going on for some time.'

'They took Route 13.'

'Yeah, I know.'

'Is it safe, without tanks?'

'They'll be OK. Kiem's safe,' Haines added with conviction.

'But that route's always getting ambushed. Are they really OK?'

Haines glanced at me with a vague grin. 'Don't worry about Kiem.'

He said no more and, hugging his pillow listlessly, set about patching up an interrupted nap. He found a comfortable dent in the pillow and, tossing once, fell straight back to sleep.

Every day, there was a three-hour ceasefire. It was a Vietnamese custom to request an annual ceasefire of forty-eight to seventy-two hours for Christmas and New Year, but a nap after lunch was an important daily custom for everyone, both Vietnamese and Americans. As if simultaneously taken ill, they retired to their respective huts and collapsed into bed. Some generals took advantage of this for their coups, and occasionally there would be a skirmish during siesta. But, for the most part, both sides honored the rule of silence for at least three hours. Saigon was a dump-yard capital of two and a half to three million people crammed into space enough for half a million. Yet, despite its teeming population, the streets turned white at siesta time. Voices and sounds disappeared as though a plague had swept the city. Midnight came at midday. At the front, our outpost, rubber groves, highways, rice fields – all lapsed into a coma and house lizards dozed on the ceiling. The gate, the guards, the barbed-wire fences and minefields became meaningless. And why didn't the Viet Cong take advantage of this paralysis and charge right in, I wondered; but it never happened. Our warriors lay sound asleep, their faces open and relaxed, and the scene in the jungle was probably the same. If there were only days and no nights, no one would have been dying in this peculiar country. Pascal referred to people of the same race and language killing each other merely because they were separated by a river. Here, the same absurdity had reached the point of naked cheerfulness. Soldiers stretched out practically side by side, woke up, and promptly started killing each other. I seemed to have misunderstood the nature of nihilism: I realized now that it wasn't a thing of darkness, meanness, misery. And I fell into bed soothed by a surf of transparent flame that filled the sky, and sank luxuriously into velvet sleep.

There had been a bizarre incident at lunchtime.

Captain Wain, Doctor Percy, Corporal Haines and I sat at the table. After finishing off one of Jones's indigestible treats – Southern fried chicken and macaroni salad – I was smoking a cheroot that Lieutenant Colonel Dô of the Vietnamese Tank Corps had presented me with. Doc Percy began telling us an interesting story. He was a tall, slender man who played a good game of ping-pong; he had a habit of dropping cynical remarks, but he was kind-hearted and kept an eye on me, gave me malaria pills or a small bottle of mosquito repellent out in the trenches.

'The peasants around here are shrewd, but they're so ignorant. No one's taken the trouble to educate them. They've had no experience of newspapers, magazines, the radio, television, anything. They've never seen neon lights; they don't know about running water.

They're a forsaken people in a godforsaken country.'

He told us of the time he went to a hamlet as part of a group teaching the Ogino method of birth control; but for people who had no calendar, therefore no knowledge of dates, of the day of the week or the month, it was useless. On his next visit, he took along a large supply of BCG, with the aim of helping rid them of tuberculosis. TB was rampant among the Vietnamese peasants, though barely noticeable in this blazing climate. One in about five was tubercular.

Arriving at the village, the good doctor took out a syringe and told the people to line up, but the villagers all ran off. He discovered from a Vietnamese interpreter that they had never seen a syringe in their life. Moreover, they said that a doctor who charged neither rice nor money for curing illnesses must be a witchman. The Americans rained fire and killed the jungles; so a drug given by an American must kill them too. The doctor tried to convince them that the medicine would cure chest diseases, but the interpreter shook his head and said it wouldn't work: someone had already told the villagers that BCG was an abbreviation of 'Birth Control Government'; and they all believed it. So Percy had had no choice but to put away his medicine and beat a retreat.

I burst out laughing and blew ash all over my ice tea, and Percy looked at me, satisfied, narrowing his eyes. He tapped me gently on the shoulder and told me to switch to a pipe if I didn't want to get lung cancer.

Captain Wain smiled wryly and said, 'Those Charlies are smart!'

No sooner had he spoken than an explosion ripped the air, pounding the roof like boulders in a rockfall. The bright, hot, quiet noon was blown to smithereens, the hut shook, glasses rattled; splinters of sound ran through our bodies, pierced our eardrums. The din died away instantly, but I had leaped out of my seat; Doc Percy had cupped his ears, face flat on the table; and Haines was scowling, yelling something. It hadn't been either a 105 or a 155; we had grown used to them. It might have been a mine.

Captain Wain was calm, laughing delightedly. He picked up his glass, gently tinkling the ice, and said three words:

'An air gorilla.'

When a jet suddenly plummets toward earth from a height of 33,000 feet, then jerks its nose skyward and soars back to its original height, the sound waves crash into the ground, creating a tremendous shock. This he called an 'air gorilla' attack. An American pilot had mistaken our camp for a VC hamlet in the jungle.

After explaining, Captain Wain said contentedly, 'Go on, give 'em hell!'

My eardrums had not recovered from the shock. I thrust my fingers into my ears and massaged them. The trauma of having been pushed in an instant to my physiological limits still convulsed me. Part of my brain was numb, and I felt as if my guts had blown away.

Wain smiled at Haines and said, 'Doing a good job, those air gorillas!'

I scarcely managed to raise my head and ask, 'What for?'

The captain answered kindly, 'The pilot's making sure Mr. Charles doesn't get his sleep. They say that the shock waves sometimes kill chickens. If the VC can't nap, it'll show in their night activities.'

He laughed happily and followed with pleased eyes the small flash of aluminum disappearing beyond the white cumulus clouds. He seemed to have changed. For the first time I saw crass brutality cross a face that had been gentle, discreet and patient. It was a spine-chillingly strange expression: eyes moving behind the eyeholes of a mask; only the eyes.

At about three o'clock, I escaped from the hut, unable to cope with the heat.

I looked for someone to talk to, but everyone was asleep, so I took a walk along the trenches. I peered into the east bunker and saw laundry hanging from the ceiling, ammunition boxes scattered, meat wrapped in bamboo leaves hoisted on a bamboo pole. A young soldier in a hammock opened one eye and smiled at me, then went back to sleep.

I picked up a carbine leaning against the wall and looked through the sights toward the rubber trees. I had never fired a gun in my life, but knew enough from watching other people to release the safety catch. The spring worked smoothly. Bullets were in the magazine. I put my cheek against the cold metal and looked through the sights at a rubber tree. I aimed at its white marking, a large gash on the trunk, cut for gathering latex.

The thin barrel was strong enough to withstand any internal explosion. The trigger was smoothly resilient, and a pleasant resistance bit into the flesh of my finger. Had I pulled it just one millimeter closer, the bullet would have been released. The rubber tree stood deserted in the afternoon heat, hushed, with no moving object in view; for a moment, I longed for a human figure. I wanted something to move beyond the muzzle sight; I wanted someone to point his gun at me and shoot. I just wanted to pull the trigger. I wanted to use this silent instrument that was filled with deadly energy and yet indifferent. The distance was only just over a hundred yards – enough to turn a man into a silhouette at a shooting gallery. A craving moved in me. At that instant I knew I could have killed a man for fun, then put the gun down and taken a nap with no guilty conscience. The gap between us would have allowed me to pull the trigger with the same ease as one might tear the tab off a beer can. It wasn't murder; no crime, therefore no punishment. Suddenly, confidence rose in me. The man over there, if there'd been one, would have felt the same about me. The weapon was absurd: it couldn't even make me a murderer!

3

Until a few minutes ago, buses passing on the highway had seemed like deep-sea fish blinking red and blue lights; now the sun was up to the treetops. The sky was suffused with saffron, and two or three streaks of vermilion streamed out between the clouds and the trees. It was a time when monks began begging for alms. A time when I could read the lines on my palm. A time when the new leaves on a tree stood out from the old.

Now we could see rice fields, forests, the highway, see the smoke of cooking fires rising above the thatched roofs of distant hamlets. The soldiers in front of me, wash basins and soup bowls on their backs, led off the highway into a rice paddy. The harvest was over, and the field had been drained dry. About three hundred small soldiers, shouldering carbines and bazookas, heavy with grenades, divided loosely into three groups, right, center and left, crossed the fields, and entered a village surrounded by forest. The road was pocked with large and small shell holes, and mounds of rubble stood on both sides in readiness for quick repair work. Four soldiers held mine detectors, advancing slowly.

Captain Wain and I were watching them when a Vietnamese NCO holding a transistor radio came over to us.

'I know soldier who can find mine with lemon. He put lemon at top of stick, he walk road. Lemon get sucked on road. You dig and find mine. If there's mine there, lemon move there; mine here, lemon move here.' Pieuuuuu pong! Pieuuuuu pong! The man made sucking sounds, moving his hands to imitate the motions of a mine-detecting lemon-stick, looking deeply puzzled and impressed.

The captain nodded and said gently, 'OK, OK. Where's the soldier?'

'He went somewhere. No here now. But he find mine with lemon. Only he can do.'

Wain tapped the small NCO lightly on the back and nudged him in the ribs, chuckling. The soldier left with a look of vague dissatisfaction.

A large convoy was expected on the highway that day. All outposts along the highway had been ordered to patrol both sides of the road to prevent any guerrilla activity. Our team had been sent out to search the area between two neighboring towns. We'd left at six in the morning; we were to confirm the safe passage of the convoy and return home in the evening.

The night before, Captain Wain had explained our itinerary on an acetate-covered map, marking areas with a red grease pencil. All the villages in the vicinity had been 'liberated' by the Viet Cong with varying degrees of success. Until recently, men had been seen working in the fields for the rice harvest; now that it was over, they must have returned to the jungle, taking large quantities of rice with them. There was no sign of any impending ambush, but we wouldn't know until we were actually attacked.

'What do you want to do? Go with us?' the captain had asked me.

'Yes, please.'

'If you need a rifle, you can have one. Anything from a knife to a bazooka, if you like. Take something. A flak jacket, too, if you want.'

'I don't need a gun. If I had one, I might have to kill somebody. Anyway, I don't know how to use the things.'

'There's nothing to it. You just pull the trigger. You can get killed even if you aren't carrying a gun, you know. I realize that under international law non-combatants aren't permitted to carry firearms, but this is war. You can claim self-defense.'

'Can you let me have a helmet and a canteen?'

'Use mine.'

The captain brought me his own equipment and we toasted each other quietly with his prize whiskey, Jack Daniel's. He didn't mention guns again. He never pressed me about anything.

But I had declined the gun without conviction. When the first ripe drops of Jack Daniel's trickled down my throat, what crossed my mind was not what I had thought the other day: that no crime even attached to my using a gun. No, I sneered at myself for clinging to a precarious neutrality, trying to keep my hands and nose clean even out here – allowing the curse of elitism, of pallid intellectualism, to follow me even this far. Surrounded by bloodstained men, I'd been sneaking away without a scratch, feeling pleased and proud that I'd been part of the battle-weary crew. For whose benefit was I trying to prove my innocence – hoarding a conscience that had grown rusty with disuse? And why drag it out now into the light of day? Hadn't I been itching to pull the trigger, back there in the bunker, thinking I could easily shoot a man for fun from a hundred yards away? No inner voice had prevented me from playing with the trigger then. Perhaps I had chosen the wrong battlefield. I might have been with the Special Forces, creeping into the night jungle to find an enemy and fight him hand-to-hand and hack at him with knives. A knife, or some wire. Yes, these might have allowed a fuller knowledge of what killing means.

We crossed rice fields, tramped through a small grove of rubber trees, and passed through a number of villages. The rubber plants were young and supple, and we marched on a thick carpet of their leaves. Every time we reached a village, the soldiers systematically searched the thatched huts for arms. Captain Wain had been proved correct: not a man was visible anywhere; they had all retreated into the jungle. Nor were we welcome anywhere. Old women and young girls turned frostily away, without a trace of a smile. The soldiers stole nothing from the fields, tortured no one for the fun of it, only peeked casually into the huts and left; but the old women looked vague when questioned, mumbled their answers, scuttled away as soon as they could. Their eyes remained coldly vacant in a stubborn web of wrinkles.

I kept my eyes peeled as I walked. Despite the absence of all the men, the fields had been weeded and cropped clean; and the ditches were neat, not overflowing with muddy water. In one hamlet, behind the dilapidated shrine of a war god, stood a thatched schoolhouse. A young girl teacher in blue slacks was leading a bevy of children in song; and without even glancing at us, though the rifles clanked noisily as the soldiers passed, she went on resolutely with her work. In some villages the children slunk into their houses the minute they saw us; in others they followed us unafraid. Wain walked over to me every so often and whispered that this village needed watching closely or that one was all right. Clean, well-kept hamlets were dangerous; dirty, neglected ones could be ignored. Villages where children met us with smiles were safe, those where they shrank away were not.

As we walked from one community to another, I was reminded of the so-called Rostow theory. Professor Rostow, an economist and a special advisor to the President, had recently given a commencement address at a Special Forces school. After expounding various theories about guerrillas, the professor stated that the reason why guerrillas are so hard to subdue is that their objective is to destroy, and destruction is always easier than construction. For him, therefore, they were bandits, armed robbers. In fact, of course, it is precisely the opposite reason that makes victory so elusive. I was astonished that, in an era that had witnessed the revolution in China, a learned academic could misread the facts in quite such a primitive, almost awesomely innocent way. It amazed me even more that this rudimentary error in the basic laws of guerrilla warfare had been broadcast at a graduation ceremony for guerrilla specialists. Just one glance at these trim villages proved how simpleminded his analysis was. The professor had obviously let his theory take flight and, airborne, kept his eyes tight shut.

Again it was a dazzlingly brilliant day. The day before had been the same. The next would be identical. People in this country didn't talk about the weather when they greeted each other. Yesterday's cumulonimbus clouds reappeared, unchanged in shape, above the jungle at about the same point on the horizon.

We walked slowly for six hours, sweating, panting. Smashed houses. Burned fields. Shrubbery scorched red. Passing evidence that 'air gorillas' had been this way, we arrived at a small village. It was noon and the soldiers were dismissed. Chattering in piping voices, they dispersed, threw their rifles on the ground, and as soon as they'd finished their meal, which they ate in their wash basins, quickly went to sleep. Walking into a thatched house with Wain and a radioman called Mayer, I stretched out on a bench. The bamboo poles supporting the room were marked with bullet holes.

Around three o'clock, when I woke up and lit a cigarette, a Vietnamese radioman came over.

'You understand Japanese?' he asked.

'Yes, I do. I am Japanese.'

'Come,' he said.

With a worried look, he led me to a radio set placed in the shade of a tree, and put the earphones over my ears.

'This not Vietnamese. Japanese?'

Beneath the dark surge of static, I could make out a rapid exchange. The voices were muffled, harsh, but firm and virile. Cantonese? Ch'ao-chou? I couldn't understand it, but knew it was southern Chinese.

'It's not Japanese. It's Chinese.'

'No Japanese?'

I returned the earphones and stood up.

With a shock I realized that we were being watched. I felt their sharp eyes slithering all over me. It was as if my clothes had suddenly been peeled off. The eyes must have been following us since we left the post in the morning, but only now did I sense their sudden presence. The VC were somewhere nearby, telling each other about us. For reasons known only to them, we weren't being slaughtered. They seemed to be leading us by the nose.

When I returned to the house, I found Captain Wain awake and polishing his Armalite. I told him that 'they' were communicating with each other in Chinese. He nodded, unfazed, and told me that he had often listened in. He put down his weapon and calmly lit a cigarette.

'They have Chinese military advisors,' he said.

'Have you seen them?'

'No, but there's no reason to disbelieve it. I've heard that a Chi-Com advisor died somewhere in combat and they cut off his head and took it away with them so he couldn't be identified. The conversation you heard was definitely in Chinese, was it?'

'Yes, but just because they speak the language doesn't mean they are Chinese. Lots of Viets speak Chinese.'

'I guess so.'

Yawning briefly, the captain rose from the bench, picked up his Armalite, and left the house.

We stayed in the village until sundown, drinking tea, loitering. Mayer, the radioman, taught English to the NCO who had a lemon-stick mine detector in his platoon, and was pestered into exchanging watches with his student, reluctantly unfastening his dime-store watch.

The Vietnamese soldiers gathered around me, staring, commenting, saying 'same-same' and '*joto, joto*' – fine, fine. When Wain filled a basin with water and began to shave, they all moved away from me to watch. They encircled him, keeping their distance, and gawked at the tangle of golden curls on his chest and cheered each time he moved the razor over his cheek. Like children, they had no beard at all; their cheeks were as sleek as polished stone.

Suddenly a shot rang out, and others followed, the sounds echoing across the sky, the forest, and rice fields soaking in the red-and-gold evening. The volleys sounded as if they came from a hill near the neighboring town and from some nearby shrubbery. Fierce waves of compressed air resounded in the empty tropical sky. The captain raised his face from the wash basin and listened.

'M-16s,' he said.

Mayer came over and reported. 'The convoy got as far as the next town, sir, and stopped. They say they can't get out. I lost contact. I'll try again.'

He hurried back to his radio and began to call out 'Whiskey, Lima, Sierra . . . Whiskey, Lima, Sierra . . . Whiskey, Lima, Sierra. . . .'

The soldiers looked disappointed when the captain put on his shirt and they gradually dispersed. I returned to our hut, which had begun to darken, and found our Vietnamese company commander, Captain Tong, stretched out on a bench in the dim light. He was a gentle, taciturn man. He had hardly spoken all day, perhaps because he was ashamed of not being able to speak English very well, and a faint smile had lingered on his face as he led his three hundred men through forests and rice fields. I groped about in the gloom, trying to lie down on a bench. Tong, supine, handed me a wooden pillow in silence and, folding his arms, spoke briefly in a faltering voice.

'My soldiers said rude things to you. "Same-same" and "joto-joto". Bad words. I am sorry. Forgive them.'

'It's all right. Don't worry. I like them.'

Captain Tong said thank you under his breath, sighed an amazingly long, deep sigh, and turned over. After a while, he sighed again and shifted. While I watched, he turned over about once every ten minutes.

I went out and found Wain in the dark.

'What are we waiting for?' I asked.

'I don't know . . . an order from Captain Tong. They may attack our post tonight because we aren't there. The radio's out of order and we can't get through. What's Tong doing?'

'Resting in the hut.'

'What's he thinking about?'

'I don't know. His eyes are open.'

'Shit!'

'We'll all be killed here.'

'You'll be killed. Mayer will be killed. Tong will be killed. But not me. I'll live.' He snickered cruelly in the dark.

'Don't say that, sir!' Mayer complained, then groped his way back to his radio and began whispering his call letters again.

We crouched in the dark until eleven and finally got on the move when Captain Tong abandoned his endless tossing and turning and emerged from the hut. We crawled in the fragrant shubbery, passed several unlit hamlets and, reaching the highway, trudged along the verge like a drove of cattle. Along our path was an immense forest that had been defoliated by a shower of chemicals, the trees ghostly under the moon. The desiccated trunks looked like a forest of pale bones. It was endless, and I felt as though we were walking through the ribs of prehistoric animals. One would have thought that in destroying the balance of natural cycles over such a vast territory some new disaster must result. The jungle is a dehumidifier in the tropics. Wouldn't this form of devastation create a torrential sea of mud in the rainy season?

After several hours, we reached a field of barbed wire protecting a small encampment on top of a barren hill; we saw camp fires and heard voices. I broke out in a sweat, feeling faint. But for some reason we weren't shot at. If two or three heavy machine guns had roared out a barrage of fire, our toylike patrol would have been wiped out in five minutes; but we were spared, despite my premonition of death. Under the moon, on the white highway, the tall figures of Wain and the other Americans were conspicuous, made good targets for snipers; so I kept away, feeling a little guilty about deserting them. I was still sure I was going to be shot, so I put the canteen over my stomach. If I were shot in the legs, it wouldn't be so bad, and getting hit in the head and dying instantly would almost be welcome; but I didn't want to die in agony, after hours of suffering. I knew the canteen wouldn't stop a close shot, but the hard metal resting against my soft, boneless belly helped alleviate the fear that ravened me in the dark. The moment we arrived at a trench, my legs collapsed like straws. I was soaked with sweat, gasping for breath, and it was some time before I could speak.

A loud tirade abruptly cut across the night air. As I peered through the dim moonlight, I saw Captain Tong shouting and flailing at a couple of barefoot soldiers. The men rolled on the ground silently, then sluggishly got up and were gone.

Mayer came and whispered in my ear: 'Those guys got beat up for gambling in the trench. Now they've got to put up barbed wire all night over the other side of the minefield.'

'But everybody's gambling.'

'Tong was making space for us because we came unannounced – that's what I think. I'm not going to sleep in that trench.'

'What happens if there's an attack?'

'*Fini*,' Mayer said and went away.

Captain Tong came looking for me, fumbling in the dark. He found me sitting under a mortar and urged me gently, almost plaintively, to get into the trench and sleep.

One can murder without a gun or a knife.

For my sleep, two men may die.

4

'Chow! Chow! Come on, you guys!'

Jones bawled his message into every hut and I stopped playing ping-pong. Captain Wain came in and told me that there had been a telephone call from the USIS – the United States Information Service in Saigon – and that I was to head back immediately. Tran must have run over with the message to the USIS building. I asked Wain what could have happened, but he didn't know.

'Is there a chopper coming in this afternoon?'

'There's no flight scheduled.'

'There'll be one tomorrow morning, won't there?'

'Yes, the milk run.'

'Can I hitch a ride?'

'No problem.'

'I'll go back to Saigon, then.'

'OK.'

'I reckon the job in Saigon won't take long,' I added after a moment's thought. 'I'd like to come back here when I'm through. I haven't seen any real action yet. Is that all right?'

The captain's face broke into a slow smile. 'OK. Sure. Very good!'

I sat at the same table as Wain and Percy. I mentioned the fact that there might have been a coup in Saigon. Wain nodded several times, then told us that the cost of living had skyrocketed in the States, that no sooner had he sent a month's pay to his wife than she wrote back asking for more. Doc Percy smiled good-naturedly and said that 'skyrocket' was about the size of it: 'Just shoots up and never comes down.'

There was nothing to do until evening. I hurried through lunch and returned to the hut, anxious to get on with the last chapter of Twain's fantasy. A black-market money changer called Krishnan had sold me the Garnett translations of *The Idiot* and Chekhov's short stories, but in mid-soliloquy Prince Myshkin or Chekhov's 'Darling' would smother in this heat that turned sweat to steam. Only Twain's free, simple, debonair chatter managed to break through. I found his bizarre story fascinating, and the discovery was fortuitous, rather like growing unexpectedly fond of a pipe and lighter that had once meant nothing much to one at all.

I'd found the book among some cowboy and detective stories in a wooden box sitting in a corner of the hut, and started reading it to kill time; but as I plodded along, stifling yawns, I gradually fell under its spell. The story had grown on me, putting down roots, developing tendrils and branches, until today I expected it to rise to treetop heights. It was first published in 1889, but there were so many parallels to the situation in Vietnam that one couldn't simply shrug them off as coincidences. Every chapter so far had astonished me.

A Yankee, the head foreman in a great arms factory in nineteenth-century Hartford, Connecticut, is assaulted by a worker wielding a crowbar. The blow knocks him out. When he comes to, he finds himself sitting under an oak tree in sixth-century England, in the reign of King Arthur. Taken captive, he is led to Camelot, the site of Arthur's court.

By the shrewd use of an eclipse of the sun and various other contrivances, Twain has the American – who remains nameless, but later acquires the title

'The Boss', or 'Sir Boss' – become Arthur's 'Perpetual Minister and Executive'; and in this capacity he begins to plan improvements in the state. On taking a closer look at conditions in the country, he finds himself outraged by what he discovers. The Church, the king, the nobility, and the landlords all treat the illiterate peasants like slaves, like worker ants. The American decides that there can be no saving this country unless its peasants are saved, and that he himself will have to acquire power if the feudal system is to be destroyed and England modernized; and so he issues a challenge to the Knights of the Round Table, most of whom are an ignorant and boorish lot, jostling for the king's good graces. Armed with a lasso and a pair of six-shooters, he defeats them all, including Launcelot and Merlin, the evil magician who dominates the court. He proceeds to build military and naval academies, so that young men can be taught modern military science as well as democracy. He publishes a weekly journal for the edification of the people, introduces the telephone and telegraph at court, and builds factories. The people slowly awaken to the virtues of democracy and science and begin to trust and love the American. So much progress is made that a naval expedition eventually sails out on the Thames in search of America.

But a crack develops in the system and widens till the whole structure comes down; and it appears in a quite unexpected place – in the stock market, which the American had introduced to Arthur's court. When Launcelot starts dabbling in the market, the brokers, who resent his prestige and his love affair with Queen Guinevere, sell him stocks for much more than they're worth. Realizing that he's been taken for a ride, Launcelot lashes out, killing not only the stockbrokers but other courtiers as well. From this point on, the country splits in two, with Launcelot's forces pitted against the king's; and in the ensuing bloodbath the king, with scores of knights, and Launcelot himself, all die. In an attempt to recover its former authority, the Church then issues an Interdict and destroys all the modern amenities that 'The Boss' had introduced. The remaining knights, nobles, landlords, peasants and halfwits all respond to the Church's command and rise up against the American – whom they'd loved and revered only moments before. Cries of 'Yankee Go Home!' resound throughout sixth-century England. Even the poorest of the peasants, when summoned by the Church, return to the fold, rejecting the foreigner who had risked his life to save them from the evils of landlords, taxes and epidemics.

Only fifty-two boys, who have been educated by 'The Boss' and who still believe in democracy, remain with him. They shut themselves up in a cave, surround themselves with minefields and walls of barbed wire, and electrify the wire. The boys, however, are haunted by the vision of all England marching against them, the thought of having to kill their own flesh and blood. The American vacillates, unsure of himself, but mustering his courage persuades his young followers that they need only destroy their cavalry, the thirty thousand knights who dominate the country. Once the horsemen are beaten, the rest will give in and peace will return. Given the option of fighting on or surrendering, the boys choose to fight, for peace and freedom.

In the evening, the massed lines of cavalry slowly advance on the cave, but some are blown up by the mines and others – helmeted and armor-clad – writhe and sizzle on the wire; and from the roar and carnage of the battlefield the boys emerge victorious. The American, however, is wounded by a dying knight as he's scouting along the barbed wire; and though rescued and on the mend, he finally falls victim to Merlin, who appears in disguise and feeds them all poisoned food.

The magician, roaring with laughter, exults: 'Ye were conquerors; ye are conquered! These others are perishing – you also,' then staggers out of the cave, only to touch the wire and, with his mouth still open in a delirium of idiot laughter, perishes too.

I put down the soiled paperback and rolled into bed. Captain Wain had come unnoticed to the adjacent bed and, in his shorts, one leg bent, he was already snoring. I could see one plump pink sac hanging limp, quietly bobbing up and down.

I was deeply moved. Drawing on a bitter-tasting GI cigarette, I felt a refreshing exhaustion, felt deliciously drained. I had followed Twain's story, idly comparing Arthurian England with South Vietnam, mainly noting the differences in my mind – until today, that is, when I reached the end and my resistance broke. The similarities overwhelmed me. Americans, French, English, Japanese, the Left, the unaligned, and Right: from almost every conceivable angle, people had written about the United States, its foreign policy in Asia, its military policy, and I had read many of them and been impressed. Yet none had had the devastating reach of Twain's fantasy.

I found all my answers in his amazing book. The Americans were spending astronomical amounts of money here, perhaps as much as six million dollars daily; and yet we'd known the outcome all along, from a novel written seventy-five years ago. The war – its beginning and its end, its details and essentials, its accidents and its inevitable course – was all there, encompassed in this tale that combined Don Quixote and Gulliver.

Mark Twain perfectly exemplified the good American writer. And I had to come all this way to understand why he has been called 'a true American' and the 'Lincoln of American literature'. I felt like laughing – there, in bed. I had told the captain that I wanted to return to see a major operation, but now that I had seen the end, what springboard could I use to catapult me back? Shouldn't I just pack up and leave the country? I felt an indescribable sadness as I watched the large man stretched out beside me in peaceful, healthy slumber. The cheerful little pink sac rose and fell with his snoring. And I felt lonely.

Late in the afternoon, I went to say good-bye to Colonel Kiem. When I entered his hut I found him getting up after a nap, yawning in the dark room. He called his orderly for some beer. We talked, drinking from flyblown glasses, and I told him I was looking forward to some action on my next visit. Kiem suddenly dropped his voice and confided that he'd been deliberately stalling all strategic operations because of the possibility of a coup. The implication was that he couldn't command a combat operation without knowing the government's next move. I asked if he was planning to run in the next presidential election, but there wasn't a flicker of a smile; he merely observed that soldiers shouldn't meddle in politics. With the second bottle of beer, I casually commented on the rumor that the government forces frequently tortured their prisoners. He answered curtly that they did what was done to them.

'Do you know what it means to "take a walk"?' he asked.

'No.'

'Americans. When we start torturing prisoners, they disappear, say they going "take a walk". And how can *they* talk! They don't mind to drop napalm, but can't stand seeing torturing. They're hypocrites, sentimental hypocrites.'

'I heard that Ngo Dinh Diem once said the same thing to the American ambassador.'

'Right. It's famous. We all say the same thing: Americans are soft-hearted. But they're still devoted to war. . . . Strange people,' Kiem said languidly, coldly, and looked at me. 'We're friends, so I tell you these things. But don't tell Wain, OK?' And he hooted with laughter.

I went for a stroll after dinner and in the process found that the nervous excitement the book had aroused in me began to wear off gradually, was slowly absorbed into my body. Twain – that American thoroughbred – had given me irrefutable evidence, and notions that had once been vague had now taken firm shape. I was fascinated by the fact that his funny, lively story, which was almost the reverse of Utopia, ended in devastation. I don't know what unhappy events in his own time had fired Twain's imagination. In all probability, absorbed in the pleasure of creation, he was unaware of the prophetic truth of his vision. The fact that he did not give any specific name to the hero of his tale, thereby representing all Americans through him, also moved me. One should avoid matching a literary work against reality, but in the reality of that tropical evening, where sudden M–16 shots thundered and faded in the forest beyond our trenches, I couldn't help being impressed by Twain. Good will, he showed us, couldn't forestall *it*. The Caucasian fraternity couldn't prevent *it*. Anglo-Saxon kinship couldn't stop *it*. The absence of communism couldn't hinder *it*, And King Arthur died, Sir Launcelot died, the Knights of the Round Table died, Merlin died. And the American died.

The war died seventy-five years ago.

5

A child was singing somewhere in the street outside.

'*Mot, hai, ba.* . . .'

The voice was high-pitched, birdlike, rising at the end. It must have been a children's song. She was counting 'one, two, three. . . .' – that much I could understand. If only Binh had been there to explain. It was he who had translated the 'loo, loo' lullaby for me into English.

'*Mot, hai, ba.* . . .

'*Mot, hai, ba.* . . .'

I'd had a nap. I pulled on my trousers and put on a shirt, pushing aside piles of newspapers, magazines, and whiskey bottles scattered on the tiled floor. There was a small garden outside the window, and the hibiscus flowers floated like huge red butterflies in the tranquil dusk.

Twilight veiled the red scrolls that hung on the wall.

One of them read: 'Happiness visits where birds live.'

The other: 'The Official from Heaven brings happiness.'

I had bought them on the backstreets of Cholon. I'd been squatting on a street in Chinatown, eating hot gizzard gruel, when I noticed an old Chinese calligrapher. Gripping a large brush in his narrow hand, he was writing these auspicious phrases one after another on sheets of paper that he'd laid out on the ground. He did this with such ease and mastery that I bought two scrolls before realizing what I was doing. He didn't deign to glance at the money put in front of him and continued to wield his brush in silence.

On leaving my room, I took a cyclo to Bach Dang Quay for a short walk. Several M-24 tanks were parked with their guns pointing at the white building of the Department of the Navy, but the soldiers stood around chatting idly, their laundered shirts hanging over the gun barrels. There had been an incident not quite amounting to a coup earlier that afternoon. It was what the correspondents had dubbed a 'coupette', and was the reason why Yamada had sent his assistant Tran to the USIS to summon me back from the front.

One rumor had it that the chief conspirator was a General so-and-so of the Army; another that it was General such-and-such of the Air Force.

I'd bustled around all afternoon and got no other information than that the prime minister had been ousted and a provisional military government was being formed; no one knew exactly what was up. Tran had run off somewhere, and so had Yamada, so I ran around with students, children and old women in a demonstration, and we all ran into a heavy dose of tear gas. It was reported that, at that moment, the young generals were in conference at the resort of Vung Tau. Not true, others said, it was in the cool highlands of Dalat. Scuttlebutt had it that the American ambassador had fled to Bangkok; and someone swore that the Cholon Chinese were betting seven to one there would be peace talks before Tet. There was even an eccentric but convincingly whispered rumor that the VC were going to launch an attack on Saigon in red Triumph sports cars. And if I had forecast a nuclear war for tomorrow and a holocaust for the day after, all Saigon would soon have been swearing by it.

At Bach Dang Quay, the 'Tour d'Argent' began to set out its tubular chairs and an MM Line passenger boat lit up its white-rimmed portholes. The evening sun canted on the yellow Saigon River and the water, trees and hotels were shrouded in saffron haze. Foodstalls opened on the riverbanks and the smells of fried banana and toasted squid mingled in the air. On the ferry pier, a few children were fishing and a young couple sat holding hands, looking up at the sky. Two cyclo drivers, smiling broadly, crouched under a flamboyant tree pitching coins with children. Somewhere in the grove of date palms across the river, artillery fire hammered occasionally, as annoying as a stubborn toothache that one has learned to live with.

A sheet of Chinese newsprint lay half-dissolved in the dirt. Apparently, a French ecdysiast had paid us a visit: 'Thrills!' 'French body bomb arrives!' 'Striptease ecstasy!'

A boy wearing a monkey mask danced on the stone pavement along the riverbank. Another boy, a beggar with atrophied legs, watched him with peals of laughter, applauding enthusiastically. An islet of water hyacinths, as large as a small room, came floating slowly by, its purple flowers quivering.

The bar 'Plaisir' in the square was filled with American soldiers. As I walked into the well-chilled room from the stifling air outside, my linen shirt seemed to revive instantly. It was some time since I had been near airconditioning and that licked-tin taste it has; and it had been a while since I had heard the wailing songs or seen the desolate red liquor shelves and their array of gleaming bottles. I looked for some Jack Daniel's, but couldn't find any, so I ordered a Pernod and asked the bartender to call the proprietress.

She came, dressed in an *ao dai*, pushing through the

bamboo curtain – a plump middle-aged madame who ruled her domain with elegant manners and cynical eyes. I would have to pay for To-nga for the night. If one wanted a rendezvous with one of the dancers, one had to buy her time for so much per hour.

'We're friends, are we not?' the madame said.

'Yes.'

'To-nga is a very beautiful girl.'

'Yes.'

In her faultless French she murmured an exorbitant price, then picked the money from my palm with elaborate disdain, as though picking feathers off her clothes. She was a study in how to dignify vulgarity.

'When she comes, send her over,' I told her.

'Of course.'

'Too many Americans here.'

'I'm afraid that can't be helped.'

'They're good customers, I suppose.'

The madame shrugged and arched her eyebrows. 'Look at them,' she said, 'all they drink is "33"! One beer for the whole evening. They know how to make their dollars last; but it's not fair on the poor girls.' She shrugged again, pouting her lower lip scornfully, then sailed away to her room in the back.

I sipped my Pernod and looked around; GIs were packed around the bar stools, laughing loudly and shouting. As the woman had pointed out, they all had one small bottle of '33' beer in front of them – almost by agreement, it seemed.

Vietnamese girls were twined around them, flirting like kittens. But though their mouths laughed and white teeth flashed, their eyes were cold.

'*Chao-ong!*' a young woman's voice called.

A girl with large eyes and heavy lips stood before

me. It was To-nga, smiling in her pure white *ao dai*. Her eyes were furious.

I put down my Pernod and said, '*Chao-co.*'

She spoke rapidly, and I couldn't follow. I assumed that she was telling me off for having left her without any explanation. Early one morning I had said good-bye at the dark entrance to the Catholic cathedral. I had left a note about my trip to the front with her brother Tran and expected her to find out sooner or later; so I hadn't told her anything. After watching her walk into the somber nave, I'd found myself a cyclo, shaken its driver awake, and left for the airport. I hadn't any excuse, really.

I said '*Chao-co!*' again.

She looked resigned and smiled decorously.

The room was completely dark except for a pea-sized bulb on the ceiling that cast only the dimmest of light. One could hardly move in the crowd. It was all I could do to stand in one spot, swaying with To-nga like strands of seaweed. The place reeked of American flesh and perspiration. A Vietnamese singer, eyes dazzled in the spotlight like inlaid mother of pearl, moved with the simpering charm of a male prostitute and, after 'Never on Sunday', started crooning a sad ballad.

> The sky turns pink and
> Shadows blur the jungle road.
> As I change into warm clothes, I remember
> My love who's gone far, far away.
> A young man at the front thinks of home
> And hugs his memories, full of love.
> But ahead of us, many winds and many rains.

To-nga leaned against me lightly, humming close to my ear and whimpering faintly. Sweet, clear breath huffed through her small teeth. My throat felt painful, constricted.

After a while, we left 'Plaisir' and turned off Tu Do Street into a small alley to have dinner at 'Napoleon'. Behind heavy black velvet drapery was a small room with dim red lighting, and the 'haves', drawn from French, American and Vietnamese high officialdom, were dining. In the silence of a deep water tank, the occasional sound of a fork touching a plate, muffled giggles, and waiters' whispers were all absorbed by the thick curtains. I ordered chilled potage and an escalope; To-nga chose onion soup and lobster thermidor; and we decided to have pineapple soufflé for dessert. She was still a bit rigid, but when we began to eat after a Cinzano, she finally opened up. Spooning out her soufflé, she glared at me, feigning anger, and rolled her eyes, but waves of radiant contentment drifted on her face, and her smiles swayed in the red light.

I put a small bottle of 'Ma Griffe' in her hand. I had bought it at an Indian perfume shop on a corner of Nguyen Hue. It was the first shopping I had done since arriving in Saigon that day.

'Pardon, pardon!' I put my palms together sheepishly, and To-nga giggled. It wasn't only an adult with a resigned smile sitting there opposite me, but a little girl, exhilarated. Her slender neck, erect in the high collar of her ao dai, had dignity and elegance.

After dinner, we went for a stroll.

The river was periodically lit by flares; the date palms and the water glinted; but the boulevard was bright, decorated with long, horizontal banners reading 'Tet, Tet, Tet' strung out between the trees. Pedestrians riding the night tide jostled along the street. On a dark corner, a storyteller strumming on a coconut viol wailed a forlorn tale about the rise and fall of some ancient dynasty. On roadside stands, Dunhill lighters were being sold along with condoms. There were shamans hawking tiger claws and elephant's hair. Perched on the shoulders of a man selling pets, a monkey and a parrot stared around with goggle eyes. The motor of a juicer whirred, squeezing sugarcane. In Cholon, the din of gongs mingled with the voices of young women moaning to the night sky, '*Aiya . . . ho! . . .*'

The air one breathed was oxygen, nitrogen, and Tet.

The flower merchants on Boulevard Nguyen Hue were already setting out their jars, pots and barrels for the Tet season. Chrysanthemums, narcissus, peach and plum blossoms, roses, carnations, hibiscus: a mass of flowers from the temperate and tropical zones were displayed in oil drums. Who grew these flowers in this land where a hundred men were dying daily on each side? Did bombs make good fertilizers? Did napalm water the soil? About a thousand Viet Cong had appeared recently in a banana plantation and the groves nearby; the ARVN countered with about three battalions, and they were locked in combat for four days. In two days, I was told, the explosives that showered down in that area came to 290,000 machine gun rounds, 1,500 rockets, and close to seventeen tons of bombs. This happened only forty miles from Saigon. But here, showers of red, yellow, white and purple petals fell from flowers, and continued falling, and yet the gardens of flowers in oil cans didn't seem to diminish by as much as even a bouquet. The streets were strewn with petals as if a parade had passed in a storm of confetti. And still endless lines of bicycles came into town, loaded with mounds of flowers. The tropics are fecund and bountiful; but they're remorseless in their abundance, indifferent to the glut of honey, the ooze of putrefaction.

★

'*Kiku,*' I said, pointing to some chrysanthemums, using the Japanese word for them.

'*Kii kuu!*' said To-nga.

'*Ki ku.*'

'*Kie kou.*'

'*Suisen.*' I pointed at some daffodils.

'*Shui shen!*'

'*Sui sen.*'

'*Shui shen!*'

I bought the daffodils and a vase and handed them to her. Suddenly she put her cheek against mine and whispered:

'*Chez moi.*'

'*Chez toi?*'

'*Chez moi! Chez moi!*'

Standing against the dark, yellow plaster wall of an alley, she smiled like a flowering tree.

We took a Renault taxi with a large hole in the floor, passed the Botanical Garden, crossed a bridge, and entered the walled Gia Dinh district. Beyond this point I always lost track. We twisted and turned through the dank slums, and Malraux's 'lichenous Asia' surrounded us. Now and then, candlelit cavities opened in the black wall and figures stirred in them like shadow puppets.

To ease the unbearable heat, a lot of people stayed outdoors, crouching in the dark, slowly moving fans. Artillery bursts sounded much closer now and they were joined by the staccato clacking of heavy machine guns. Just beyond the wall, immediately outside this district, stretched rice fields. There was a rumor that three or four VC companies had infiltrated this community for a number of months, awaiting an opportunity to stage an uprising. It was also rumored that members of Cells 65 and 67 of the Special Volunteer Task Forces, who were responsible for terrorist activities in Saigon, had been smuggled into this area.

We got out of the taxi and stepped into a dark alley paved with what I thought were rags but soon realized were refugees from outlying villages. The smell of rancid bodies and foul breath mingled with the stench of the gutter, of rotten fish sauce. Feeling twinges of fretful guilt, I groped my way over the bodies.

In the pitch dark, a mound of mud muttered lazily, '*Di . . . di*' – go away, go away – and turned over.

To-nga disappeared into one of the houses, jangling keys, and I followed. There was a click in the dark and a tiny bulb lit up the ceiling. I found myself standing in the garage. Here, the walls and floor were completely bare, and a bed stood in the center, with a large earthenware jar in one corner. The scene was as painful as ever. I walked slowly along the wall. On the windowsill were two bottles of cosmetics, lipstick, a celluloid soap box, a cracked hand-mirror; on the wall, two *ao dai*. Nothing had changed. Nothing had been added or taken away. The girl lived surrounded by all her possessions; and they would scarcely have filled a hatbox.

She put the daffodils in the vase and laughed and cheered, clapping her hands.

Then, slowly, she took off her *ao dai*, removed her brassiere, and got into bed, smiling secretively. I took off my shoes and left my trousers in a heap on the floor. The mosquito nets fell around me like clouds.

Why do women's eyes look so large in bed?

My cheek close to hers, I smelled her clear breath and heard our teeth click faintly. Her tongue moved quickly between her heavy lips. After a while, I descended from the mountain to the plain, tarried briefly at the navel, and wandered off to a nearby hillock and its tufted crown. In the nest below, the dark lips were half open. The quickening touch of her hard, sharp nails loitered at my belly, and hesitantly found me, and began to caress. The hard crust that had formed over my skin like lime, from trench life, sweat and jungle fatigues, dissolved without a sound and my body felt reborn, as vulnerable and tender as a larva that has just sloughed its first skin.

She was, as usual, simple, unpracticed, and, for a long time, hesitant. A shamelessness in me urged me on. Suddenly I buried my nose and lips in the moist dark mouth and placed her resisting hands on me and made her suck me. She submitted timidly. Her thighs opened, arching like a bow. The sheet grew furnace-hot. I rose, turned, and in one thrust penetrated her.

To-nga gave a low moan. '*Char*. . . .' The sweat lapped. There was the sound of ripples and billows. '*Oi . . . oi . . . Troi . . . oi. . . .*' She moaned again faintly, trying to suppress it by clenching her teeth, contorting her face. In the half-light, the face looked fractured amid strands of hair. I hugged her desperately, squeezed her, and held off the tide that upsurged.

Before long, fingers brushed the overripe fruit and it suddenly fell. I opened, exploded, and plunged like a lead weight into that tender, urgent tremor. To-nga's clenched thighs fell away from my sides. Her belly undulated and her lips smacked together. The dinning of the drum receded gradually from my hips, my thighs and belly. And I lay motionless on her, waiting for the soft night sea to slowly unfurl and envelop me.

When she had recovered, she began to chase me out busily with her little lips. I retreated gradually, then fell away.

'*Troi-oi!*' I groaned, raising my face.

She giggled in her hair and pinched my stomach tenderly.

The big guns roared and the walls shuddered. The machine guns were still drilling. Were they just a gesture, a threat? Or was it a real fight? Several house lizards had gathered, squeaking, around the little light on the ceiling. Beyond the wall – next door? – a baby was whimpering and an old woman's muffled voice was hushing it.

'*Bébé!*' To-nga whispered and, still flat on the bed, picked up my hand and began to tease my thumb into wrestling with hers. Her dry, cold finger pecked at mine and flew back, pecked and flew back. I had taught her how to finger-wrestle some time ago and she loved the game. Ever since, she was always ready to grab my thumb and start playing. Evidently it wasn't played locally.

Her brother Tran spoke French and English. To-nga knew only pidgin French, which was just about a match for my fractured Vietnamese. Tran worked as an interpreter and assistant at the Saigon office of the Japanese Press, which had sent me to Vietnam as a special correspondent. Yamada, who had come from the Hong Kong branch, was Tran's superior. I got various information from Tran and had him translate articles from the local papers. What I tried to coax out of him was the local gossip, not the editorials; I had him tell me, for example, the story of the soldier who fixed the family debt with a hand grenade, or the high-school girl whose father caught her reading pornography and shaved her hair off.

Tran and To-nga might just as well have been orphans. Their parents were in Hanoi, but where exactly was unknown. Their father was thought to be teaching history and French at a lycée there, but again that wasn't certain either. If I asked about them, Tran turned away, claimed he didn't know, and To-nga only said, 'Papa, Mama, Hanoi.' The two children, aged about thirteen and twelve, had come south from the port of Haiphong on one of the 'free exchange' ships that resulted from the 1954 Geneva Accords. Penniless, they went to their uncle's home for help. Evidently a man of principle, their uncle, his official position in the government notwithstanding, was in open opposition to the totalitarian regime of Ngo Dinh Diem, and his association with an anti-government faction was rewarded by exile to the island of Poulo Condore. After a time, a coup ousted the Diem tribe, and a fair number of political prisoners were released from the island; but their uncle never returned. Their aunt was forced to earn a living and bought a permit to open a general goods stall in the market, where she now sold pots and plates. Tran left his aunt's home and, because he knew French, was able to find work in the Saigon offices of various foreign newspapers; he had learned English on the side. To-nga also left her aunt's place and went to work in a bar.

They lived separately. Tran lived in a pension near the start of My Tho Boulevard and roved the city all day on a motor scooter. To-nga's garage was in the opposite direction, in the Gia Dinh district, and in the evening she would cross the bridge and follow the fence around the Botanical Garden as far as 'Plaisir', which was on the edge of Hai Ba Trung Square. Their means of living were worlds apart, but it was evident that both lived from hand to mouth. Tran's room was like an attic cupboard, with only a curtain separating it from the landing at the top of a dilapidated staircase. The floor was always littered with months-old copies of *Paris Match* and *Newsweek*. Rats skittered behind the walls; and the only utensil was a wash basin. Nothing could hide the naked poverty of the place.

Why their parents had sent them south and themselves remained behind was a mystery to me. Tran never volunteered any details about their past and seemed to prefer not talking about himself at all. About politics, especially about the war, he was even more discreet; he never committed himself to a frank point of view. He'd tell me how many had died and how many were missing on each side, but not which side he thought was right. There was always an alert but ambiguous look in his eyes when he was near me. In terms of a painting, his gaze fell neither on the foreground, nor the background, but somewhere in the middle. He seemed determined to avoid a focal point, or letting others know that he had a firm opinion about anything. And who could blame him for developing this protective coloring in a country where one day's friend might be another day's enemy – though sometimes I felt that I was holding a walnut shell. I couldn't seem to smell or reach in and feel what was inside. I could only scratch the hard surface.

I remember a peculiar scene I witnessed back at the outpost.

One morning, around ten, I was reading Mark Twain in the shade of a tree near the 'Waldorf-Astoria' when a Vietnamese soldier came over, carrying a heavy machine gun on his shoulder. He saw me and smiled.

'Hellooo. Gooomornin. Howyou? . . .' the soldier said friendlily and, putting his gun down in the cool shade, he began to take it apart and clean it. He undid screws, took out springs, carefully and thoroughly wiped them all with an oily rag, and arranged them neatly in rows. His fingers moved swiftly, eagerly, and he seemed to be enjoying the work. Then Corporal Haines appeared, swinging his long arms along aimlessly. He was an easygoing, good-natured Yank who spent a lot of time playing horseshoes and volleyball with the Vietnamese troops. Their officers called him 'Haine, Haine!' with a French accent.

Haines saw the machine gun and crouched down beside it, then started giving suggestions as to what the Vietnamese might undo next, and where he could go from there. They weren't orders; he wasn't giving a lecture; in fact, he was rather reserved in his demonstration of how the screwdriver might be used. But suddenly the soldier's arms went limp and his chin dropped as though he'd fallen into an airpocket that left him blind and deaf. Haines continued to talk, but the Vietnamese put his screwdriver down and walked away. The American realized after a while that something was wrong and asked me, 'What happened?'

As I tried to explain, he clicked his tongue and said, 'It's a shutter reflex.'

I leaned against the tree and picked up my book. With the soldier and Haines gone, the machine gun, now stripped down to its bones and joints, lay unattended in the morning sun until noon.

There are insects and animals that suddenly turn over and feign death when chased into a corner by a stronger enemy. It may not be a pretense, however, but something that physically happens to their body mechanism. The insect's nervous system may cause its legs to freeze in a conditioned reflex faster than its consciousness. In other words, it may actually be dead at that instant, the body's shutter closing automatically.

The soldier's face had shown no resentment, hatred, scorn or rebellion; that is, no indication of conscious resentment on his part; but suddenly he shut off, though his hands and legs still moved.

I felt an indefinable admiration and awe for that soldier. I had never seen such a subtle, innocent, yet thorough form of rejection. Only enormous fatigue, it seemed to me, could produce that kind of total denial. I had had my share of adolescent *cafard*, of touching bottom, when I was growing up, but never anything like this – not even here, in Vietnam. I had seen dozens of mutilated corpses on the dikes between rice fields, in army hospitals, and in the grasslands after a battle, but never experienced that shutter reflex. I always seemed able to bounce back and squeeze out enough words for a story and send it off to Tokyo. I was paid, had the money credited to my account in a Saigon bank, ate Cantonese food, and inexorably gained weight. The more havoc I saw, the keener my reports became – a hyena feasting on carrion. I felt the ennui and fatigue of that soldier with about as much sensitivity as a barnacle clinging to a ship's steel hull. His exhaustion was beyond me, out of reach.

To-nga was playing with my fingers. The machine guns were quiet, but the 155s still droned on. House lizards squealed on the ceiling, but the baby next door had stopped whimpering. A buzz came from somewhere in the room and To-nga rose immediately. Showing her behind and its wet underparts, she groped around the mosquito nets and loudly slapped her hands together.

'*Muoi, muoi.*'

She opened her hands and showed me a smashed mosquito. Did *muoi* mean mosquito?

'Malaria?' I said. She cocked her head and thought a little, listened, and as soon as she heard another buzz, shot her hands out, clapped, and opened the palms right in front of my eyes.

74

'*Muoi, muoi,*' she said.

'*Muoi, muoi.*'

'*Muoi!*'

'*Muoi?*'

'*Bon!*'

She smiled gently, satisfied, then bounced down beside me and sank back gracefully on the wrinkled sheet. She crooned a few snatches of song, closing her eyes, then staring at me. She was like a kitten that had drunk its fill of milk. I, too, closed my eyes and drifted, like a drowned man floating down a river, luxuriating, stretching.

After a while, I chased To-nga from the bed into a corner of the garage and we washed ourselves with the water in the large jar. It was the moment I had longed for. The skin of the unglazed pottery was drenched with condensation, the water shivery cold. In the dark she touched me and laughed, and I fondled her and laughed. The bud inside her had already tightened. I was on all fours on the concrete floor and asked her to pour water over me. I shook like a dog . . .

To-nga stood, thighs firmly apart, and washed herself, mumbling, 'Mm . . . nice.'

The water gurgled down the drain. I was aware of the river, the bay, and the vast swampland of ravaged mangroves behind me. My seed was returning to the sea, seeping through the hot earth – gone, like salmon spawn, down to the South China Sea, where giant rays and lobsters sleep.

6

At about ten in the morning a phone call came through from Captain Wain. He was back in Saigon on a five-day furlough. He was leaving for Hong Kong the following morning to meet his wife who was flying in from the States. He would be free that night. Would I like to have dinner with him? I agreed on the spot. We decided to meet at the Caravelle Hotel bar at six o'clock.

I had breakfast as usual at the 'Yin Hua' restaurant: fried noodles with vegetables and a twist of fried bread. The dining room was huge, but the 'atmosphere' hadn't much to distinguish it from a garbage dump. The spouts of the teapots were cracked and the bowls chipped; the bamboo chopsticks were black from constant use and the floor was slippery with snot and slops and vegetable scraps. A dog, glassy-eyed and mangy, roamed about sniffing at the air of the place – fetid and nutritious, characteristically Asian. The shirt on the man boiling noodles in a copper pot at the entrance was torn and grimy and his nails were black. But after trying out more than ten noodle shops, I'd settled on this place, and intended to eat there every morning while I was in Saigon. Their noodles came with bits of roast pork, a piece of lettuce, and a shrimp cracker, and the lobster broth was thick and delicious; the noodles themselves were springy, *al dente*, in the soup. Biting off bits of a vinegary red-hot pepper, I'd slurp the noodles up and soon my mouth would be on fire; but hot spices go well with tropical mornings.

Some Buddhist priests had been locked up in a temple and were protesting with a hunger strike; and their leaders were rumored to have begun talks with the military. Students had held a demonstration on the riverbank demanding the release of some comrades of theirs, jailed for advocating opposition to the draft. And they'd been marching along, with professional mourners at the head of the procession, when, on reaching Le Loi Boulevard, they collided head-on with the Army. Tear gas was lobbed among them and they scattered wildly in all directions. When I arrived on the scene, the tanks and armored personnel carriers had withdrawn, and troops lolled on the green island in the middle of the city square, dozing or drying their moldy feet in the sun. I went up to Room 309 of the Majestic Hotel and found Yamada sitting there in his shorts, sipping Cointreau and typing away.

'How is it outside?' he asked.

'Seems like it's over. There's no more street fighting. All the talk is of negotiations. Plummer from AP said the same thing.'

'More than likely.' Yamada continued tapping on the typewriter. When a fair number of pages had accumulated, Tran hurried off with them to the central post office. Yamada rubbed his eyes, bloodshot from a night's work. He was fluent in Chinese, both Mandarin and Cantonese, and had lived in Hong Kong for five years as bureau chief. He had recently been promoted to an editorial position and, on the way back to Tokyo, had stopped off in Saigon to bid farewell to Southeast Asia. Smelling a coup in the air he'd decided to stay close to the scene for two additional months. On the way to Vietnam, I had passed through Hong Kong and he had given me letters of introduction for Saigon, then taken me to a Chinese restaurant and treated me to scented green bamboo wine and crabs and baby eels from Shanghai. He even presented me with a poem of his as a farewell gift. It's still in my wallet. I've read it and reread it so many times I can recite it by heart. It's written in Chinese.

> I stand in the wind, longing for the north;
> The geese, without a word, winged forth.
> The Pearl River flows eastward to the sea
> To nurse the green paulownia tree.
> What fate, what reunion, await you and me?

'You'll get involved,' Yamada had predicted.

'D'you think so?'

'Oh, yes. It's inevitable, knowing you. In English, they call it "sitting on the fence" if you hold back and just watch, but I'm sure you'll come down off that fence. I wouldn't mind betting on it. I'm rather looking forward to it, in fact.'

'But I've got a wife and daughter.'

'That doesn't matter. I'm certain you'll get involved.'

'How do you know?'

Yamada had left my question unanswered and, with a smile on his face, looked down the wintry Hong Kong street, loud with clicking mahjong tiles. And, between sips of bamboo wine, I went on sucking at the plump white flesh of Shanghai crabs.

Yamada finished typing and collapsed onto a sofa.

'How's the coupette?' I asked.

'It's a mess.'

'It's only the skin on the milk, isn't it?'

'That's about it.'

He held out a box of cigars and, taking one himself, tore off the band with a fingernail. It was a saying of his that a man should be able to enjoy a cigar and some

Cointreau after a meal, and that his lips should glisten elegantly with a faint sheen of fat.

General so-and-so of the Army had apparently had talks with General such-and-such of the Air Force and made a grab for his position. Such-and-such had yielded it to so-and-so. The Army general then rallied the young officers who couldn't decide whom to side with and made a speech: no matter how poor we are, he said, we ought to be allowed to settle our own fate instead of having foreigners decide it for us! The American embassy took exception to the anti-US tone of his speech and called his loyalty into question. On hearing this, the general, looking astonished, had protested: 'But what are they talking about?' Pressed on the same point by reporters who rushed over for an interview, the general turned red in the face, rounded on them, and bawled, 'It's a dirty lie! The Americans and we are *tam-dong*!' then drove them out. *Tam-dong* means 'of the same heart'.

The rumor was that this man had already pocketed close to fifty million dollars and stashed it in the Banque de l'Indochine in Paris. A month ago, according to the customs officer who witnessed the scene, the general's wife had flown to Paris, and when she opened her suitcase at Orly Airport, bundles of dollar bills had fallen out with an obscene thud. This kind of gossip was rampant and it no longer bothered me much – less, even, than the fish-sauce stench of the streets. But the rumor that the same man went around *boasting* of his own corruption interested me. It was an extraordinary idea – that a person should actually spread the word that he was crooked. The reason, which Yamada pieced together from both 'reliable' and 'unreliable' sources, was as follows. The general was out to imply that his corruption was a private way of getting his revenge on the United States. The Americans would never understand the Vietnamese, no matter how hard they tried, and they would go on fighting their own war. For this, surely, they deserved a little whipping. Which made his own doings permissible, particularly since he'd never confiscated any Vietnamese property. Not only was this the way he justified himself, but he openly boasted about his ingenuity.

'What's going to happen?' I asked.

'The guy will probably run around trying to make peace with the monks and students. That's all. If the Buddhists promise not to run wild, he'll agree not to oppress them and will probably build one or two temples for them. For the students, I expect he'll ease regulations for studying abroad and so divert the pressure they're putting on him. That's about it. Everybody's walking on air because of Tet. So they'll get over the New Year, drink New Year's wine, and after the first three days, well, another coup may be on tap. I'll bet a dinner on that. Or even a thousand Ps. How about it?'

'I'd rather donate it to the Refugee Relief Fund.'

'He's got away again!'

Yamada chewed his cigar butt and, frowning, sipped his Cointreau. He was irritated that, with all his mad chasing after news, when he did secure information, he was restricted in what he could report because if it were published openly he might be expelled from Saigon.

When Tran returned from the post office, Yamada decided to make the rounds with him. While Yamada got ready, Tran quietly waited in a chair. As usual, he was calm, loose-limbed.

'Tran,' I said to him, 'I hear the Chinese in Cholon are betting seven to one on a peace treaty before Tet. I can't really believe it.'

'Some say the odds are fifteen to one. I've heard about it often, too. Sometimes I hear people talking about it on the bus or in the market.'

'Can you confirm it for me, today or tomorrow? I want to know what they base their assumption on. I don't care if it turns out to be hot air. I just want to know what's behind it.'

'I can probably find out.'

Tran wrote something on his memo pad and quietly left the room with Yamada.

I returned to my lodging house and lounged in bed, first reading a newspaper and then a book. My cognac had overcooked in the heat and turned lukewarm and cloying, and my tired tongue tasted in it a cheap perfume rather than the fragrance of real flowers. The white plaster walls were glistening, slimily hot, and in my weary brain a woman's voice returned . . . slightly breathless, a voice that held both passion and innocence. To-nga would be asleep now, curled up in the dark empty garage. My skin vividly remembered the inner softness and quivering pressure, but the sun at the window scorched my forehead, and my sweating body made a sticky sound every time I turned; desire, marred by rancid sweat, quickly soured and retreated into languor. A cigarette between my lips, I took up a newspaper from my right side and passed it to my left, picked up something else on my left and passed it to my right, letting my eyes glide over the printed words. The newspaper was full of fury. People deplored the war, cursed, prayed, refuted, advocated, appealed, shouted, threatened and despaired. Swelled with sweat and cognac, I cauterized my tongue with cigarettes and sank into a brackish sleep.

When I woke up, I thought of corpses, for some reason. It hadn't happened at the front. Why was it that

I brooded about the carnage only in the safety of Saigon? At the front, I found that I was free from any morbid self-concern, and my body and mind were always open, facing straight ahead whether I was standing up or lying down. But within these sturdy, quiet, white walls, I found myself at sea. Was it to give me some focus that these vivid recollections kept recurring? I propped myself against the wall, lit a cigarette, and fumbled through my memory. In clumps of grass, dewy in the morning air, we'd find them: faces – some beautiful, with eyes peacefully closed, and others that had run together into formless jelly. There were clenched hands and hands that had started to clasp chopsticks and been stilled. Fingers were bony, long, with white nails and small wrinkles on the fingertips. Everywhere, I looked down on the dead; my eyes never peered up from the ground, from the eye level of the dead. And the death I saw was always clotted, fly-infested, malodorous. The most disfigured, perhaps, was in the morgue of the Danang Military Hospital. A small ceramic Buddha sat in the lotus position in a yellow wall niche. The Buddha's face was white, as though made up with powder; its lips were red, and it shouldered the nimbus of a neon tube studded with red and green miniature bulbs. A fluid, precisely the color of coffee, oozed from one corner of a red-painted coffin, gradually forming an elongated bead that looked like a small lead sinker. The liquid stretched into thread and drop by drop dripped onto the concrete floor, where it spattered its terrible odor. Countless little fists of drizzle beat secretly against the walls, and I gazed at the Buddha, trembling with cold. In that desolate little room, the sickening, obscene smell lingered and burned my eyes like some chemical; incense would have smothered in it. Looking up at the Buddha squatting like a figurine in a fairground shooting gallery, I felt a sudden urge to speak to it, but quickly left the room, covering my nose with a handkerchief.

No matter how deformed, corpses don't frighten me if their eyes are closed. But the eyes were always staring, peering through a sandy, dust-dry membrane, past my own eyes and shoulders, looking beyond. From the damp grass ridge of a field, a poor father and mother had looked at me, looked at the sky, not blinking even when flies crawled over their eyeballs. Living things move, always move. Living eyes and faces are gossamer images that dissolve and reform moment by moment. The eyes are the transparency of gossamer that gleams and darkens momentarily. I don't look at the eyes of the living. Living eyes are patches of sky in two slits in the skin, fading and shifting at will. Gaze into them and they invariably move. Have them gaze back and one's own eyes move. Mine move if they're tired or because I want them to move. The eyes in the holes of a mask can seem startlingly dead, but they also glint, darken, pierce and recede; they laugh, and they close.

Lu Hsün once wrote: 'Revolution, anti-revolution, non-revolution. A revolutionary is killed by anti-revolutionaries. An anti-revolutionary is killed either by anti-revolutionaries because he is suspected of being a revolutionary, or by revolutionaries because he is an anti-revolutionary. Or a man is killed by revolutionaries or anti-revolutionaries because he is neither.'

'Revolution, re-revolution, re-re-revolution, re-re-re-re . . .'

Thirty years later, the situation was even more tangled and intricate. Any commitment now involved a readiness to kill. How easy it was to fulminate and play with dogma and offer ritual sympathy in the safety and comfort of the rear! In my own way, I was no exception.

I had eyes only for atrocities. Corpses I found atrocious because I wasn't involved. Were I in any way involved, I would have been able to see beyond them. But the fact is I didn't kill, so nobody killed me. I knew it was possible I might be bombed someday at a restaurant or a bar, but it wouldn't be because I was a revolutionary or an anti-revolutionary or even a non-revolutionary. I was only a voyeur, lurking in the narrow ribbon of a twilight zone.

Tran confirmed that the rumor about betting on the peace talks had no basis in fact. At around four-thirty, he crept up quietly to my bedside and gave me the news, then handed me a piece of paper. He had been to see some big shot in Chinatown who dismissed his question with a hearty laugh and gave him a prescription for an aphrodisiac instead.

> 7 large black prunes
> 7 small fresh prawns
> half a finger of candy sugar
> 2 small glasses of water

'It's supposed to be terrific. The man said his wife couldn't be happier, and he's been taking it for quite a while. You put them in a bowl and steam the whole thing until the sugar melts. Take it once a week. It's called "*Chang pao chien kang*". It means "good for your love life". I told him I didn't understand Chinese, so he wrote it down for me.'

He pointed at the piece of paper. Underneath the English recipe was the phrase he had mentioned, beautifully written in Chinese. I sat up in bed.

'This just means "for a long life".'

'Really?'

'He was putting you on.'

'I don't believe it.'

'He was, you know.'

'I don't believe it.'

Tran looked away and started to say something in a sour voice. When I looked up, he was disappearing through the half-open door; I had just a glimpse of the back of his handsome head. I called out to him, but he was gone.

At six o'clock, I met Wain at the bar of the Caravelle Hotel. He had ordered a Coke and was wearing a pale blue shirt that made him look like a salesman on a tropical vacation. I had a glass of Pernod and we decided to dine at 'Napoleon'. On the way, we stopped at an Indian bookstore on Tu Do Street. Krishnan, noble as Tagore, with a scholarly goatee, was sitting at the register in front of his bookshelves. He solemnly took my dollar bills, thrust them into his socks, and briskly counted out piastre notes. For the duration of our brief transaction, his eyes were those of a black marketeer, an Indian merchant who was known to leave nothing, not even a bent blade of grass, on his trail. But after handing me my piastres, he let his lofty, philosophical look return.

Captain Wain stubbornly refused to come in from the heat outside, saying that he hadn't come to this country to make money. I stuck the notes in my pocket and walked out into the evening street, where he was standing looking up at the sky.

'Now, then,' he said, rubbing his hands, and we set off.

Striding along beside him, I asked him, 'Have you really never used the black market?'

'Never.'

'Not once?'

'Not even once.'

'But it's like chucking money into the gutter! You're

an amazing person, Captain. You must be the only foreigner who's kept clear of it.'

'It's not a question of money,' he said laconically. 'It's the principle of it. I suppose it doesn't matter whether one man stays out of the black market or not. But who knows in a shaky little country like this – it might go bankrupt if one more person got involved.'

He knew that it was unrealistic, knew that he was being sucked up by this thirsty sponge of a city. I remembered that he had shown no interest in the black market value of the price on his head.

'It's on me tonight,' I said. 'You took good care of me at the front. "Napoleon"'s meat is a lot less leathery than Jones's.'

'Delicious dinner, good wine, and a nice girl, eh?'

'We'll see.'

'Napoleon' was, as usual, chilly; the velvet curtains were heavy and the thick pile cushioned the sound of our footsteps. The French spoken by the waiters, who were courteous to the point of nausea, bubbled like champagne. We crossed the golden aroma of drawn butter and took seats in a corner, behind a bowl of hibiscus that set the mood for adultery. The chairs and windows were emblazoned with rococo motifs.

Amidst all this, Wain was a threat to the atmosphere. In this hothouse of a restaurant, he was too big, too boorish, and too outdoors. This was a room for middle-aged men with plump hands and noses, with shoulders rounded from gourmet meals and womanizing. Wain pulled his chair forward timidly, hunching his shoulders, and lowered himself gingerly onto the seat, testing his weight.

Onion soup, Chateaubriand, green salad, pineapple soufflé. As an aperitif, I had a Pernod and the captain ordered an extra-dry martini. In addition, I ordered escargots, but Wain, being a rabid Francophobe, refused to touch them. Anything that smelled of and sounded French, from café au lait to baguette rolls, was anathema to him. And every time these items made an appearance on the mess table, he'd say 'Shit!' and scowl and cluck, tear bread muttering 'Goddamn French bread' and put down his coffee cup mumbling 'Fucking French coffee!' If it weren't for French colonialism, he wouldn't be out here sweating and bleeding. If the French had given this country independence immediately after the Second World War, he wouldn't be crouching in red clay trenches for night after sleepless night. The Frogs had wormed arms out of the States on the pretext of 'defending democracy' and 'protecting the free world', and all the while they were dousing women and children with napalm, and dragging us into what became an impossible position. And now they turned around and condemned *us* for the war – as if their own hands had never been dirty! Hell, some of them were still profiteering – selling electricity, running the waterworks and rubber plantations, exploiting people, bribing both the government and the VC, lying snug in their safe little beds . . .

America, albeit reluctantly, had made the decision to help France and so inherited its bloody legacy. And though Wain could, on occasion, bring himself to praise the Commie's fighting spirit, he could never forgive the French. What had once been merely a pet peeve had turned into an obsession. He hated the Frogs with the same rigid integrity as he shunned the black market. I even heard him once say that the reason why all the heroes in pornographic novels published in Saigon were Americans was because English-writing Frogs were churning them out to spite the Yanks. His eyes glittering, he'd blurted out this absurdity just after a nap, sitting up in bed in his shorts.

'That waiter's a Charlie,' I said.

'Really?'

'Can you prove he's not?'

'Let's ask him!'

'He'll put *plastique* in your steak.'

'You know, he would, too!'

Somewhere on the wall, Danielle Darrieux was singing 'Save the Last Dance for Me' in a voice that was barely credible at her age: leathery and polished, it swayed, swelled and faded away. Obediently, we drank our red Algerian wine, sipped soup, ate beef, spooned out soufflé, and grew as heavy as a pair of barges. Contented, eyes glazed, we puffed on cigarettes. Wain showed an interest in the fact that I was a novelist, so I began to explain the Japanese language to him, pointing out that there are three kinds of script – Chinese characters, *hiragana*, and *katakana* – and that a writer weaves the three like strands of rope to construct a sentence. Unlike English, where 'I' takes care of all kinds of first persons singular, there are numerous personal pronouns; so the choice of the 'I' form can determine the tone of the work. This is a difficult point, one that no other country's writers have to contend with. There is even a style in which you don't have to use a single 'I'. And there is a tendency among critics to believe that the more abstruse the work, the more effective it is; so you have to judge exactly how much obscurity and how much clarity you want to put in. The right balance is hard to attain.

Initially, Wain contributed his own comments – about the wild prices they charged at the 'Latin Quarter' in Tokyo, about Japan being an unusual country that had modernized without destroying its traditions, and about how he found purity in all kinds of things Japanese. But while I was explaining sentence craft, his eyes glazed over. Sipping after-dinner coffee, Wain said, in the tones of a man stepping out into deep water:

'You sound like a talented man. I've only kept a diary, but a novel must be hard work. I reckon you'll be writing a novel about this country when you get back to Japan, won't you?'

'I haven't decided. Actually, I didn't come here to do a book.'

'You'll be writing about us, though?'

'If I write anything, it'll be about smells. I want to write about the different smells around us. The essence of any object is its smell.'

'I wish I could read Japanese. I'd like to read your novel. Anyway, be sure to send me an autographed copy if you do get around to writing it. . . . Come to think of it, shouldn't literature be about one's mission in life rather than about smells? I mean, it's up to you, but if it was me, I'd be writing about my purpose in life. Smells disappear, but one's mission doesn't.'

'It doesn't?'

'Of course not.'

'But the interpretation of man's purpose changes with time. Smells don't. Sweat smells of sweat, and papaya of papaya. I know papaya doesn't smell of anything much, but its odor doesn't die out, and it doesn't change. I want to write about smells that don't fade.'

Teeth clenched on a cigarette, leaning back behind the hibiscus, I was thinking that novels begin to rot from their adjectives, just as corpses begin to rot at the most delectable parts: the eyes and intestines. The captain just might be right. If missions were bones, they would last, be exposed after everything else dissolved; but what bones remained after a smell had gone?

When we finally left the restaurant, we strolled over to the riverside. The broad, dark field on the opposite bank was deathly silent, and a single gunship hurried west through the night sky, its red light pulsing.

In foodstall braziers, mangrove charcoal flared, red sparks crackling. We stole behind some lovers sitting on a rush mat, gazing silently into the darkness across the river. Wain's towering body had dissolved in the dark and I couldn't see his face. I remembered the time he had loomed up like a crude rock sculpture in the morning mist of a rice field. Here, he was a large, slow-breathing continent.

'How do the Japanese look at this war?' his voice asked hesitantly.

'I don't know.'

'But you're Japanese.'

'Yes, but I'm not in Tokyo. Still, I get sent the Japanese papers, of course. I get them all the time. I can tell you the opinions I've found there.'

'Whose opinions?'

'You mean, intellectuals or ordinary people?'

'Just the average man in the street.'

'Seven out of ten feel it's an unfair war. There was a time when they believed that American democracy was based on fair play, but this war's terribly unfair. So America has betrayed democracy – that's how they look at it.'

'But we're fighting against the spread of communism and to protect Southeast Asia; to protect Japan and ourselves, too. Freedom's like good health – you only appreciate it after you've lost it. And that's too late. We're firemen in peacetime and soldiers when we're attacked. Don't they know that?'

'The point is that it's an uneven contest and ideology doesn't come into the picture. Charlie Cong is small, poor and barefoot, and Uncle Sam is huge, strong and rich. And you drop napalm and kill innocent women and children. You're a Goliath, so you should let David alone and stop killing the children.'

'The Japanese really think this?'

'Yes.'

'Seven out of ten?'

'That's my impression.'

Wain inhaled deeply in the dark.

We moved away from the river, crossed the street, and walked on to the Majestic Hotel. I could see the captain in the neon light. His head was hanging, his back was hunched, and his eyes were closed. His body looked dazed, from a pain he was unable to hide, like a man who'd just been punched hard below the belt.

He muttered gloomily, 'We've got to think.' And after a while he added, 'It's important.'

I remained silent.

'We've got to think,' he repeated.

He trudged along the tree-lined boulevard, trapped in his depression.

We shook hands and parted at the entrance to the Catinat Hotel. As usual, his feelings were unadulterated. Again, a stone that had been thrown for fun had hit a frog. In the fluorescent light, he looked as if he was bleeding blue blood, and his stern face was visibly distorted in the humid heat. He smiled bleakly and walked away down the dark corridor. Watching his broad back recede, I suddenly felt a kind of strength, as well as envy. How long was it since I'd last suffered for a cause of any kind? I had focused my energy on avoiding suffering, armed myself with frigidity, and now was drifting slowly in a coma.

1965

7

It was New Year.

The city was empty, and people dreamed behind grimy walls, panting in the heat. Families moved en bloc from street to street calling on relatives, wearing crisp new shirts, their only luxury. The shutters of shops on the main streets were down, and only a few neon lights remained bright at night. The lonely promenades were like dry gutters, like blind widows. Recorded music wafted from the occasional bar, and GIs' faces loomed briefly in the dark holes in building walls. Children ran around with incense sticks, fastened firecrackers onto tree trunks, lit the fuse, and scuttled away. The fireworks exploded and echoed like M-16s in the vacant streets. I jumped up, startled.

In the afternoon, I went to see Mori, a reporter for UPI, and played a game of flower cards at his place. I brought canned rice cakes and canned sweet-bean soup that had come from Tokyo. Mori took some canned saké from a cupboard and added canned *fukujin* pickles and canned fruit-and-bean cocktail. Several other correspondents then joined us, bringing canned pickled turnips, canned broiled eels, canned bean curd, and all sorts of other canned things as presents, so the room was soon littered with cans. We played cards, cross-legged on the tiled floor, leaning against Mori's bed. Then Kawasue turned up, looking dazed, and began to drink, picking at some fruit cocktail from time to time. He didn't join in the game.

Two of the other guys called out:

'Hey, Kawa-chan, what's the matter?'

'You look ill.'

Kawasue raised his face sheepishly and told us that he'd been to a 'licking house' the night before and had the full treatment. His assistant, a Vietnamese, had talked him into tagging along. When they arrived at the house, he was led into a room with red curtains and a leather couch. A Eurasian girl appeared and began the operation. She made Kawasue lie down and, smiling, took off his shirt and trousers as though changing a baby's diapers. Then she began to lick his baby-bare body, wriggling her tongue. Starting at his forehead, she gradually worked her way down to his nose, his chin, his throat, sucking at every part of his skin, lapping his pores, tonguing his holes. He came alive, stimulated not by any drug or liquor or even steam, but only that tongue that constantly wriggled and quivered; it was like being broiled under icy flames. Kawasue shivered all over, exhilarated, his glasses steaming. She dug into his navel, explored his bush and, holding down his trembling phallus, ran her tongue up and down it, and strayed down the 'ants' corridor', and when she reached his rectum, she suddenly dug deep inside it. Caught offguard, Kawasue was astonished, but the next moment an electric ecstasy spread from his nerve center to every inch of him. The clustered folds in the area were as innocent as an infant's skin and, tickled by the woman's tongue and lips, they twitched awake and seethed and squealed with joy. And Kawasue dissolved, with an indescribable sense of intimacy and rapture. After a while, a familiar, hot, yeasty smell approached. He opened his eyes and saw the woman just beyond his steamed-up glasses smiling and puckering her lips.

Mori asked in a hushed voice: 'And you kissed her?'

'Yeah,' Kawasue nodded.

Mizuno flung his cards on the floor. 'Oh, God, Kawa-chan, you can keep that fruit cocktail. Don't pass it around. Eat it all yourself! And move away a little, for Christ's sake!'

Kawasue grinned sullenly. 'I'm not moving.'

I put down my can of saké and asked, 'How did it taste?'

Kawasue's small eyes glinted behind his glasses. 'Yeah. Sort of sweet, sticky. Bits stuck to my tongue.' After thinking seriously he added: 'If you chew on it, it's creamy. Very good for the digestion; super enzyme. I was amazed. I felt my whole body surface expanding about a hundred times last night. I didn't know I could still feel like that. It's very nice, that licking house!'

He kept his head high and purposely made smacking noises while he ate the fruit cocktail and drank his wine. We went on with the card game, elbowing him away whenever his face came peering into our hands.

At two o'clock, Omatsu came in. His face was ashen and he walked straight through into the garden. He stripped off all his clothes and spread his shirt and trousers on the grass, then pulled out a handkerchief and a wallet from one pocket and pressed the wrinkled bills flat on the grass, one by one. This done, he crouched on the ground, arms limp, head down, and made no move to return to our room.

We soon found out the reason for this strange behavior. Omatsu had gone to Le Van Duyet Park to see the New Year's crowd. Beggars with Hansen's disease were out in full force in the thick pall of incense. It was not a scene he was altogether unfamiliar with in this country, but these beggars were mutilated beyond recognition, melting into each other, pus discharging from holes that used to be noses and mouths. Like sores that had erupted in the ground itself, they squatted everywhere, chanting their prayers, begging for alms; and in the sickly sweet smell that came from them, girls and children sat eating noodles, laughing, oblivious to the ooze around them. Omatsu had looked on amazed, moved, and in despair. As he walked along he remembered the phrase 'a kiss for lepers' and became nauseous, felt guilty about his revulsion yet also an urge to nurse his own suffering.

By chance, he had turned to look in the direction he had come from and caught sight of the cyclo he'd just left; a beggar with a can around his neck was climbing into it, helped by the driver. The man was crawling like a turtle, sodden with sweat and suppuration, his wrists and ankles already gone. Omatsu remembered the cyclo's greasy armrest and cushion and, choked with repugnance at the sight of the beggar's pus shining in the sun like oil, he'd run through the streets like a madman, telling himself 'Leprosy's curable, it isn't contagious', again and again. But by the time he reached us, the assurance was gone and all he could think of doing was exposing the germs to direct sunlight. He felt that the roads, the walls, the money, the tables, the spoons, the dishes, the trees and rivers – anything that he had ever come into contact with – must have been crawling with germs. He had a vision of a sky filled with drifting, rippling pus. He imagined his flesh already loosening, his tendons melting, his joints decaying, and spots and nodules forming on his skin. Fear, he said, had crept up from his toes to his belly and chest, and he felt that he was sinking, helpless, into a swamp.

Mizuno hurled his cards onto the floor again.

'Stop it! Goddamn it! First a man who eats his own shit, then another with creeping leprosy! God

Almighty! What a New Year! We can't even celebrate! You bastards!'

Mori put down his cards and mumbled, 'You *can* get some good medicine in Tokyo, you know.'

Kawasue was pale and muttered to himself: 'It's OK. Don't worry, it'll be OK.'

I dumped my cards and stood up. 'I'm going to wash my hands.'

Omatsu's eyes glinted. He'd turned to look at us over his humped shoulders, hiding his balls with one hand. 'It all melts. Your body'll turn to jelly, you'll see. And you'll creep along the street like a turtle. I tell you, there's no hope. God, I wish I was back home! Do you realize that it was leprosy that finished off the Khmer dynasty? Don't pretend you're tough, just go and disinfect your money and stuff in the sun. They're all crawling with germs. If it doesn't bother you, OK. But don't come moaning about it later!'

Omatsu maundered on, his shoulders drooping as he stretched his hands out on the grass and turned them, first one way, then the other. A vague melting sensation spread from the center of my body to the surface. I sat down next to Omatsu and put my wallet on the grass, spreading the bills out one by one, smoothing the wrinkles. Mizuno, Mori, and Kawasue, too, all crouched down shyly and laid out their money in the sun. The notes were crumpled and gummy with sweat. I wanted to see a swarm of germs actually chase out of the mesh of wrinkles, see them burn, disappear; but only a deep chill shuddered through me.

Mizuno sneered, petulant: 'It's too late, anyway!'

I left the card game at four o'clock and went in search of a small newspaper office behind the market. The office was the size of a printing shop in downtown

Tokyo, the kind that might do name cards and advertising fliers. It was closed for the New Year, but a man was waiting there for me, the door latch left open. Tran had contacted him. He was a novelist who wrote for two or three papers under various pen names; his address was unknown. His manuscripts were usually delivered by some waif for a few coins. It would be a different face each time, and the boy would only say that some man, a passerby, had stopped him and asked him to deliver the package. The boy would take the money for the manuscript and disappear.

'He's not a bad writer,' Tran had said.

I wandered down an alley littered with bits of vegetable refuse, fish entrails and papaya rinds, looking for the address. A woman's voice, singing, came from somewhere behind the yellow plaster, probably a cheap bar. It was a Japanese song that had been popular when I was in grade school. Its turn had now come here.

I'm a Manchurian, a girl just sixteen.
March is here at last and the snow will melt,
Flowers will bloom; it's spring again. . . .

The grooves of the record were worn and the woman's voice was peculiarly high-pitched, now fading, now panting; but the memories welled up like water in a hot spring. I lit a cigarette and listened until the song died away, then looked for the address again.

The cold fear of leprosy had receded to the back of my mind. I remembered the time my father took me to a department store. He was in an unusually expansive mood and offered to buy me a bicycle. Once in the store, however, I found the bicycle so magnificently shiny, so overwhelming, that I said I'd be happy to have *Treasure Island* instead. The book was also beautiful and came in a cloth-covered box, but when I got home I read it in one night, and in the morning thought that the bicycle would have been much better. My parents looked at me across the dining table and laughed, saying I was 'easily bought'. But they were wrong. The bicycle was so splendid and expensive that I'd thought my father must be making sacrifices for me; so I had chosen the book. The one who was fooled was my father. Being laughed at didn't appeal to me much, but I kept quiet. I remember grade schools still used to distribute red and white rice cakes on holidays then, and the song about the Manchurian girl was everywhere on the city streets.

I pushed open a door and went in. Inside a dark room full of scraps of paper, a middle-aged man was reading a newspaper.

He looked up and rose, apologizing in slow English.

'Unfortunately, I've only got thirty minutes,' he said. For a Vietnamese, he was tall and muscular, and he had a bull's neck and shoulders.

He gestured at a sofa with protruding springs, and poured lukewarm tea from a chipped teapot. I offered him my cigarettes. Sipping tea, the man began to speak in a low voice, before I could ask any questions. In his youth, he said, he had studied in Paris and, enchanted by Proust, had decided to become a writer; but on returning home, he'd developed a greater interest in Russian literature, especially Chekhov and Gorki. Without any conscious decision, he had parted company with Proust at some point. When the first Indochina War broke out, he put his pen down and joined the Viet Minh; and as a guerrilla commander in a Delta district, he'd fought against the French and the Bao Dai Army. At present, he was writing a novel for serialization in a newspaper, based on his own experiences – not of famous officers and generals, but the nameless men who fought bravely and died. The government censored any anti-government material, and it was a constant struggle to escape the net.

'Have you read Graham Greene's *The Quiet American*?' the man asked me, sipping his tea.

'Yes, I have.'

'What do you think of it?'

'Good. It's cynical, but it's a good book.'

'The movie was bad, wasn't it.'

'Terrible.'

'I gave him the material for the novel. After it came out, I realized that Greene didn't really understand anything about this country. It's a novel written to please European readers. I was very disappointed with it. There's a young woman who smokes opium in the book. I know her, too. I hear she's in Paris now.'

He looked up, narrowing his eyes nostalgically. He had piercing eyes, but they had softened, and a misty longing flickered in them. He went on talking. Greene had stayed at the Majestic Hotel and from there made periodic trips to the front, as well as to an opium den. He had contacted him in his Delta village, and my host had left his submachine gun and secretly gone to meet the novelist in Saigon. The defeat of the French had become inevitable, and 'economic observers' and 'medical aides' were the first signs of a growing American involvement. The man had told Greene all he could, on various subjects. One day, Greene had asked him what he thought of the Americans, so he'd told him a story that was popular at the time.

A young man who had studied Vietnamese history and language at Michigan State University came to Saigon 'to defend freedom'. He hailed a cyclo and in fluent Vietnamese ordered the driver to take him to the Majestic Hotel. On the way there the American said: 'Listen. I did Vietnamese at Michigan State. I know the language – and just about everything else about this country. I know you people cheat foreigners sometimes, but you won't get far with me. So just take me straight to the Majestic.'

The driver, shamefaced, replied: 'Sir, you speak Vietnamese like one of us. I couldn't cheat you if I tried.' In about thirty minutes, the young American arrived at his hotel and duly paid a hundred piastres for the ride. 'You see,' he said, 'you can't fool me. It's a good school, Michigan.' The next day, he went out for a walk and happened to pass the spot where he'd picked up the cyclo; it had taken him seven minutes from the hotel. As a test, he asked a cyclo driver in the area how much he would charge for a ride to the Majestic. The driver jumped up, clapping his hands, and said, 'Sir, I'll take you there for five Ps.'

The man smiled at me. 'Isn't it a nice story?' I nodded in silence. They were a shrewd people. Even ten years ago, when there'd only been a handful of Americans here, this was the sort of comment that had been making the rounds. I could imagine Captain Wain scowling and a smile on Mark Twain's face.

'Are they still like that?'

'Who?'

'The Americans here.'

'Not as bad as they used to be,' the man answered. 'I must admit they try to learn, and they work hard at it. But they can sweat away at it for as long as they like, they're still too young. They're too young to understand people in old countries like Vietnam and Japan.'

'But these old cultures don't necessarily understand

themselves! It's not a question of old and new. Take me, I'm Japanese, but I don't understand the Japanese at all.'

'That's a different matter.'

The man suddenly peered at my watch, raised his head, and mumbled that he had to go. The sharp look had returned; alertness and a sense of danger had replaced the poise of that powerful body.

'Can we meet again?' I asked.

'Yes, sometime.'

'What should I do?'

'Let me contact you. Please don't look for me. I'll choose the date. Wait until you hear from me.'

His tone was modest and cautious, but a look of intense, ruthless energy flashed in his eyes. He rose nimbly from the sofa and shook hands with me. Even this brief contact left me aware of a strength that could have crushed my hand. There hadn't been a word to suggest it, but hadn't he perhaps kept his links with that Delta village?

I found an electrical goods shop that was open in Cholon and bought a light bulb. I also bought some fruit and a *lap-xuong* sausage and struck out for To-nga's place, crossing from one end of town to the other. With the bright bulb, the garage looked more desolate than ever, but To-nga shouted and clapped her hands, gushing laughter like a fountain and rolling around on the bed. She kept looking up at the ceiling in rapture.

'You happy?' I asked her in my halting Vietnamese.

'I'm happy, happy, happy!'

'This, first time?'

'Yes, I've never had a big bulb in my room before! My aunt and Tran have got oil lamps. I've never seen such a bright room. It's like the Gia Long Palace!'

Later, when I got out of bed to wash, I noticed a rich, hothouse smell in the air. It was the ripe pineapple I'd tossed into a corner: like a bottle of perfume that had been left open, it had exhaled a fragrance that now permeated the garage.

8

In the afternoon, I went to see Tran, who was ill. Papayas are thought to be good for the digestion, so I stopped at the market on the way there. The evening before, when I visited him with To-nga, I took along some Chloromycetin as well. Tran's wound was infected, and he'd been shivering with fever then, unable to get out to a café or the hotel or my place. I'd urged him repeatedly to see a doctor, but he only went on shivering, with the blanket drawn up to his chin, and asked how to take the medicine. To-nga had put a damp towel on his forehead, and he lay there obediently, staring at the ceiling.

His lodgings were near the highway to My Tho, in a lichenous slum where the sewage overflowed and pigs wallowed in mud. There was a tailor's shop with one rickety sewing machine, and Tran lived on the second floor. One climbed a dark, dilapidated staircase to the top, and behind a ratty curtain was Tran's home – more like a cell than a rented bedroom. The wide bench that served as a bed was usually strewn with dictionaries, newspapers and books.

I found Tran dozing on it, a small, shrunken figure in his shorts. When I entered, he listlessly raised his fever-glazed eyes.

'How do you feel?'

'A little better, thank you.'

'You're still feverish.'

'Yes, but I'm not chilly any more.'

'That's good.'

I sliced the papaya with a pocket knife and Tran sat up, favoring his right hand, and ate the orange fruit, numbly, without any enthusiasm. His tongue was coated with a yellow-green fur. The bandage on his right hand was a dirty rag that smelled of medicine and bloody pus.

He had been sent an induction notice not long before. It was about half the size of a postcard and ochre-coloured, I think, and it told him when and where he was to report. He had about ten days to go. He'd taken the thing along to Yamada's hotel and silently showed it to him. Yamada had been expecting something of the sort, but was still not quite prepared for it, and was shocked. Losing Tran meant losing a pair of sharp ears and light heels. And so, the next day, he'd made the rounds of people he thought might help, trying to set up a deal.

South Vietnam was notorious for the way money ruled. You could buy anything from a visa to a bazooka, and the draft dodgers and deserters who hung around Cholon were said to have piastre notes stuck in the back of their ID cards, so that when they were stopped for questioning, they could thrust some money into an officer's hand and scamper away like lizards leaving the tips of their tails behind.

College students were exempt from military service for three years; they could also study abroad. The sons of generals, high government officials, and rich businessmen escaped to Paris in such a steady stream that the Air France flight was known as a sort of air-conditioned Noah's ark. But Tran had none of their qualifications. What's more, the government had just tightened up its draft policy. Virtually everyone was eligible, including cripples, tuberculars, men with criminal records or a history of attempted suicide, homosexuals, phony lunatics, even people with missing fingers. They had also clamped down on officials, doctors and draft officers who were found guilty of accepting bribes; they too would be sent to the front. Still, Yamada was convinced he could find a loophole, and he tramped all over the place, without getting anywhere. In desperation he went to the Japanese embassy, but was briskly rebuffed when he hesitantly broached the subject there. And Tran? Tran hadn't hidden in his garret or crept away through the rice fields; nor had he committed sodomy or suicide. He'd merely borrowed a kitchen knife and unceremoniously chopped off two fingers.

On my first visit, he'd let his sister fuss over him while we talked. He was fighting the chills and shook violently, and throughout our conversation he kept the blanket up to his chin. As I listened to him, I could almost see germs riding in on waves of heat, soaking through the walls and windows, invading his body through the two festering wounds, rampaging through his veins. Tran had talked in a low murmur, suppressing the quaver in his voice. The government was absolutely corrupt, he said. The Army was rotten to the core. The officers were like vultures tearing at carrion. The family of a dead soldier was supposed to get compensation from the government, the amount depending on his rank. An infantry private felt his mother might just as well have miscarried, swore he'd be better off dead, that the condolence money would pay off his father's debts, and the family could then buy seed for the next spring planting. But when that soldier died, his company commander deducted part of the allowance, saying so much was for the coffin, so much for the soldier's gambling debts; and the bastard ended up putting most of the money into his own pocket. And we called ourselves Buddhists and Confucianists! It was common for commanders to pad their lists of active soldiers, but they did it to the casualty lists, too. And that ghost money also disappeared into their pockets. How many times must a man die for his father? How many deaths would buy him a pig?

'All officers above major should be exiled to Poulo Condore or just dumped in the sea. They toadied to the French. They squeal that they had no choice, that they had to work for the French just to eat and keep the Commies away. But they're ass-kissers, all of them – down on their knees in a flash!'

Tran had become more and more agitated and his head rose above the blanket. His voice and face were distorted with hate. I had never expected to see him bare his feeings so visibly. Then he abruptly fell silent and slipped under the blanket, his shoulders shaking. To-nga whispered something and moved quickly to his side, lit the lamp and put it on the edge of the table, then crouched in a dark corner.

After a while he peered out, with only the upper half of his face showing. He stared at me. In the lamplight, I saw deep shadows under eyes like holes gouged out by a knife.

'I've got no guts,' he muttered weakly. 'I don't want to kill anybody.'

His young voice moved me. Suddenly the ceiling felt lower and the walls closer. His mumblings sent out soft tendrils that reached into me and groped inside.

'Why did you cut off those fingers, Tran?' I lit a cigarette. 'With or without fingers, you'll still be sent to the front, you know that. Even if you can't pull a trigger, you'll still be in uniform. It's the same thing.'

'No, it isn't!'

Something had changed. Tran's voice sounded irritable in the half-light. His face had closed, and the familiar look of focusing on the middle distance had returned.

'If I'm captured, I'll be interrogated by their cadres. I'm not a regular soldier. If they find out I'm an intellectual, I'll be charged with moral responsibility. I have to prove that I never wanted to kill anyone.'

'Are they that hard?'

'Yes.'

'That's the first I've heard of it.'

'I'm sure that's what will happen.'

'Are you sure you're not overreacting?'

'I'd do the same if I were them.'

I felt rebuffed. Tran lay there, outwardly much the same, but instead of his usual courtesy there was a desolate alienation about him, something insidious and compelling – a recognizable odor, one I'd observed in other men – the odor of conviction.

Tran had always been extremely cautious, yet he had never acted coldly or indifferently toward me. He was just painfully discreet, slipping in and out of rooms without registering a presence.

I wasn't even sure of his real name; he merely insisted I call him Tran. Knowing shouldn't have mattered, but for some reason he was secretive about it. To-nga's name, on the other hand, was no longer a mystery: I had visited an old scholar in his thatched hovel in the suburbs and heard him explain that *to* meant white silk thread and *nga* a fairy butterfly. (He was an anachronism, devoting most of his time to a Vietnamese-Chinese dictionary that he was editing.)

The only time Tran ever let himself go was on his motor scooter, his second-hand Velo. I'd often seen him flying down Le Loi Boulevard and stopped to stare, amazed. He rode extravagantly, hair blowing in the wind, body twisting lithely to left and right. He looked utterly different then, like a messenger of the gods.

'This is an unlucky country, Tran, isn't it?'

'Oh, but what an unlucky, unlucky country,' he sneered behind his blanket. Then, cracking his whip, almost cheerful, he added: 'But it's heaven for journalists.'

I was silent.

'The West pities us, bewails our poverty, and the East applauds our courage. What passes for the truth here is untrue there, and their truth doesn't apply here, just as Montaigne said. But it's a paradise for the press. You look pretty happy yourself.'

'I know.'

'It's true.'

'I know. There's no excuse. I'm enjoying it. Most people are, I'm sure. Unanimous in condemning the war, but not satisfied unless the paper shows them the usual gore. I sometimes think they'd be bitterly disappointed if it came to an early end.'

'C'est la guerre!'

Tran looked up at the ceiling wistfully. His passion melted and the bitterness disappeared; an adolescent loneliness showed on his face. He started to get up and stopped, bit his lip, and let his head drop limply on the pillow.

To-nga stood up swiftly. 'Stay still,' she said, 'you're ill.' She rinsed the towel in the basin and replaced it on his forehead, tucked him in, and gave the blanket a gentle tap. Tran closed his eyes, shivering. He murmured something under his breath and submitted to her care. To-nga seemed suddenly ten years maturer. The childish girl who had finger-wrestled with me happily in the midnight garage was transformed. I watched her, amazed.

On my afternoon visit, we talked again and ate some papaya. Tran sat up against the wall and spoke quietly, drawing slowly on a cigarette. I now realized that he feared the anti-government people just as deeply as he hated the government party. Fear and suspicion. Secreted in some intimate part of him, they had spread over his skin and calcified, and one couldn't crack the crust without hurting him.

His opinions weren't new to me. I had heard similar thoughts often enough from Buddhist monks, from scholars, from newspapermen. But the sight and smell of bloody pus gave Tran's voice poignancy and force.

The Communists were taking a low profile, he said. In order to win over as many collaborators as possible, they were bending over backward to be accommodating. They didn't proselytize, they didn't exhort; they were magnanimous, for the time being, and ready to welcome anyone – even dogs – as long as they were anti-American.

'You know what *doc lap* means, don't you?'

'Independence. That magic word.'

'Suppose a dog barked at some American soldiers, going "*doc lap!*" instead of "bow wow!" The Commies would come at night and shake its paw, pat its head. But after taming it – "liberating it" – they'd chain it to a doghouse. And if the dog barked at them then, they'd kill it, club the chained animal to death. They'd kill it for just barking or turning its head away.'

Tran slowly raised his good hand and suddenly slashed it down, then picked up his cigarette again and inhaled deeply. His distrust was so profound that no other emotion flickered in his eyes.

'You're saying they're ruthless?'

'People, to them, are disposable; they use everyone they can, then throw them out when they've served their purpose. Mao said any intelligentsia that couldn't accept Marxism was utterly useless. Did he say the same sort of thing when he was fighting Chiang Kai-shek?'

'It's a theory of evolution,' I said. 'They believe in progressing constantly from one stage to another. They don't think in terms of betrayal. They say animals that can't adapt will die off. So exterminating them isn't inconsistent.'

'But that's just semantics. Betrayal, evolution – it's shuffling words. They're always saying "in this phase of the revolution". Friends of one phase are untouchables in the next – and disposed of. If they find out they've made a mistake, they apologize in print, and they're always saying "the party must sincerely and energetically tackle the various problems we face in this phase of the revolution." They kill sincerely and apologize sincerely. What are people supposed to do?'

'The National Liberation Front includes democrats and radical socialists. There are also Catholic priests, Montagnard leaders, and Buddhist monks in it. If you're right, these non-Communists are all window dressing. Are they so unsure of themselves?'

'You may well ask. But I think they're sincere in their own way. They all have ideals that depend on the Americans being chased out. But in our political system the only large, well-organized, and firmly united party is the Communists – the People's Revolutionary Party. The Greater Vietnam Party and the nationalists on the government side don't amount to anything because they're all looking out only for themselves. You'll even find some parties that are one-man bands. It's the influence of the French, their individualism and pluralism. And then you have the democrats and the radical socialists in the NLF not knowing how many members they have or how they're organized. They're all minorities, tokens. Pawns in the scheme of democratic unification. As with any political platform, they can revise their positions any time.'

'Will any of them survive the revolution?'

'They'll be killed, or exiled, or manipulated like puppets. I think they'll disappear one by one, party by party.'

Cross-legged and resting against the wall, Tran was breathing heavily, but he talked unemotionally. He had lost the bitterness and petulance of the day before. Coldly, he sought to follow the thread of his thoughts through to its conclusion. He no longer sounded obsessed.

Some time ago, I interviewed an abbot who was on a hunger strike and heard him state a similar opinion in a more concise form. The monk lay on a mattress rolled out on the bare concrete floor of his temple. On his fifth day of fasting, with only fruit juice to keep him alive, he had become a twist of old rope, dozing in a white mosquito net. His shoulders and hips were like brittle, wrinkled tar paper. I squatted by his pillow and, with my palms pressed reverently together, asked him questions. A bespectacled young monk translated my English for him, and the abbot's face, skin drawn taut like a plucked thrush, moved slightly to left and right as he answered in a thin, feeble voice. A small novice with one lock of long hair on his smoothly shaven head sat nearby wafting a lazy breeze toward us with a palm frond. With his eyes tight shut and the set of his neck and shoulders declaring his resolve, the old monk told me that he had sworn to fast until the government fell. When I asked about his relationship with the NLF – was

it one of active collaboration, resistance or neutrality? –
he was silent for a few minutes; then, muttering something briefly, he raised his strawlike arm, opened his
hand, made a fist, and limply let it drop.

The interpreter-monk whispered: 'Until the Communists grab power we're friends; after that, we're all
slaves. That's what His Reverence the Abbot says.'

The abbot's eyes remained closed and he didn't
speak again. The novice approached on his knees and
gently mopped his master's forehead with a towel. The
old monk's eyelids, sunk deep in their sockets, looked
like small brown shells. I had made a painful discovery.
These people could protest against the government to
the point of self-immolation, but only offered the NLF
a sort of icy acquiescence. I felt as though I were looking
at a giant who, rising to his feet, began to totter, sagging
at the knees.

One man on an up-escalator and another going
down may see eye to eye at one point, but the next
moment they're already gone their separate ways. Was
it this truth that the abbot saw so clearly?

When I left him and walked outside, I passed into
incandescent sunlight and a swarm of Buddhists chanting prayers amid the reek of sweat and betel.

Tran was saying: 'If you open and close a door often
enough, the hinges won't rust. For the time being,
the Communists are opening the door wide, shaking
everyone's hand, but when the war's over, they'll slam
that door. They'll shut people up in a closed room and
chuck a grenade in.'

'Are you talking about the Hundred Flowers movement?'

'Not just that. Everything will go that way. Can't
you see? It's not only intellectuals who can expect to

suffer. Before, I used to think a revolution would benefit the peasants here, but they'll cheat them, too.'

Tran took out a Bastos from its red pack and stuck it between his lips, then blew out a heavy cloud of smoke with a sigh, scowling.

It was characteristic of Ho Chi Minh that he should distill the hardships of his youth into humorous poems – simple, skillful pieces filled with open laughter, poems that touched and softened a reader's heart. If only the tone of the politician's poetry could have set the tone of the society he led! Utopian fantasy, I know, but my mind drifted in this direction sometimes when I was out wandering the streets.

After eight long crippling years of war against the French, hordes of people, mainly starving peasants, poured into the South. When Ho realized the extent of the exodus, he told a Catholic priest, sobbing, 'It's all my fault.' Ten years later, this story was still being told among Saigon intellectuals. Even people who despised communism seemed to cherish anecdotes about Ho. Ho's subordinates condemned the clergy as 'reactionaries and provocateurs collaborating with the American imperialists', but their attacks merely served to confirm the enemy's strength. The episode may have been apocryphal; Ho's countrymen were natural aphorists, quick to invent shrewd and witty captions for any notable event. Still, it was eloquent testimony to the probity, the powerful charisma Ho possessed, that it existed at all and took the form it did. Even if it was pure fiction, it is significant that people had this urge to honor Ho by keeping such anecdotes alive.

But two incidents that occurred in 1956 had no poetry or sentiment in them. Emulating Peking and the Hundred Flowers movement, the Labor Party that year granted intellectuals the freedom to criticize.

Immediately, charges that party members were taking bribes were leveled by emboldened critics. Fingers pointed angrily at members, accusing them of corruption, totalitarianism, fanaticism, bigotry, cliquism and dogmatism. An evil smell arose from the iron generation of Dien Bien Phu. At first, blame was placed on Ho Chi Minh, but this was eventually replaced by general skepticism about the merits of the party itself. The Labor Party had probably begun its campaign to air current problems hoping that, by virtue of its own resilience, it could turn the public outcry into a mood of constructive change; but in fact it inaugurated a period of slaughter – laid a trail of rice that lured unwary chickens to their death. The Hundred Flowers died in three months. Frighteningly, writers, poets and journalists disappeared, died suddenly, died mysteriously, committed suicide. Leaders who only yesterday had been tigers in a revolutionary war turned into kittens, afraid of their own shadows, now that their power had been established. Japanese intellectuals are a cautious and sensitive breed, veering constantly, reacting like statoscopes to shifts in the political climate; for me, the Vietnamese who made their suicidal protests in that hermetically sealed political atmosphere shone through like beacons in thick fog.

That fall, Hanoi had to swallow a painful humiliation. It started with a quixotic revolt by starving peasants and ended with bloody suppression by units of the North Vietnamese Army. To make matters worse, the bloodbath took place in Ho Chi Minh's home village in Nghe An Province. This region had become sacred during the war against the French. Ho and many other revolutionary heroes had been born there.

On November 2, an international observation team

passing through the village was mobbed by villagers pleading to be taken to the South. The local militia attempted to disperse them with guns, but met with furious resistance; the riot spread like wildfire, and by evening the entire province was ablaze with rebellion. Hanoi sent in the 325th Division, and in four days the uprising was bloodily subdued. About six thousand peasants were arrested; many were executed. No one knows how accurate the figures are, but it is a fact that the rebellion was serious enough to require the intervention of an entire army division; and it is a fact that the 'People's' Army was mobilized to put down the people. It is an unconcealable fact, too, that revolutionaries cut down barefoot peasants equipped with neither guns nor doctrines, neither organization nor leaders, only wooden clubs and a voice with which to scream.

That was the year of Suez and Hungary. Hanoi hushed up the incident so quickly that the world never found out that only two years after Dien Bien Phu another unspeakable and cold-blooded crime had been committed. In Budapest, the Russians crushed the Hungarians, but in Asian rice fields it was the Vietnamese slaughtering Vietnamese, and mounds of nameless, shoeless corpses piled up in scenes reminiscent of colonial days and the wars of liberation.

Ho Chi Minh wept and publicly apologized, and Truong Chinh, Hanoi's Saint-Just or Beria, was ousted from his position as secretary of the party. But his gloomy, ruthless face disappeared only temporarily from the scene. He was indestructible and, for whatever reason, was later readmitted to Hanoi's inner sanctum. No other member of that hierarchy had emerged from obscurity to command such unpopularity, such an arrogant and threatening presence. He was a figure tiptoeing in the wings of government and yet he was always present when important decisions were being made, though even then his power was largely hidden. And it was this man who drove the peasants to rebellion by imposing a relentless quota system, by the enforcement of land reform according to 'wealth', and by his almost comical obsession with dogma; but when he was dismissed from public life, there was not a word of apology from him.

Ho broadcast a grief-stricken speech after the uprising and, blaming himself, begged forgiveness from both the party and the people and swore that amends would be made, that the slain had not died for nothing – though nothing would bring them back, he added.

In the South, Diem's tyrannical reign continued, punctuated by pogroms which effectively sealed the eyes and mouths of critics. And though they went by different names – the Can Lao Party in the South and the Lao Dong Party in the North – they both deceived their people. An unqualified, uninformed and unprincipled bunch they were; and their citizens were probed, examined, spied on, commanded, legislated, ruled, classified, educated, lectured, scrutinized, evaluated, judged, reprimanded and convicted. At every business transaction and fluctuation of the price index, they were registered, written up, investigated, fined, stamped, measured, appraised, taxed, exempted, confirmed, permitted, addendumed, admonished, interrupted, reformed, reoriented and rehabilitated. In the name of public welfare and the benefit of the system as a whole, they were used, trained, robbed, blackmailed, monopolized, embezzled from, squeezed, deceived and cheated; and if anyone showed a hint of rebellion or dissatisfaction, their arms were confiscated and they were oppressed, indoctrinated, scorned, censured, cornered, slapped, struck, bound, incarcerated, shot, strafed, sentenced, indicted, exiled, sacrificed, sold, betrayed, manipulated, sneered at, humiliated and dishonored.

I remember a conversation with a university professor. After buying a cigarette from an old woman at a roadside stand and lighting it with an incense stick, he asked me if I knew who had said something to the effect that 'When the people rise, support the people.'

'No, I'm afraid I don't,' I confessed.

'Really?'

'No.'

'It was Lenin.'

He spoke quietly, dragging on his cigarette with tiny puffs. His gentle brown eyes blinked forlornly, looking past me, beyond the trees.

Tran's voice was soft.

'You know, after that incident, they despised Truong Chinh but sympathized with Uncle Ho. No matter what happens, North or South, Uncle Ho always comes out on top. Apparently, for some Communists Saigon is "Ho Chi Minh City".'

'He's a living legend.'

'He really is.'

Tran leaned against the wall and picked a speck of tobacco off his lip and scrutinized it, his face like a beautiful dog with ears cocked to the sound of fluid dripping endlessly in an inner recess of his body. His eyes seemed lost, bewildered by what had happened to him.

He spoke again suddenly, as though tossing a riddle at me:

'We have a saying: "If two water buffalo collide, a mosquito dies." It's an old phrase, not something thrown out by the war.'

He laughed feebly. In my mind's eye I saw a large hole suddenly open in his face. I looked away. The thought that this boy was dying flashed through my mind. Perhaps his flesh was already disintegrating; maybe the smell of death was already on him.

'By the way, some writers are going to get together the day after tomorrow. They're neither left-wing nor right, but it's an unauthorized meeting. Would you like to join in?'

'Sounds interesting.'

'I've got the address here.'

'Thanks. I'd like to go.'

'I'll let them know.'

I took the piece of paper and, briefly touching his crudely bandaged hand, descended the dank staircase. When I emerged into the street, the white glare of three o'clock stung like red-hot pepper rubbed into my face and arms.

In the evening, I went to 'Plaisir'. I paid for To-nga's time and took her off to see some Thai boxing in Cholon. Through the clamor of Tran Hung Dao Boulevard, immersed in a gray fog of exhaust fumes, we jounced along in a cyclo for two. To-nga, released for the evening, was sweetly playful. The gym was packed and shabby, harsh with cheers and clapping hands. Children peered in, standing on dustbins, clinging to every window. And two young men, one in navy blue shorts and the other wearing red, climbed into the ring and began to lunge at each other; skinny, sinewy, tilted back in a half-crouch, gloved hands outthrust, they circled, dancing like praying mantises, and kicked and jumped, splashed sweat.

I bought a Coke for To-nga and a coconut for myself and sipped the milk through a straw inserted in a hole in the hard shell. Still unripe, the liquid smelled and tasted green; it was like chewing grass.

'Taste good?' To-nga asked.

'Too young, still too young.'

'Is it true you'll eat anything?'

'Yes.'

'I hear you've even had rat.'

'Who told?'

'My brother.'

'Rat's delicious.'

'But that's soldiers' food.'

'No matter.'

'Dog, too?'

'What?'

'How about dog?'

'Dog's not delicious.'

To-nga laughed indulgently, showing her small white teeth. Her simplicity comforted me. I needed a place where I could hide from discussion, from words. An irresistible lethargy had settled on me, stagnating darkly in every part of me. I felt myself choking on a vinegar of aimless disgust. I would have collapsed if anyone had come up to me and even breathed at me. Wrapped in a shirt, cinched by a belt, and tied up in shoes, it was all I could do to stay upright.

Leaving the gym, we rode back along the boulevard and went to the 'Tour d'Argent' on Bach Dang Quay. We took seats at the end of a terrace jutting out into the river. A gentle breeze touched our cheeks and the river glinted as flares floated down every few minutes. The water quivered with the pounding of artillery, but the diners seemed oblivious, eating and chattering around charcoal braziers and cooking pots. To-nga spread a rice-flour pancake on her palm and put shrimp paste, fresh herbs, and several other condiments on it and neatly wrapped it up for me.

'Hot pepper put!' I demanded.

'Hot pepper put?'

'Put!'

'Hot? You like?'

To-nga giggled softly, mimicking my pidgin Vietnamese. She used her chopsticks like a sandpiper's beak. I watched a plateful of leaves and roots disappear in her small, quick hands as I sipped my beer.

The river's warm breath smelled of the salt tide and seaweed. Inertia paralyzed me, choked me. I felt chilled, drained, like a dry riverbed. I was caving in. The blast of flares, the noise around me, seemed far away, sluggish. Had the lanterns on the pillars been any brighter, To-nga would have seen my face and stopped eating. I could almost describe how I looked, slumped in my chair. Mirrors had often shown me it before: a cringing, frowning, fish-eyed face, with something brutalized about it that made me turn away from other people's eyes.

Why does solitude spawn such degradation on a human face? These spells come suddenly when I'm alone, and occasionally in other company. All sense of purpose and time recedes. There's no trigger, no premonition that might allow me to prepare for them. I can't tame them, domesticate them; so I slink away, out of sight, and let myself sink in as far as I can go. I can stand at a street corner or in a theater, a restaurant, an office with the sound of footsteps or whirring computers all around me, and I can sniff out fellow victims, spot the face of someone in mid-crisis. I've seen veterans waiting for it to pass, eyes closed like a patient on an operating table. And in each of these faces there's something mean and chilling; I find I can't look, can't bear to think that we probably look alike. We don't commiserate, but feel contempt, aversion. We're all untouchables.

Curfew came and the diners stood and headed home like soldiers returning to barracks, like cattle returning to their barns. A dark river breeze swept onto the empty terrace, and dead leaves scuttled across it like open hands. Impatient waiters hastily began upending chairs, and we felt we had overstayed, so we rose and left. The town was like a palely gleaming graveyard; not even a dog's shadow roamed on the riverbank. The leafy tamarinds seemed almost a jungle. Night after night I had gazed out on this scene and should have found it familiar; yet I had to stop and look. Some monster might have been lurking somewhere in that strange quiet.

The wind blurred To-nga's eyes.

'I'm cold,' she said.

'We go home.'

The garage was, as usual, dark, so dark that no shadows formed. A single flyblown bulb was the only light. The hundred-watt bulb I had bought her just the other day had been used for the New Year holiday and quickly stored away. I complained that I couldn't see her face, but she obstinately refused to change the bulb, and it would probably remain this way until next year. She stinted on light the way peasants stinted on salt. Light was a special treat here, used freely only twice a year: at New Year's and the Festival of the Dead in summer.

'Dark, dark,' I complained.

'It's not that bad.'

'Book. I can't read.'

'You haven't got a book.'

'Tomorrow I bring book.'

'But you have to sleep at night.'

'Me not owl.'

She turned over in the mosquito net. Her breasts were round, her thighs long. She twined herself around me like a young vine and with the lightness of a feather began to scratch my body with her hard, sharp nails, small hands crawling up and down from chest to navel, navel to bush, bush to thighs. With each stroke, the skin – grown thick and coarse again – revived and quivered faintly like the thin new skin that forms over a healing wound.

A river rippled and coursed through me. Fatigue came. Enervated, chilled and depressed, I feigned a paroxysm of passion and found myself aroused. I was crude, and shameless. I forced the hesitant girl to hold me and, pressing her small, resisting head into submission, I made her suck me, then thrust her thighs apart and licked the split fruit hidden inside. It was soaking wet and hot, but somehow vulnerable and childish. I chased the bobbing float and trapped it with my lips and tongue. My nostrils choked on the smell of urine and sex. I rose and penetrated her. The hot young fruit-flesh trembled, and the tremor passed into my phallus. Veiled with long hair, To-nga's small face was blurred. She began to moan between clenched teeth, shoulders moving vigorously, eyebrows dimly visible but twitching with a greedy will. She rose, ripened, and overtook me. And when I finally dropped my forehead on the pillow, the feeling of abandon was delicious, like sinking up to one's neck in warm mud or stretching until every joint in one's body cracked.

To-nga's broken cries rose in the air.

The day was over.

I lay in the dark mosquito net and listened to the squeal of house lizards playing their usual games around the miniature bulb, hunting for mosquitoes. To-nga lay panting, her belly heaving, her throat purring, with her face buried in the pillow. I pulled the blanket up and covered her shoulders, and she managed to lift her head, smiling broadly. I reached for my shirt on the concrete floor, picked out a Bastos, and lit it. The cigarette was damp and the smoke bitter. Everything got damp in this country, even the water.

After a while, gazing at her nails, To-nga murmured: 'I wonder what'll happen to my brother.'

9

On my way back from the garage, at the foot of a bridge, I saw a stall with a smoked pig's stomach hanging from an iron prong. I bought half the meat and two baguette rolls and made a sandwich in my room. I took a swig from a bottle of Smirnoff vodka that I kept on hand and went to sleep. I got up shortly after noon, ate the remains of the sandwich, and drank more vodka; and while I was reading some newspapers and magazines sent from Tokyo, I fell asleep again. When I finally awoke, the afternoon was over; dusk was quietly gathering in the room, and the air was stale with the odor of sweat and alcohol.

The vodka smoldering in my body flared up from time to time, blue flames flickering, and my swollen tongue felt hairy. The sun went swiftly down and the hibiscus in the garden faded. I lit the lamp and, putting it on the table by the window, cut the rest of the smoked pig into slices which I then tossed, one by one, into my mouth, rinsing the fat off my tongue with vodka. My chair was rickety, and I had to brace my legs against the floor. I forced my bleary eyes open and began to read Twain's Arthurian saga again, but I couldn't get beyond the first page and a half. The columns of small print paraded like dried ants. The pages, marked with fingerprints and sweat stains, were faded, like pressed flowers. Twain's acuteness and prescience were gone; I could feel nothing. Even the hut back at the outpost seemed on the other side of the world.

Two round pieces of cardboard that a Vietnamese radioman had given me lay next to the ashtray. On the night of the highway patrol, when we couldn't get back to base, I'd slept in a trench on Plateau 24, and in the morning, creeping out of my hole, I asked someone where the latrine was. A little soldier, who looked like a schoolboy, silently pointed beyond the minefield. A line of rubber trees formed a distant backdrop and not far away was a pit. I found an army of maggots in it, dancing and wriggling. Afterward, I was sitting smoking absently when the little soldier approached without a word and handed me something. I looked at it and recognized the cardboard top of a mortar canister; on it was written, in ball-point pen: *'Cher Capitaine, permettez-moi d'aller à la forêt, merci.'*

I raised my eyes. The little soldier sidled up again and, keeping his eyes averted, gave me another piece of cardboard. He crouched a few steps away and glanced at me now and then out of the corner of his eye. The second message read: *'Cher Capitaine, je voudrais beaucoup vous aimer, merci.'*

He had probably asked an officer to write them for him. I laughed briefly. I remembered his face. He had been with us throughout the previous day, toddling along beside the company commander, almost crushed by the weight of the radio he carried. We had eaten rice from the same wash basin and walked through the scrub in the night together. It had been too dark to see, but we might have slept in the same trench. We hadn't spoken, though, so we'd remained just bits of flotsam drifting together and apart. This was our first communication, as it were. The soldier's small, sallow face, puffed from lack of sleep, returned my smile with a modest, satisfied grin; then, shyly turning away, he picked up the radio, anchored it to his back, and toddled off toward his comrades, who were banging wash basins around. As I watched his back disappear in the crowd, sudden tears welled up and trickled down my cheeks.

Even that memory had faded. The cardboard was now spotted with sweat, the surface furry, and the writing rubbed off. The vodka burned in my eyes, but I was airtight; cold and alienated and withdrawn. Neither affection nor nostalgia stirred in me. No casual passion or sudden impulse caught fire in me. Here it seemed like ripe, virile, festering August, but I was at the end of October. Lolling and smoking in bed, I felt multitudes of words and images materialize under my skin like schools of fish, wheeling and vanishing, but no amount of trolling with my fingers caught anything. No sooner did I address an idea that began to take shape than it melted into thin air. Death didn't make my belly tense, make me sweat cold blood or creep across dead leaves on tiptoe. No object or sound filled me with quiet dread. I was a prisoner of alcohol, strapped to the bed, unable to budge. The fruits of my journey had ripped open and gone dry. Why I was here was beyond me. My bibulous, swollen face was heavy with vodka. Dank walls. Newspapers scattered on the floor. Ashtrays heaped with cigarette butts. Everything was bulky, remote and irksome. The war had receded, was being fought elsewhere, on another continent, in some hinterland beyond my reach.

10

It was New Year in Tokyo a month ago. I went to the Japanese embassy and picked up a package from my paper containing books, malaria pills, a can of toasted seaweed and – probably forwarded by my wife – New Year's cards from a bookseller and some friends. I returned to my room and, sipping vodka, arranged the cards on my bed, one by one, then shuffled them and set them out again.

•   RESPECTFULLY WISHING YOU
         A HAPPY NEW YEAR

I would like to express my deep gratitude for your special patronage over the years, and hope to be favored with its continuance this year.
Yohei Todo, 'Suigyobo'

   MAY THIS SPRING BE A TIME OF JOY!
   Damn it, I'm thirty-seven already!
         Mikako

Last December, my doctor took me off saké and cigarettes, and my horoscope at the Ikoma Shrine gave me the blackest of all prospects. How can I wash down the New Year meal with *water*?

         Ken

Ts'ao sê ch'üan ching hsi yü shih	Grass budding, rain drizzling,
Hua chih yü tung ch'un fêng han	Spring breeze the blossoms chilling.
Shih shih fou yün ho tsu wên	Oh, weary – yes, worn out am I!
Pu ju kao wo ch'ieh chia ts'an	Lolling, lounging, New Year in bed.

Wang Wei, Bin Mukai, Motoko, Hun, and Haru

HAPPY NEW YEAR!

O foolishness of man to seek
Salvation in an ordre logique!
O cruel intellect that chills
His natural warmth until it kills
The roots of all togetherness!

Masao
(From W. H. Auden's *New Year Letter*)

HAPPY NEW YEAR!

Suminobu Yasutake

SPRING GREETINGS!

The sky's complexion is returning spring,
The light is lambent, still without a speck of cloud.
Inside the humble fence around my home, the grass
　amidst the snow
Begins to color tenderly, and herald mist
Steals in to make the buds on tree twigs blur
And of its own accord, man's disposition seems
　to ease, unbend.

Taketoshi Inui

A DAY OF JOY!
AND MAY YOU HAVE MANY MORE OF THEM!
Ichiro Matsumoto
Akiko Matsumoto

II

I emerged into a cluttered alley behind the Gia Dinh district market and looked for the address Tran had given me, peering at the numbers in the light of my cigarette lighter; it was like going down into an almost pitch-dark well. Old women squatted in doorways in flickering candlelight; children played in puddles; and men huddled around foodstalls, eating, smoking.

I was standing by a wall comparing the white number on a blue plate with my slip of paper when, suddenly, a barefoot boy appeared and poked me in the side with a skinny finger. The child motioned with his chin and began to walk briskly and confidently away. I snapped the lighter shut and followed him. What I had thought was a dent in the wall or a pool of shadow was in fact a hole, and in the hole were buckets and basins, and in the soft, prying shadows were a father, a mother, and a baby. I crept through the hole, groping with hands and feet, and all of a sudden I was standing at the door of a small house. When I turned around the boy was gone.

I tapped lightly on the door and it opened a crack.

'I'm the Japanese novelist who . . .' Before I could finish, the door opened wide and a lean middle-aged man confronted me. Whispering *'Bienvenu'* behind a bamboo curtain, he smiled, then politely asked me whether I preferred French or English. I mumbled that English would suit me best. The man clutched my elbow and, whispering 'Welcome, welcome,' led me to an inner room. He appeared to be the host.

The room was plain and several men sat, or stood, drinking tea. They were all painfully thin, their dress not noticeably different from a cyclo driver's, but their high foreheads and glasses suggested they belonged elsewhere than on the street. Introduced by the host, I shook bony hands, both young and old. The host took me to a corner and sat me on a stool made from a stuffed elephant's foot. Pointing at the faces dimly floating in and out of the lamplight, he explained that one was a novelist, another a playwright, and he commented briefly on their work. One wrote Taoist occult stories and was an expert on esoteric nonsense; another wrote heroic novels, modern variations on the *Shui-hu chuan* – *The Water Margin*. Yet another produced romantic novels about young girls rebelling against feudalistic parents and leaving home. The host himself had recently finished a book about a girl searching for a missing lover. She follows his trail across fields and mountains, dodging jets by day and tigers by night, until she discovers that he's in a Viet Cong village. But fate won't let the two lovers reunite. Weeping, she pins a letter to the railing of a bridge and leaves her village.

'It sounds a bit like *Evangeline*, doesn't it?' I said.

'I know. It's a potboiler.'

'Why doesn't the girl just move into his village?' I asked.

'Because I don't want to go to prison,' the host answered, scowling. He added bitterly that everyone present was writing Gothic novels or love stories for a living; they couldn't write about subjects that really interested them because the censorship was so strict.

A young man in a leather jacket came in and shook hands with the host and was then introduced to me. He told me he'd like to talk later and disappeared.

The host watched the leather jacket go and said, 'He's

a critic. . . . He pulled off a big deal the other day,' he added. 'His life, for fifty thousand piastres. He dodged the draft. Not a bad bargain.'

'Is that really true?'

'So the rumor goes.'

'Can you really buy yourself out for fifty thousand?'

'Yes, usually.'

The host spoke casually, pouring tea from a flower-patterned pot. I sat on the elephant's foot and searched the room again for the leather jacket, but he had gone. I felt a bitterness begin to seep in, a bitterness that was close to anger.

A monk in a yellow robe entered. In a whisper, the host told me that their new guest would read an open letter to André Malraux. They couldn't publish this sort of thing in any magazine, he said, but they enjoyed discussing each other's work among themselves. Sooner or later, the letter would be published in pamphlet form – one abridged version and one fake, he explained.

'Do you understand Vietnamese?'

'No. I'm still learning it at the moment.'

'There's a translated version. Would you like to see it?'

'Yes, please.'

The host brought me several sheets of typed text that had been mimeographed. The monk stood by the wall and hunched over the paper he held in his hands. The writers fell silent, slouching, heads tilted to one side. The host carefully stubbed out his cigarette in an ashtray and adopted a humble, attentive pose. The monk began to read in Vietnamese; it sounded like the chirping of a bird. I took off my glasses and scanned the paper in the lamplight.

. . . I thought at first that I ought to address this letter to you in your capacity as minister of state.

I felt I had to choose, you see, whether to write to you as minister or artist. But then what could I say to a public official, short of presenting one of those proposal sheets that relies on quantities of circumstantial detail to state its case? I realized, therefore, it was best that these words of mine be addressed to you as an artist.

In prefaces and postscripts you have stressed in declamatory tones the defeat of mankind, and I must say that the essential theme of your work is being proved correct. And so you have appealed to the West's collective intellect, which must indeed find a solution to this great problem. It is a problem uniquely worthy of the attention of intellectuals, and even if it is not solved, their efforts will remain with us in works of literature.

Dear M. André Malraux: Until the end of the Second World War, all the actualist systems of thought, including those of Confucius, Lao-tsu, and the other great masters of Oriental philosophy, dealt with mankind in the abstract without, normally, embracing a clearly delineated concept of man. Consequently, these systems of thought were bereft of moral contours which could be grasped by our sensibilities and were without the sort of intellectual content that could be perceived by the intellect. We had no choice but to wait for the reemergence of an atheistic, existentialist current of thought in order to place one type of human being in a context of dialogue and debate. This human being is concrete, he really exists, he is tangible, can be understood, and is the direct object of study for his improvement, be it anthropological or, simply, scientific.

As far as we are concerned, all systems of

thought have ended in failure. The philosophers of our country possessed all that is best in human motivation from the point of view of moral intentions. However – and this has been thrown into sharp relief by a number of incidents – their systems have never become definitive, and have now wound up as material for academic inquiry. But until existentialism throws up some conclusions, and until the call for the salvation of man is made audible, I personally will not act as unquestioning advocate of atheistic existentialism based either on purist arguments or those of Sartre. Mankind is now, and will continue to be, confronted with the specter of mass suicide. However creative the imagination or refined the intellect, no one can picture in his mind the vileness and tragedy of it all.

Dear Monsieur Malraux: Maybe I am mistaken in putting it this way, but you have, haven't you, your own system of ideas. What I think is mistaken is that, now as in the past, you are a novelist, but the way you marshal your ideas is constricted. The word 'system' as applied to philosophy, or rather the very power inherent in that word, surely does not deny the clear existence of your message.

I picked up my teacup and drank a mouthful of the cool, strong, bitter tea. At this point, I really couldn't understand what the monk was trying to say. I couldn't understand properly his use of the words 'system' and 'existence'.

. . . Now let me summarize. Man, for you, while seeking his outward identity and inner salvation, is in fact searching for his own self and, in so doing, he gives it concrete expression. Man's search has been carried on even in the midst of archeological expeditions that delve far into the depths of the great forests of the Far East. Now, however, the forests of the Far East are the scene of a bold but dangerous quest for man's spirit. So it is that danger and adventure occur in even the most delicate repositories of man's soul. And man's soul is, after all, one of the tools of knowledge. This can be seen reflected in your early works.

The next stage is that man finds concrete expression for his self in those of his historical machinations that are called revolutions. Garine, Kiyo, and Chen, like Narcissus at the clear water's edge, were searching for their own reflections in revolution, asking questions of themselves in the midst of their actions, with the difference that they had tears in their eyes while Narcissus had a smile on his face. However, man has not been successful on his own account. So I believe. Whether man can, according to the Hegelian system, meet with success in the flux of history, I do not know. Man stands alone, feet planted on the ground, overwhelmed, existing, as he always has, back to back with despair, a truly existentialist despair which cannot shirk the thought of suicide. Garine himself never hinted at this, but Garine's creator, the author of *Les Conquérants*, thought it appropriate to allude to the subject.

The thunder of artillery fire began again. The musical sound of women's voices and the cries of babies could be heard drifting up over the undulating tumult of the vast slum. Despite his rather stiff, wordy, pedantic style, the monk had captured my attention. Even in his confusion he had grasped Malraux's meaning well enough. I could picture him absorbed in his books of sorrow and passion, sitting bolt upright in a mosquito net in some impoverished temple, dry as a piece of old rope, forbidden meat and marriage, self-gratification, sexual intercourse, and drink; a man bound by precepts so strict that he couldn't dig a stick into the ground for fear of killing a worm, but devouring stories about assassination, the collapse of morality, revolutionary war, and people who, vacillating between reflection and resolve, struggle on though almost torn apart by feelings of isolation and hatred.

. . . As many historians of ideas realize, Buddhism is a great therapy. For the world of man is beset by spiritual afflictions. If revolution can be likened to a form of social surgery, and if a careless scalpel, used by some irresponsible leader to perform part of a political maneuver, results in mankind lapsing into a coma, in danger of collective death, then a moralistic, a metaphysical kind of treatment is called for. I am referring to the treatment offered by Buddhism. We Vietnamese have waited with restraint for our turn to proclaim our opinions, as we have done in all the historical conferences of mankind. War – and what a war! – is being waged on our soil. We have given up relying on the strength and capabilities inherent in mankind even when it comes to broadcasting our own grief. Our opinions are not considered worth listening to.

The monk went on reading. Indifference was the accomplice of evil. Malraux should make his voice

heard. Artists had always been fighters for peace and
freedom. Plato was mistaken only in defining the historical role of poets. Maybe, in the writer Malraux,
man's 'last clarion call' lived on. But Minister Malraux
was bound by the interests of his own country.

. . . Could it really be that you do not have the
time to lend your ear to the lonely voice of one
Vietnamese? These are benighted times, so please
forgive my many *faux pas*. And having said that,
I lay down my pen.

The monk finished reading, handed the manuscript
to the writer of Taoist oddities, and pressed his palms
together. The writers crowded around him, chatting
in whispers. The monk, sipping his tea, talked with
them for a while. But soon he quietly got ready, bade
everyone farewell, and left. The threads of his essay
were loosely woven, the rhetoric failed to cover his
confusion, and a lack of any real leavening spoiled
the total effect; but a keen intellect peered through
in parts and his transparent melancholy discharged a
kind of power. He was learned, obviously competent
at examining his own wounds. His free hand and yellow robe floating dimly in the dark room, in a high,
disembodied voice that sometimes rose to a squeak, he
sounded like a child earnestly protesting evil. Looking
at the text again I saw that the monk had only used
the word 'war' three times: the rage and resignation
of a neglected people were all the more dramatic for
his restraint. It was excruciating that a man of his
caliber, of his sensitivity and erudition, could only
state his views in whispers . . . that would eventually
fade into silence. He was caught up to his hips in the
jaws of disaster, yet he could feel, and think, and

understand. But not act. Perhaps understanding in itself implied defeat.

The host reappeared, holding a grubby bottle filled with a thick purple wine that looked like moonshine and tasted just like Japanese saké with a sting to it.

'You weren't bored, were you?'

'Not at all. It was very interesting.'

'Does it surprise you that we've got our own intellectuals, too?'

He glanced at me with a kind but slightly sarcastic smile. He was no fool. I protested, then stopped and, sipping the rice wine, nodded deeply two or three times.

'Eighty percent of the population are peasants,' he said, 'so the problem lies with them, as outsiders are always telling us. And they're absolutely right, as I'd be the first to admit. But it's also true that the leaders and chief opponents of a revolution are all intellectuals. They forget that. This country probably has too many intellectuals. As a percentage of the total population, we've a larger share of them than pre-revolutionary China. I'm not exaggerating.'

'To be honest, I used to think there were only a handful of intellectuals here – until today. I'm convinced. I was amazed that that monk, for example, had read Malraux so thoroughly.'

'We used to get together every Thursday evening, but it's not often nowadays. Next time, we'll be reading a public letter to René Char. After that, one to Henry Miller, Martin Luther King. . . . We've got quite a few things lined up. Sometime soon, when you've the time, perhaps you'd like to tell us about Japanese literature.'

'I'd be glad to. I mean it.'

'I understand there's a psychological novel of the old Japanese court that's comparable to Laclos or Proust. You know, we've a classic of our own that's just as good as the *Chanson de Roland*. . . . It'd be interesting if we could talk about this sort of thing and compare notes.'

'Here, in Saigon.'

'Yes.'

'What have you been reading recently?' I asked.

'I don't read much nowadays. If anything, Camus and Simone Weil. I've had the poems of René Char recommended to me by young friends, but I prefer Camus. Camus and Weil are overwhelmingly popular here with us. Weil is wonderful, a real shining light. There'll never be another woman like her!'

His lined, longshoreman's face broke into a broad smile, and a great sadness rose slowly in his eyes and spread over his scrawny features. And with the chipped teacup at his lips, he murmured 'Weil . . . Weil. . . .' several times, smiling gently, as though it were the name of a pet bird.

'Do you know what a *retour* is?'

'Someone who's come back from France, isn't it?'

'Yes. The radical ones are called *évolués*. I was an *évolué* myself once – about two generations ago, of course. I was with the Viet Minh. I've lived in the U-Minh forest and on the Plain of Reeds. I wasn't always writing cheap novels, you know – it all started after I left the forest.'

The man sipped at his wine and began to reminisce. Those distant days of fire and purpose lit his wine-glazed eyes with sad regret. It was a past much like that of the writer who had given Greene his local color. About twenty years ago, immediately after the Second World War, he had returned from Bordeaux, where he'd been studying, and joined the Viet Minh to fight against the French. His main assignment had been agitprop, writing and handing out leaflets and underground newspapers. During the day he ate and slept with the peasants, worked with them, helped plant the rice and harvest it; and at night he traveled from village to village, creeping through the lines, organizing meetings, lectures, festivities. He hadn't belonged to any political party, but in those days the Communists kept their affiliation so dark a secret that even among friends no one knew who was a party member. Besides, politics and art were kept distinct, so he wrote and fought with equal freedom. And the peasants were helpful. When a village was attacked, he would jump into a tunnel, wiping the lid with an orange to fool the dogs; German shepherds weren't stupid, but an orange would throw them off. What's more, there were decoy tunnels, and if Moroccan troops crept into a nearby tunnel, just a foot away, he could lie there, quite relaxed, listening to their faint voices through the wall.

'When we moved in the jungle, we used to walk in creeks so that our footprints wouldn't show. It's not a good idea to break off twigs all over the place, either. A simple hint like that can attract the enemy's attention. The Delta wasn't too bad because there was plenty of rice and fruit, but the jungle was hard living. My urine turned red once from malnutrition. We ate bamboo shoots and cassava roots.'

'Cassava?'

'It's a carbohydrate. You beat the roots and wash the starch out in water. It tastes terrible, but we made dumplings with it. They're probably still eating it out there.'

The man had given four unstinting years to the revolutionary cause before finally parting company with the Viet Minh. When the revolution in China won through and the Red Army reached the borders of North Vietnam, the local Communists let their colors show and took control of the entire Viet Minh network, from its heart to its fingertips. The national independence movement abruptly turned into a national communist movement; indoctrination and self-criticism – above all, self-criticism – became the order of the day. People were sticking their hands down their own throats and pulling out their guts in their impatience to confess all, to prove their loyalty to party dogma. Intellectuals like himself, however, were now regarded as 'establishment lackeys' and began to desert the Viet Minh in droves, despairing, refusing to be turned into robots, running from a dark forest that they had sworn never to leave until the French had been driven out – back along paths that had once led them into battle, across rice fields and plains, back to the city.

And this man, too, after four years of willing sacrifice and struggle, with little food and sleep, his spirit broken, had finally come down from the highlands, sleeping in woods and paddy fields during the day, and moving by night to avoid the roadblocks set up on highways and in villages by their security police. He had always accepted the need for some sort of redistribution of land after the French were run out; and he had always supported an all-out war of independence, involving the whole nation, in which he too would fight, come what may. But the threat to freedom itself had proved more than he could stomach.

In Saigon, factionalism and corruption had run cracks right through the administration, and the French seemed doomed. The Americans, on the other hand, were arriving in increasing numbers, and Diem's return from abroad was rumored to be imminent. One war was already preparing for another.

In desperation the man had begun to write potboilers

and, with the income from them, smoked opium. The news of the fall of Dien Bien Phu had come to him like a gleam of hope in a smoke-filled den, but when eight hundred thousand people came south, that hope evaporated. When news of the Hundred Flowers campaign reached him, he thought at first that he might have misunderstood the Communists, but it was all over in three months, and the disappearances and mysterious deaths chased out all hope for good. So when he heard not only of the Nghe An uprising but the bloodthirsty reprisals that followed and Ho Chi Minh's tearful apology, he merely listened and, when his informant had left the room, took up his pen and got on with the rubbish he was writing.

Grabbing the neck of the wine bottle, my host poured some more of the purple brew into my teacup. I could see his hand in the lamplight. It was raw-boned, strong; it held the bottle like a metal claw.

'Have you ever smoked opium?' he muttered dully, eyes filled with sorrow and remorse.

'No, not yet.'

'You ought to try it.'

'I will – soon, I hope.'

'There isn't much around any more. There's a good house on Tran Hung Dao. The peasants hoard the stuff; it's their only thing of value and they won't part with it for love or money. It's the first thing they rescue in a fire. But they never smoke it themselves.'

'I'd like to try it once.'

'You won't really appreciate it unless you've had it more than a couple of times.'

'Ah. I see.'

'I tell you, I crave the stuff during the rainy season. I can't help it. I hate that season, feel as if I'm choking.'

The writer's voice was dreamy; he paused to drink.

But he looked strong, not slipping or degenerating. After a while, he stood and quietly left the room. His bearing, however humble and polite, was too virile, too dignified, for a man whose smashed hopes were now pulling him down.

The critic, his leather jacket now slung over one shoulder, appeared in the lamplight. He was young, slender, loose-limbed. A cigarette dangling from a corner of his mouth, he looked thoroughly bored.

'Are you ready to leave?' he asked.

'OK.'

'I'll take you somewhere interesting.'

'To smoke?'

'No. An Indian stripper. You ever seen one?'

'Not yet.'

The host was now talking with the occultist, fingering the bamboo curtain at the entrance. I thanked him for his hospitality and for an interesting time and asked him to get in touch with me again. He saluted me playfully with palms pressed together and said he would let me know when the next meeting was scheduled. A smile had returned to his face and he looked at ease, but the impression of strength was still there; there was a firmness in him that he hadn't lost along the way.

We meandered through a warren of streets for what seemed an age. At the mouth of one dark alley, men were cleaning pigs' intestines in a large metal tub of hot water in the middle of the passage, drawing them through their fists as though wringing silk sashes. Blood, fat and feces – the giddying odor filled the air. The critic guided me into a small adobe house on the riverbank. A middle-aged Indian came out and said something, vanished, and immediately reappeared with a lantern and a phonograph. The phonograph was an old broken-down wooden Victrola with a horn shaped like a morning glory; it would have been hard to find another even in a flea market. The Indian wound it up and put a record on, then readjusted the lantern on the floor.

'It's a museum piece,' I said.

'Bronze Age,' the critic laughed mirthlessly.

The Indian stood and said in English, 'This is Tamil music,' and vanished again.

The wooden box began to hiss. Then came a jumble of sounds, the clamor of markets, empty cans being scraped. Concentrating, I could make out a shrilling of string and wind instruments beneath the surge of other sounds; it sounded like a festival of lonely souls in distant treetops.

'Here she comes,' the critic said, leaning against the mud wall.

An Indian woman entered, dancing, and slowly unwound her silk sari, layer by layer, until she was completely naked, then moved into a coital position. Her ripe breasts, belly and muscular back, anointed probably with olive oil, shone like bronze in the lantern light. Abruptly, she spread her long thighs and, at the bottom of a valley that was quite defoliated, a small animal raised its ruined face and burst into laughter.

The critic whispered in my ear, 'The eyes and fingers.'

I was puzzled.

'Watch her eyes and fingers.'

The woman's fingers moved exquisitely. With every change of posture, they folded and unfurled, sowed and gathered, softly, tranquilly forming a language of fickle shapes, now flowers, now rings of water. How could fingers with bones bend so freely?

Soon, pearls of perspiration began to trickle down her body and an unfamiliar fragrance hovered in the mud-walled room. As I leaned against the wall, cross-legged, staring in the dark, I began to feel that she no longer moved alone but linked, and saw the outline of a naked man, and watched them wrestle, engrossed in each other's flesh. The valley opened and closed, the mound moved in and out. With her huge buttocks facing us, she arched her back and opened her thighs, and light splashed on her rump and radiated on the undulating waist, and the heavy, drooping lips swung like figs. And I suddenly noticed that she was staring at me over her shoulder with deep, ferocious, perfectly almond-shaped Indian eyes.

'Look more?' she asked.

I nodded.

'Give money,' she said solemnly, stretching out her hand.

She snatched the proffered notes and, wetting her fingers on her tongue, she counted them one by one, then put them by the lantern and resumed her act. Her breasts, her belly and shoulders coiled and uncoiled, undulant; the rectum twitched inward like a sea anemone; and the fleshy labia dangled, limp.

The critic suddenly raised his head.

'You can buy this woman.'

'No thanks, I'm all right.'

'You want to go?'

'Yes, why not.'

Hearing our voices, the woman stopped and took the record off, picked her sari off the floor, and quickly wrapped it around her body. Matter-of-factly, like a housewife, she took more money from me and hurried out, leaving a fog of perfume and perspiration behind. The deep bags under her eyes made her look terribly old. The lantern fizzled forlornly on the floor.

'She's a Tamil. Most Indians are moneygrubbers,

but that woman is incredible. The man we met before, he's a Tamil too and just as mean.'

'Are they married?'

'No, not even living together. He fetches her from somewhere for the show. Tamils don't marry, don't drink, don't smoke, don't eat meat, don't even kill mosquitoes. They just save money. They want to go home and be respected.'

'Then they're exceedingly normal.'

'Too much so.'

The men were still squeezing pig intestines when we passed. I followed my companion back through the labyrinth and, reaching a boulevard, found a small noodle shop on the cluttered sidewalk. We sat outside and drank beer. The critic asked me to tell him about Japanese literature, so I began to talk, but he seemed inattentive, letting his quick eyes shift idly to right and left, looking at the trees and pedestrians. He had made the same request on the way to the Indian's house and I had talked while we walked along, but he had responded with halfhearted, unfocused comments. When I got onto postwar literature, he frowned, a cigarette in his mouth, and fixed his attention on a bald dog under the table chewing on a sick-looking chicken's foot. I stopped talking and, swirling the ice around in my glass, drank a little of the watery beer.

After a while, he threw his cigarette away and announced that a German orchestra would be arriving in two days' time. The Goethe Society, which included most of the city's university professors, had arranged a concert of Bavarian folk music under the auspices of the West German embassy. Performances would be given at the City Hall for four days, and tickets would go on sale tomorrow.

'I'm invited on the opening day. They say the

orchestra's pretty good. Would you like to go? If you want a ticket, I'll arrange to have a good seat reserved for you.'

'Thanks.'

'They're from Munich. They use medieval instruments, and the program includes some old folk music as well as modern Bavarian stuff. Saigon's got everything, hasn't it – a real *petit Paris*. Horse races, golf, opium dens, scientific baths, fashion shows, even mass suicide – which is one thing they don't have in Paris, of course.'

'I can't go.'

'Oh, what a shame.'

He sat in his metal chair, aloof, slightly tired, full of arrogant disdain, peering vacantly at the beer glasses, the dog, the hanging carbide lamps. A powerless antagonism moved in me as I sat there, senselessly hating the man. He stuck another cigarette in his mouth and began to tap on the table with his fingers. Softly, in French, he sang 'Save the Last Dance for Me'. . . .

12

There was a small round island in the square facing the market. Four boulevards drained into the square, spitting out and sucking in throngs of people: Ham Nghi, Le Van Duyet, Le Loi and Tran Hung Dao. The square must have been a French legacy, for the French are fond of the radial scheme where arms shoot out in eight directions from a central *rond-point*. Vietnamese streets are a mixture of France and Asia, an octopus sitting on a chessboard, some intersecting in a grille pattern and others radiating from an open hub.

I went out late in the afternoon to follow up a current rumor. Crowds had gathered on the green island like people gawking at a fire, spilling over into the street. Those who couldn't squeeze in had clustered around the bus terminal, the entrance to the market, and the mouths of the four boulevards. An Army truck was parked in front of a railway company building and soldiers were busy piling up sandbags in several layers, forming a wall; the wall was U-shaped and in the open space a stake – an ordinary post of roughly shaved wood – was erected. The crowds were cordoned off, watching from a distance, but the familiar faces of foreign correspondents and cameramen began to collect around the stake. I showed my press pass to the policemen and stepped over the rope.

The press had been there for hours, waiting in the glare of the afternoon sun, sweat forming large wet blotches on their shirts, some sitting on the street, heads down, some standing with humped backs. I walked over, asking questions, answering questions. Various brief comments resulted:

'Some say three, others five.'

'I heard two.'

'Most likely tonight or tomorrow morning.'

'They say it's a college student.'

'I heard it's a twenty-year-old from a private school.'

'He was carrying a mine, apparently.'

'Hand grenades, I heard.'

'He had some documents on him, too.'

'Hang around, we'll know soon enough.'

I squatted at the edge of the sidewalk, watching a scrawny chicken pecking at vegetable scraps. Two Eurasian girls, arm in arm, inched up to me timidly. Their pale, unstockinged feet peeped through the straps of leather sandals. Both were small and slim, and had Asian skin and European eyes. They weren't pretty, but their eyes sparkled with intense curiosity. One of the girls asked me if I was a journalist; when I answered yes, she begged me to let them stay with me or the gendarmes would chase them off.

'Tell them we're your friends,' she said. 'If we get in your way, we'll go.' Her voice was modest, soft and sweet, but she spoke with animation. I said it was all right, I'd warn the cops off. The girls whispered to each other delightedly and huddled beside me.

'How old are you?' I asked.

One murmured, 'I'm eighteen.'

'I'm seventeen,' the other giggled.

'Do you know what's going to happen?'

'Yes,' they answered simultaneously.

'This isn't a place for girls like you.'

'What's wrong with it?'

'What if a ghost comes knocking on your door?'

'We don't care,' said one girl.

'I'll tell him he can't come in,' the other added.

'He thinks he's dying for your sake.'

'It's nothing to do with you,' the taller girl replied, turning to her friend. 'Is it?'

'That's right,' the younger one said, nodding, with shining eyes. She was biting her nails. They were both dazzlingly alive, smiling, flashing their white teeth.

'What school do you go to?'

'Marguerite.'

'Catholic?'

The girls were pointing at some people behind the cordon and whispering, giggling. After a while they ran off, but their faces soon reappeared in the second-floor window of the railway company. They spotted me and waved cheerfully. The wooden post stood just below them. I turned and looked at the crowd, roasting in the cruel sunlight, tired, chewing sugarcane, drinking fruit juice, slurping up noodles, and all the while turned silently toward the stake. A boy was going to die for these people, and all they'd come for was a free show. The girls had wanted a closer vantage point and now were hanging out of the window, looking forward to the grim event, smiling broadly and gaily waving their hands. And countless eyes, twisted with hatred, stabbed at me from somewhere in the crowd or behind some yellow plaster wall nearby; eyes glazed with fury, boring into my shoulders and the back of my head.

On the following morning, I got out of bed at five. I went to the toilet, brushed my teeth, and washed my face. The Cantonese dinner I'd stuffed myself with at the 'Rainbow' restaurant in Cholon the night before, laughing greasily with some fellow journalists, had packed down close to my rear exit, mixed in with talk of international politics and amateur notions of military strategy, gossip about personnel changes, and obscene stories loudly told. I lit the lamp and in the haze of a small mirror found the puffy cheeks of a man bloated with food. I was disgusted and quickly put out the light.

The town before sunrise was dark, quiet and chilly. The river flowed past in silence as I crossed from the riverbank to a nearby street, lamps casting intermittent rings of light. I rolled up the neck of my polo shirt and, passing through the light, I suddenly saw my shadow extend across the street like a long arm, creep up the wall of the house on the other side, and just as suddenly disappear. On garbage boxes and at alley entrances slept refugees like heaps of black rags. A mother held a child, a sister hugged a younger brother, their tangled bodies a defeated, sleeping animal that lay on newspaper on the sodden sidewalk.

The area surrounding the square had been sealed off by Army trucks and paratroopers, heavily armed. Hundreds of people seemed to have passed through and stood like herds of cattle behind white barriers and rifles with fixed bayonets. The morning was still cool and crisp, the pavement not yet festering, and the fish-sauce stench hung low, no higher than one's knees. There were two tanks, one loudspeaker truck, one fire engine and an Army truck. Clots of shadow moved about, muttering with sleepy, shivery voices, now lapsing into silence, now chattering and stamping feet.

I heard whispers in Japanese.

'Incredibly tight security.'

'They could mortar this place, you know.'

'D'you think there's a chance of it?'

'Well, maybe not here, but in a hotel or a restaurant somewhere.'

'We'd better watch it for a few days.'

'Got any cigarettes, Kawa-chan?'

'This is my first execution.'

'Hey, what about a light.'

A white station wagon entered the square. The voices hushed. A young man with his hands tied behind him was tumbled out and dragged into the dazzling flood-lights of the Army truck and tied to the wooden post. A plump clergyman put his hand on the boy's shoulder, whispered something, and walked away. Someone put a strip of black cloth over the boy's eyes. He was pitifully thin, his skinny neck drooping in bewilderment, his mouth pouting. His shirt hung partly out of his dirty trousers and his bare feet were muddy.

A voice shouted.

Ten MPs took aim . . . and a child died. The child's knees gave. Small black holes bored through his chest, his stomach and thighs. From each hole, fresh red blood slowly welled out, and branching rivulets soon soaked his trousers and spilled onto the paving. The boy's head, hanging, swung silently to the right, then left. An offic-er approached and, pulling out a pistol, shot him in the temple. Blood spurted and the body sagged, hanging away from the stake but held by the rope, immobile. His cheeks and neck were drenched with blood. Blood dripped from his nose like a lead sinker at the end of a long light line. Reporters and cameramen clattered toward the dead boy, lights flashing fitfully. In the dirty twilight, a bugle moaned twice and died away. Fellow prisoners carried the boy away and laid him in a coffin lined with a plastic sheet. A coroner examined the body and the lid was fitted over it. Nails were driven home. I heard, for the first time in my life, the 'echoes of a coffin being nailed down'. And the sound went ringing across the square, across that poor corner of Asia.

A great fatigue descended on me. I felt chilled, my

knees shook, and yet my body was soaked with hot sweat. The sweat evaporated almost instantly, but the chill came up a shaft sunk deep inside me. My stomach twitched and nausea stirred. I opened my mouth and gagged in the dark, but nothing came. The firemen began to hose the place down; soldiers threw the stake into the back of a truck; the tanks turned, their heavy bodies rattling on the pavement; and the paratroopers clambered into their trucks and were driven away. With the *cordon sanitaire* now off, the mob broke up into vague shadows that streamed across the square. No one shouted, no one sobbed. Some of the shadows moved fast, making a beeline for their destinations, and some shuffled as though going home from market. My knees shaking at each step, I trudged along a street rank with scraps of food.

When I got back I reeled into bed. My sleep was shallow; there were flashes of light and blood and my limbs twitched uncontrollably. I had blocked out the windows with the blackout curtains, but I felt I was looking at the sun behind eyelids that were almost clear. It was like drifting in bright water somewhere, with no impression of shapes or images or scenery lingering in my mind, only a glittering translucence that enveloped me, the dazzling gossamer of a summer beach.

Was it the floodlights whose glare had not quite dimmed? Or was it shell shock, as if the lid of a shelter had been left open? In sleep, my body jerked, my legs kicked suddenly, and I was soaked with sticky sweat. I clung to my pillow in the pitch dark with my eyes tight shut. The glittering vacuum reappeared and I let myself drift in it, not sinking, not floating up. Again, I felt a sudden jolt and jumped up, eyes wide, then fell back on the bed.

It was nearly twelve when I opened the curtains

and lit a cigarette. The steamy light of tropical noon shimmered on the walls. Threads of smoke rose toward the ceiling, twining. The glare and shock were gone. Exhaustion and a sullied feeling, as though semen had been smeared on my face, had taken hold; and a dull but menacing fear still crouched somewhere, sneering. But something had already changed. I could sit cross-legged and puff calmly on a cigarette, letting my mind drift in a haze of association and reflection, indolent. I had more room now, felt somehow secure, as if protected by strong bulkheads. A savage mob had almost broken through but, barred by the wall, had stamped about outside, then gradually withdrawn and melted away. I realized that being awake was being shut off, and was seized with the idea that a true observer might be someone who could sleep with one eye open.

I went to Yamada's hotel and had lunch with him in the dining room. I ordered a red 'product of Algeria' and a Chateaubriand. The wine was coarse and sour. The table water smelled of disinfectant. Still, I seemed to have no trouble enjoying my meal.

I got going on my steak, ate the French fries, and even bit off part of the stem of watercress, enjoying the way it stung my tongue. When I first drew my knife across the rare meat, fragrant with garlic, a puddle of pale red blood oozed out. I put my fork down and stared at the red liquid spreading over the white plate. The pink cross-section with its blackish crust was exactly like a wound – a wound where flies would swarm, sucking, feasting, fucking on some peasant's body found abandoned in high grass. I speared a piece of meat and chewed it slowly. It was succulent, delicious. There was no physical revulsion. No resistance on the way down.

I seemed to have come through unscathed, and went on slicing the beef in silence.

After lunch, Yamada showed me a piece of paper.

'It seems they're going to have a repeat session tomorrow morning. Same time, same place. This morning's kid was twenty, but tomorrow it's an eighteen-year-old. They're getting younger and younger.'

'Another *kamikaze*?'

'Probably.'

'Part of Cell 67?'

'I don't know. The boy this morning was a student at some private school and was caught carrying two mines and a grenade. He looked as if he'd come straight out of Maquis D.'

'Did I tell you? I was with two Eurasian girls yesterday who were there to watch. They looked *happy*. And some of the crowd just went on eating and drinking. And then look at me! – putting that steak away as if nothing had happened.'

'It was the same in China, you know, years ago. Women and children were the ones who really enjoyed it. I was stationed in central China, and that sort of thing happened all the time. At first it made me sick to my stomach, but I got used to it pretty soon and it became routine. But this morning was the first time in twenty years and it really shook me up.'

'You know, those girls were sweet, like a couple of children, completely innocent. I told them the boy's ghost would come and get them because he was dying for their sake. Do you realize – they actually told me off, said it was none of my business! They had no qualms at all. They were so sweet I couldn't feel shocked. I was close to admiring them for it.'

'It's the same everywhere.'

Yamada lit a cigarillo and, making a face, tipped

up his balloon glass and drank the rest of his red wine.

By the time we left the hotel, siesta had begun; the shops had their shutters down and the tree-lined walks were empty gullies. Young women on bicycles, their long dresses fluttering in the wind, rode out toward the north and east and west. I took my overloaded body and its cargo of wine, meat, bread and watercress to the market. The square was boiling in the sun, deserted, comatose. Behind the sandbags, a girl who sold noodles was sound asleep, leaning against her bamboo basket. The wooden post had been carted away and only the hole remained. Twenty years that boy had lived, and all he'd left behind was a handful of books, perhaps, and brothers and sisters. He'd taken his trousers and shirt with him, but he might have left a candle holder or a lamp, though probably not a bed. A small puddle, colored like diluted wine, glistened near the sidewalk. The water was tinged a smoky rose, and a piece of onion skin floated in it. The chicken I saw the day before was paddling, pecking at the pavement with its chipped beak.

The next morning, I got up at five again.

The homeless mother and child were sleeping huddled behind a garbage box. The square was dark, cordoned off and encircled by paratroopers, tanks, the trucks and fire engine. Everything was the same. And a boy of eighteen walked calmly into the floodlights, was tied to the post, and shot. The only difference was that he cried out defiantly at the end.

His childish voice soared.

'*Da dao de quoc My!*' Down with American imperialism!

And someone echoed his cry.

The rifles roared, the explosion carrying the boy's

voice across the square. He died instantly. His small body sagged and blood gushed like sudden incontinence and spread over the paving. The same officer as before quietly approached and shot him in the side of the head. The journalists began to run, clattering along. The boy was laid in a coffin and firemen began to spray the ground. A bugle sounded low, twice. The cordons were taken down and the soldiers got into their trucks. The tanks turned around and shadows began to cross the square.

And nothing happened. I didn't sweat, didn't shake, didn't feel nauseous. There was no disgust or euphoria. Like a person seeing a movie for the second time, my eyes focused on details, on the background. The boy's shirt was white, his trousers khaki, and when the barefoot prisoners picked his body off the ground, his legs stuck out through his comrades' arms like spindly chicken legs. After seeing it all to the end, I crossed the square and went into a large restaurant that had just opened its doors. The bleak pallor of the fluorescent light gleamed dully on the wet floor. I saw Yamada sitting with a couple of other journalists, his eyes dark and his cheeks as pale as a frog's belly.

'So you were there!' I said.

'Yeah.'

'I didn't know.'

'Sit down.'

Yamada asked the waiter for another glass and poured a Coke for me. I picked up the glass without trembling and took a sip of the medicinal-tasting drink.

Exactly twenty-four hours before, I had sat in exactly the same place, bathed in sweat and shivering with cold nausea. In the space of a day, I had had two meals, drunk a bottle of wine and several shots of vodka, walked in the streets for a while, and read a little. That was all I had done, yet I'd changed completely. Respiration normal. Pulse normal. My eyes could see, my ears could hear. No fluster, no panic. I was as serene as a thicket of waterweed in an old pond. I was a voyeur. Some echoes of excitement or exhaustion, hot or cold, might have lingered on, but I didn't feel any; I just sat there, holding a strange calm like a parcel on my lap. Since no one spoke, I drank my Coke in silence.

When I returned to my room, I ate three pieces of salami, drank some vodka, and got into bed. As I lay in the shrouded room, sleep came without my having to wait for it. The drifting feeling was gone, though a lid must have shifted, for something slipped into a dream. The glitter, too, was gone, but an opaque gleam was visible. I saw a whirlpool of slowly churning slime and in it shapeless objects, tangled and heaving. Things rose sporadically to the surface and sank again, for it had no funnel, but whether they were human figures or animals, tools or buildings, I couldn't tell. Before, I had looked on with my eyes open, but now I watched face down in the ooze, with my eyes closed. I felt two or three shocks, at short intervals, but my legs didn't kick out rigidly, my body didn't jerk; and not once did I wake up. The shocks were like squalls, moaning at the windows and gone. I went on sleeping, moving between semiconsciousness and oblivion, hugging my pillow. In my mouth, sweet spirits and nicotine fermented while I slept.

In the evening, I went to Tran's place to deliver some Chloromycetin. The wounds had stopped suppurating and seemed to have begun to close. Tran could get out of bed and move about. Pale but no longer feverish, he leaned against the wall and read aloud from the crime page of a local paper.

'Do you want stories about the market area again?' he asked.

'Yes.'

'You really like this junk, don't you?'

'There's no propaganda in it, that's why.'

With a cigarette in his left hand and the newspaper pinched between the three fingers that stuck out of his clumsy bandage, Tran read in the even tones of a patient schoolteacher. The night before, for instance, at about nine o'clock, a group of young hoods called the Evening Stars had got into a fight with another teenage gang, and both had thrown homemade hand grenades at each other. Any conflict in this city was liable to end that way – with a grenade, or a match and gasoline, or a machete. A soldier, insulted by a newspaper seller, let fly with a grenade; gamblers quarreled and threw grenades; political bosses had henchmen who threw grenades. Only a few days ago, a soldier who had been pressed to pay off his debts had chucked one into the house of a loan shark, a widow; and the widow and her four children, as well as the soldier, were blown to bits.

I went to the window after a while and stood there sipping lukewarm, bitter tea. The rice fields were already steeped in darkness, and several red spots moved, blinking, eastward in the sky.

'Three more days, Tran.'

'That's right.'

'Have you packed?'

'I haven't got anything to pack.'

'They say the war's getting worse.'

'Yes, I know.'

'I wonder that To-nga will do?'

A cigarette between his lips, Tran raised his eyes and looked at me, smiling cheerlessly.

'She'll be all right.'

'But you won't be here.'

'I'm sure she can take care of herself. She's managed so far. She's much stronger than I am, she really is.'

With admiration and pride, he told me how obstinate she had been as a child and how she had never cried since then. He also told me again about their aunt and how grateful To-nga was to me. I caught a whiff of a familiar smell – the harsh odor of misfortune; and as he relaxed and talked on about her with a brother's affection, the smell grew stronger. He knew everything about To-nga and me, but, until today, he had never said a word; neither had I ever broached the subject. I always felt that my mentioning our affair might insult them both. In that way, I dreaded touching them, dreaded stepping into their lives. And I didn't know what to say, or if there was anything to be said. I could feel my face clouding with an irritable sense of guilt.

On a thin rush mat unfurled on the concrete floor of the garage, I was drinking wine and studying Vietnamese. To-nga sat with her legs crossed on another mat and spread a meal of ham and cheese on a sheet of newspaper. She didn't have a bottle opener, so I wrapped my trousers around the bottom of the bottle and, keeping it level, tapped it against the wall. If you repeat the motion as accurately and slowly as a pendulum, the wine becomes a piston and should slowly push out even a stubborn cork. The sediment at the bottom clouded the cheap wine; it tasted like a cousin of vinegar. I took a swig from the bottle and handed it to To-nga, who drank it a sip at a time, frowning, coughing. I cut the ham and cheese with a knife and offered them to her. She lifted a piece of Camembert to her mouth, opening her eyes wide. I went on drinking.

I remembered an evening like this in Warsaw, at the

small apartment of a couple of young Hebrew scholars. I had sat on a rag rug, cross-legged, drinking wine. It was a Hungarian red wine with a strange name: 'Ox Blood'. Poets, writers, painters and scholars crowded the room, drinking, discussing all sorts of subjects. There was no ideological polio in the air; everyone was relaxed, frank, cheerful. Around midnight, we began to amuse ourselves by reciting the names of streets honoring heroes. 'Boulevard Lenin!' someone would shout, and 'Lenin's ass!' another would promptly add. And so it went on: Stalin, Chopin, Conrad, Apollinaire, Paderewski . . . all had asses.

'To-nga.'

She looked at me questioningly.

'Two children murdered.'

'So I heard.'

'I saw.'

'This morning?'

'This morning and yesterday morning.'

'Was it frightening?'

I didn't answer. To-nga was thoughtful for a while, then murmured: 'A lot of people are dying.'

Hands on her crossed legs, her head tilted slightly to one side, she possessed an extraordinary serenity, an equanimity shared, perhaps, by people who had to expect death at any time, even in bed.

Sipping wine, I sketched all sorts of pictures in a notebook and showed them to To-nga, and she wrote words under each of them and taught me their pronunciation. As I struggled with them, one word at a time, mouthing and gesticulating in a light so murky that we could barely see each other's eyes, I began to feel as if I were kneading clay. It was the task I had of condensing shadow, crushing, pressing, squeezing it into words. The words grew like clumps of mushrooms inside me, around me, in odd corners of this cave with its mosquito net and earthen jar.

To-nga pointed. 'That's a bat, isn't it? . . . This is a basket. They sell these on Nguyen Hue. . . . Fruit bats. . . . They suck the juice out of fruit. . . . Some people say they suck human blood. . . . You feel tired after a nap, don't you? That's because of the bats. . . . Owls are bad, too.'

To-nga went on talking and, soon tipsy, pushed the notebook away and softly began to sing, snorted, shoulders quivering, and sang as rapturously as when we danced in the dark of 'Plaisir'.

There was a sadness in the melody that seeped out like water from the minor key and bred like colonies of fungus on every wall of this widowed capital. And grieving drifted and coiled around everything, to merge with the screak of lizards and the roar of artillery, and float over pavement and promenade, morning and night. Elegies echoed in the sky, moaned in the gutter, sobbed behind garbage pails. Sorrow and passion rose hand in hand from the center of the earth, from the muddy banks of yellow rivers, and from the thatched huts' earthen floors that feet had stamped coal-hard.

I remembered the banyan trees I saw at Angkor Thom; trees with octopuses' arms. Immense stone palaces had been devoured. The trees had multiplied and intertwined and fused, and formed a vast jungle of a single tree. The roots crept over stone and into it, wrestling, wriggling into every crevice and corner, fumbling, swelling, crushing the corridors and breaking gates loose, picking up stone pillars and hurling them sky-high. Local heroes, phallic symbols, a leper's god, and features melting in old stone were ravished, overrun, and torn apart by that ravenous tree until all form disintegrated. And Saigon, too, would be transformed some day. Perhaps the sorrow and passion of this country were themselves a tree that fastened onto rock without a speck of nourishing soil or water on it. Perhaps Asian revolution was a banyan tree that tamed the men who sought to tame it, wore them out in endless conflict with a greedy incubus and left them wishing they were stone themselves. A tree that even then fed on its victims and sent out tentacles to snare and suck in more . . . and kill . . . and crush their backbones, shrivel their livers in the sun. Overwhelm. Prevail!

The garage was warm, dark and solid. To-nga was warm, dark and fruit-sweet. I was full of alcohol, sour and sweaty. I felt a dull desire stirring in fumes of wine, felt safe but frightened, and this induced an aimless, brutish mood. I thought I'd shaken off that other self, but it still clung and sapped my strength. I rolled around her on the bare, gritty, concrete floor, licking her forehead, eyebrows, eyes and cheeks, and then her lips, her chin, her breasts and navel, and in the nest below I licked the open fruit.

'I wish I had a new handkerchief,' said To-nga serenely.

And after a while, 'I wish I had two.'

13

The NCO in the guardhouse put the phone down, raised his head, and handed me my press card, saying that only Yamada and I would be admitted, and that before entering the barracks we'd need the company commander's authorization. I pointed at To-nga and asked him to let her in since it was her brother who'd been inducted that morning, and we'd make sure she left as soon as she had seen him. But the NCO had already begun a game of cards with his subordinates and ignored us.

'Wait here,' I told To-nga.

'Don't worry.'

'I come back soon.'

'I'm OK. I'll be over there.'

To-nga nodded, raised the collar of her *ao dai*, and walked away toward some stalls selling noodles and coconuts. Standing or crouching by the stalls, gazing at the barracks, were clots of humble-looking people – mothers, sisters, fathers. The entrances to hospitals, cemeteries and army barracks always seem to spawn a crowd. One old woman squatted by the fence and, tucking up the hem of her outsize skirt, revealed a wizened rump that suddenly splashed urine.

Yamada glanced sideways at the crowd and said:

'God, that brings back memories. I was drafted into the Kurume Division. My parents packed a lacquered lunch box with sweet bean-paste cakes and red-bean rice and came to see me off. You know, the MPs guarding the gates wouldn't let anyone else in, so my parents just stood there, looking at me. They told me to walk straight ahead. If I turned around, the NCOs would lay into me, they said. So I walked away, shoulders back.'

'That must've been pretty rough.'

'I know. But Army boots are only made to march forward. So I just kept on straight ahead, and before I knew what was going on I was packed into a troopship. And when I realized where I was, I was already in Hankow, and I kept going all the way to Chungking. The Imperial Army did nothing but march, you know. The next time I stopped to look around, I was back in Japan, defeated.'

Yamada sucked at his cigar stub in the flame of a Zippo, and as he walked along he told me stories of the battlefields of China twenty years ago.

Machine guns in a training ground nearby suddenly let rip, clattering frantically like old sewing machines, clawing at the tropical morning, bouncing between the yellow plaster walls of the barracks. We walked from barrack to barrack looking for information about where the new draftees were quartered. A young officer, alert, clean-shaven and polite, told us that the recruits were being X-rayed and showed us where the infirmary was.

The night before, we'd had dinner at the 'Rainbow' restaurant in Cholon; there were any number of Chinese restaurants to choose from, but only one served a particular bean-curd dish. Yamada had heard a rumor about another 'coupette' and had gone off to hunt up some information. Tran, To-nga and I sat around the table and drank beer, cracked pumpkin seeds, and picked at steamed river crabs. A little color finally rose to Tran's cheeks. Around us were American officers in varying states of gloom and animation, each with his little woman, head held high, laughing and shouting in brand-new English. 'Damnit!' and 'Take-leezy!' one heard them saying. On the wall, Melina Mercouri was singing 'Never on Sunday'.

Tran kept his right hand under the table and, with his chopsticks in his left, made awkward progress until To-nga had a waiter bring him a spoon; and while she pecked at her own food, she kept darting keen but unobtrusive glances at her brother, and seemed relieved to find him outwardly relaxed and enjoying his meal. Tran talked about the mandarin intellectuals in Vietnam's distant past and how they shut themselves away and wrote poems and read all day. On clear, moonlit nights in Hue they boated on the Perfume River, and entertainers sang and played for them. A taste for opium in moderate quantities was considered elegant, and cockfights were tolerated with a sort of scornful amusement. Going into the kitchen and meddling with the cooking was out of the question, utterly taboo, and this attitude had survived among contemporary college students. It was considered correct at table to behave as though the chopsticks were too heavy, too awkward, to handle, and so one held the long ivory sticks at the very top and daintily manipulated them.

'It sounds pretty much like old Japan,' I said. 'Confucius's influence. It was his idea to ban intellectuals from the kitchen. The only difference is that, though ours also read and wrote poems, they handled their chopsticks with as much finesse as cyclo drivers.'

'There was *harakiri*, too, wasn't there?'

'Yes, lots of it. Samurais were studying how to die as soon as they were old enough to read. Weighed on the scale of loyalty to one's lord, one's life was about as light as a feather.'

Tran drank his beer slowly, munched the crab meat

with a chilly weariness, and stared around at the diners near our table. There was still a certain casual strength in him that showed in his forehead and fingers, but his usual sharpness had broken up like a stranded ship; he made me think of the monk and the writer I had met the other day. The loose and confident set of his shoulders was assumed. A donkey. Buridan's ass, as in the allegory, a Frenchman would have said: hungry and thirsty, torn between a hay box and a water trough, and dying in the middle of the yard before making up its mind. No, Tran wasn't vacillating, though. He was cowering, caught 'between the devil and the deep blue sea', and the choice had been abandoned. They were alike, the monk, that writer, and Tran – all moving in the center of a whirlpool and still outsiders. And I stood well back, safely outside.

'I would have liked to have seen Tokyo,' said Tran.

'Really?'

'I've never been anywhere. I wanted to travel just once. Anyway, tell me something about it. You never talk about Tokyo.'

'It's a big city.'

'And?'

'It's full of people, cars and houses.'

'I know that.'

'People blow hot and cold. They snap up new fads, new gadgets, but get tired of them in three months. Everything has a three-month deadline. They're unreliable.'

'And?'

'They talk about themselves from morning to night.'

'What else?'

'They're clever and cold-blooded.'

'And?'

'That's all.'

Tran smiled wryly and slouched over his soup bowl. I leaned an elbow on the table and lit a bitter-tasting Bastos. Abundant and poor, grand and ugly, frivolous and energetic, Tokyo was two thousand five hundred miles away. It was a tiring and relentless city. It was the only capital in Asia where none of the many protests and demonstrations of the last twenty years had ever resulted in martial law. Its crises never developed into an armed silence after 11 P.M., either in the streets or in the minds of its inhabitants. Set against the standards of Saigon, where curfew had become a ritual as familiar as breathing, it was questionable whether Tokyo was really part of Asia at all. Tokyo was a stranger to barriers and bans. Time there was amorphous, as finely ground as graphite, with no real boundary between day and night. Again, if it was Asian to have the twin choice of government and anti-government, Tokyo, offering a third, a fourth, a fifth and limitless other choices, was only arguably Asian. But Tran would probably have found all this offensive at the time.

We worked our way through crab, pork, chicken, vegetables and soup, sometimes putting our chopsticks down to wipe away the sweat, then starting in again. Our eyes glazed over and our cheeks shone. Leaving the table much heavier, we decided to take a stroll by the dark My Tho River.

'I'm going to see you off tomorrow,' I said when we parted.

'No, don't,' he replied.

'It's a Japanese custom.'

'How sentimental!' Tran spat out the words. Then, muttering something to To-nga, he turned on his heel and walked away along a wall in which urine had worn green holes.

*

Back at the camp, Yamada asked, 'Is that him?'

'Looks like it.'

There was a barrack painted gray-green and beside it stood a cluster of shirtless young men. A card hung from each youth's neck and everyone was waiting to be summoned, aimless, slouching. Some wore sandals, others rubber slippers. They looked like the motley haul one might get if one threw a net over a crowd at any nearby market. From time to time, a doctor would stand at the entrance and call out a name, and a boy would disappear into the building, leaving the rest gazing at the ground, heads hanging on their chests. At the tail of this melancholy herd stood Tran, half naked, glowering at us as we approached.

'What did you come here for?' he demanded reproachfully, narrowing his eyes.

Yamada searched in his pocket and took out a little charm, the sort of thing that Tokyo girls use to decorate their wallets with. It was a little frog man sitting on top of a small plastic ball, and inside the ball was a die that moved around. It must have cost about twenty cents. When I left Tokyo, my newspaper gave me a bagful of them, as well as some Chloromycetin and malaria pills.

The charms had caused a memorable episode. It was during the siesta on a highway patrol. Quite casually, I distributed some of the little balls among the soldiers. And from the commander, Captain Tong, down to the trooper who carried our lunch, they all began to cheer, some standing on their heads, some clapping, all fascinated by the sight of the moving die, roaring with laughter and then gaping again in amazement. They were too neglected, too deprived, had never been given anything in this exhausting war save that vast, arid plain. And so they were excited and went on laughing, heads back, looking at the sky. I was dumbfounded.

Yamada shook the charm in front of Tran's eyes and shyly, seriously, explained it to him.

'It's a good luck charm, a mascot. Anything will do. When I went to fight in China, I took one along myself. If you don't want it, give it to someone else.'

An emotion passed across Tran's eyes.

Yamada stepped back a little and bowed deeply. 'Thank you for working so hard, Tran.'

I took out the red Chinese scroll that I'd peeled off the wall of my room that morning and translated it for Tran, who couldn't read Chinese. 'The Official from Heaven brings happiness.'

Anger faded from his eyes. Troubled, flustered, he had lost the inner clarity and ambiguity of that afternoon when he'd murmured something about a mosquito getting squashed between two buffalo; and it was a poor, skinny youth with narrow shoulders and hips who stood there, lost for words.

'This is lucky, too,' I said.

Tran cast his eyes downward. His hands, still holding the red paper, hung limp; he hadn't thought of putting his presents in his pocket. He licked his lips and gasped. His pale, flat belly convulsed lightly and the navel moved in and out. He began to murmur: I misunderstood you people . . . I thought you were just having fun . . . foreign journalists are like that. They pretend to sympathize, but they're all here for the thrill of it. . . . I know you gave me some medicine that helped get rid of my fever, and you talked with me a lot. But I thought the medicine was because you didn't want to see anything that might upset you. No one really seriously sympathizes with us, because if they did they couldn't bear this country for another day. But you people were . . .

The doctor appeared at the door and called a name.

Tran took a deep breath and whispered, 'My turn.'

I grabbed his arm and hissed, 'Run away, Tran!'

He nodded, like a marionette with broken threads.

'Write to me.'

'I will,' he said.

'It's a waste, this war . . . people killing and dying for nothing. When it gets too close, chuck your gun away and run for it.'

'Tran,' said Yamada suddenly in a low voice. 'Say cheese!'

Whether he heard him or not, Tran didn't smile, didn't turn; his cheeks pale and taut, he slipped out of my grip and disappeared into the dark building where an X-ray machine purred. The doctor, with slick, neat hair and an unctuous face of polished stone, turned sideways to let him pass and, glancing at me with weary fish-eyes, went inside.

Yamada and I walked away toward the sound of gunfire. In the training ground was a machine gun fixed on a wooden rack, and under its long trajectory was a swarm of crawling soldiers, dragging their rifles along.

'They're not blanks, they're real,' Yamada muttered. 'Christ, what a waste.'

The muzzle of the machine gun flashed nonstop, and the cartridges spattered like firecrackers. The schoolboy soldiers zigzagged, lugging rifles with one hand and helmets with the other, hauling themselves forward with their elbows. And when they reached the safety of their goal, they rolled over, panting, faces mud-smudged.

'Yamada, what was your lucky charm?'

'The hair from a woman's you-know-what.'

'Oh. The usual stuff?'

'Well, it's better if it's a professional's, and not plucked by her but someone else . . . that's what they used to say. It was pubic hair that protected us soldiers of the Emperor as we marched through China. Everyone had some.'

'I've got a bit, too.'

'Your wife's?'

'Not exactly.'

'It doesn't work if it's your wife's.'

'I've even got a shirt stitched by a thousand women.'

'You really are old-fashioned, aren't you? – despite appearances.'

'The stitching's in the shape of a hard-on.'

'That's good,' Yamada nodded seriously. 'That sort of thing really works.'

'Are you sure?'

'Absolutely. It's guaranteed to.'

The soldier loaded the machine gun with a new cartridge belt. An officer brandished his baton and the gun began to rattle again. One by one, as though diving underwater, the men plunged under the stream of bullets and, faces inches from the ground, began to crawl. We could see them trembling, lips dry, eyes shining, as they crept to left and right like ants. It may have been a mistake to give Tran a lucky charm. It was wrong to comfort him; I should have encouraged hate instead, even if he had no focus for it. Fear is useful out-of-doors since it makes one watchful, but pity is like leprosy, it softens people, rots them. When Tran turned to look behind him, he'd die.

The swelling sun approached the meridian.

14

I had a routine. I'd brush my teeth in the morning,
then go to a café, bouncing along in a cyclo. I sat in
the third seat from the right beside the picture window that faced the boulevard. I read the newspaper
while I ate, dipping a croissant in café au lait. Unlike
Parisian croissants, these were heavy, sweet and sticky.
I watched the pedestrians through the glinting window,
reread the newspaper, smoked, and in no time it was
noon. I left the café and went to Yamada's hotel to
have lunch with him. Sometimes I ate at 'Don Kan'
in Cholon: steamed dumplings. Then it was back to
my room for a three-hour nap. When I woke up, I
brushed my teeth again and bounced all the way back to
the café. If I was at 'Brouillard' in the morning, I went to
'Jeunesse' in the afternoon; and if it was 'Jeunesse' in the
morning, then I turned up at 'Brouillard' later. I drank
Pernod before dinner. At five-thirty, the news briefing
wound up and reporters appeared in one or the other of
the two cafés for drinks. After a while, I left for dinner
with some of the Japanese correspondents. Dinner over,
I accompanied one of them back to his hotel or lodgings
to play poker, flower cards or mahjong. After that I
went to 'Plaisir' and danced with To-nga. We slept in
the garage, and in the morning she went to Mass. I
took her as far as the church door and returned to my
place.

Over the past few weeks, scores of reporters had
arrived in Saigon from every corner of the world and the

two cafés had turned into conference rooms where end-less talks proceeded without a chairman; but the mood was also of a busy railway station with its steady under-tow of murmuring voices. American, French, English, Japanese, German, Korean, Thai and Filipino: the new-comers listened, rapt, when bored and blasé veter-ans held forth, then gnashed their teeth and headed out through the door, hurrying toward paddy fields, mountains and jungles. Nine out of ten returned silent, deeply tanned, eyes shining; some of them disappeared unnoticed. And it made me feel I'd turned into a fish as I sat there smoking by the window, thinking of their faces and voices and names. Fish rub against each other as they drift down creeks, and sense when one of their number leaps up after food and leaves the group; and it never seems to bother them if he doesn't return. Anyone who has cast a fly into a school of feeding fish will know this nonchalance, this cool indifference to departing friends.

The café was air-conditioned, Parisian in style, with a rich fragrance of espresso coffee, and yellow, black and red plastic panels that glittered in the sun; and here the correspondents tablehopped, appending chapters of their own experiences to Giap's book on the 'people's war'. No outsider could hope to understand this war or have it well conveyed to him. Yet all these journalists used to fret that the odor of a red clay trench at night was hopelessly, irretrievably fading in the chilled air and coffee fumes; and, eyes glinting, in hushed tones, they'd rummage in their little bags of words and strain to give some tangible meaning to their experiences, though they knew it couldn't be done. And in the end, invari-ably, they'd draw a snap conclusion; and when the ver-dict was out, their look said somehow they'd betrayed themselves, lost face; but they couldn't resist the urge.

Some said that guerrilla warfare was a form of judo, where a big man's strength is turned against him by a smaller opponent. Vietnam was variously a struggle between haves and have-nots; a battle between human beings and machinery; a war between yellow and white, with help from yellow and black. Some said it was night wrestling day, and others a contest between an elephant and a mouse. It was called a conflict between primitive force and atomic power, and a struggle between men seeking change and others clinging to the status quo. Some saw it as a war between virtue and evil; others as a crusade against crusades; and some, a boxing match, with one side using the Queensberry Rules and no low blows, and the other fighting Thai-style, where almost anything went. (When this particular view was launched, one of the guys snickered and shrugged and said, 'Go fuck yourself.') All these people read daily statements from Moscow, Peking, Hanoi, Washington, Paris, Seoul, Tokyo and the jungle; all of them felt they must approve or deprecate; and each new day they started from scratch, pushed sheepishly through the glass door, smiled at each other wryly as they took their seats, and mechanically began to stir the same pot of topics; and another gray stew resulted, the same tasteless, odorless muck as the day before.

I nibbled time the way termites gnawed at wood. The difference was that they worked, demolishing a house to build their own, while I just sipped Pernod, subsiding slowly in my chair. Words dropped out of people's mouths like legless ants that wriggled and twitched and soon curled up. Inside me was an empty warehouse full of faded words collecting dust. A lion was an indefinable, feral source of fear before it was called 'lion'; once labeled, though no less fierce or frightening, it shrank, became another quadruped and little more. When people defined war as 'a struggle between haves and have-nots' or said 'Go fuck yourself!' the war stopped, wounded, in its tracks, in full view for a moment; but new heads formed from gaping wounds, and it snaked out through the window, spread and sprawled across the fields and mountains, and not a trace of blood or a whiff of death remained behind.

Yasuda, of UPI, who had taken himself off for several days to inspect some refugee camps, reappeared in 'Jeunesse' with a new suntan, his black eyes more unforgivingly solemn than ever.

'You know,' he said, drinking beer, 'pretty soon the refugees are going to break America's back – if nothing else does. All they have to do is beat the ground with empty cans, moaning "I'm hungry, I'm hungry, *troi-oi, troi-oi*," and Uncle Sam bends down and they all swarm aboard. They may still starve to death, but they'll bring down America with them. Do you realize, those refugees are fed California rice! Just imagine, peasants in Southeast Asia's leading rice-producing country eating California rice! Can you believe it? When I saw that, I thought *they've won!* A million, two million, three million refugees are coming out and they're all leaning on America, half starved. How in the hell is the US going to take the strain? The North may lose the people's trust and just run dry, but who knows? – it could all be part of a plan – to keep sending them down here until the government cracks under the strain!'

I sipped my Pernod in silence. What he'd said wasn't all that sinister, but the tone was dark, infected with despair. His anger was slightly stale. Three months earlier, when he arrived, he had been determined to shake off the aura of Tokyo and suffer the war, and had written article after article in his own caustic style.

But he'd overloaded, like a man who'd eaten himself to a standstill. And the horrors had blurred, as they did for everyone.

'Anything happen while I was away?' he asked.

'The black market rate shot up ten Ps.'

'That all?'

'Another Turkish bath opened.'

'That's encouraging.'

'It's called a scientific bath.'

'What's scientific about it?'

'They clean you with alcohol after blowing you.'

'Must be painful.'

'I suppose so.'

Yasuda narrowed his eyes and, sipping beer, seemed sunk in thought. A blunt energy rose from his square chest and shoulders. There was an odor of nakedness about him, of the outdoors, of sunshine, of smoldering earth and the faint echo of wailing peasants. I used to feel bullied, threatened, by that smell whenever I was near it; and it brought out a keen irritation in me. I dreaded it, but also – secretly and passionately – I envied it, and used to bitch about my life, at night, alone. I had a growing presentiment of death, which heightened my awareness of life; and when obsession with myself reached bursting point, I leaped out of bed, put on my shoes, and somehow hoped they'd let me step outside myself, lead me beyond myself.

And so I'd chased the rain clouds, moving through the wilderness at night, damp with chilly sweat. Havoc and crisis filtered through into the mud inside me, stinging and spreading. My senses lay open to the corpses that I found in meadows in the resonant dusk, and I devoured the physical world.

But I had changed. The only aura Yasuda now had was of someone just back from a grueling weekend trip.

And in the morning, he'd slough it off and I'd return to my comfortable routine – show up at the same café and sit at the same table by the same window; read my newspaper, eat a croissant, and think about those hungry peasants with only a dim awareness of their misery.

Was I in Saigon?

Or in a café in Tokyo?

Yasuda wiped his mouth with his hand and grinned greasily.

'Gia Dinh tonight,' he said.

'A 105?'

'No, a 155. More kick to it.'

'Another grandmother?'

'Yeah, in her fifties.'

'I don't understand it.'

'How could you?'

'I honestly don't.'

'A fifty-year-old's is flat, all wrinkled up. All they do is piss, so it's rusty, sour and salty. You keep your eyes closed and just concentrate on teasing it into life, and soon the house starts shaking and you've an earthquake on your hands. That's what makes it so good, you really feel you're achieving something. You've never seen an old woman sob with pleasure, have you? It's a terrific, chilling feeling.'

'Something like rape?'

'No comparison. Entirely different. I give an old woman confidence in life. She realizes she's still female – it renews her will to live. And I get the pleasure of rummaging through her fifty-odd years like a box of toys. It doesn't take much to make a younger woman cry, does it? And what's so great about making her come? What's there to crow about? There's no challenge. But this, if you like, is a matter of self-respect.'

'My God, what an intellectual!'

Screwing up his savage, smoldering eyes, Yasuda suddenly grinned like a Cheshire cat, gulped down his beer, and, leaving a sharp whiff of body odor in his wake, made his way out. He exaggerated, but he didn't lie. Journalists who'd been out looking for women with him had been stunned, even appalled, to see him only pick up prostitutes old enough to be his mother. Tonight, stirred up by the chaos he had seen at the front, he'd probably pursue his goal with added zest, and in a thatched hovel somewhere, under the bloodshot gaze of an attendant pig, he'd tease some hag into tears of joy; and in the light of a lamp hung on a bamboo support, those small red eyes would peer at them at eye level, like a predator with fangs and claws. A pig's sperm is pungent, murky yellow, squirted from tumid hips.

When was it that I met the old man?

One morning, at about ten o'clock, I went to change some money at Krishnan's store and was browsing among the shelves, looking for new titles, when I bumped into an elderly American. He was short and bald as an egg, but everything else about him – his neck, his bottom and his chest – was massive, built like a stevedore. A grubby shirttail hung out of his wrinkled khaki shorts and his obvious poverty and unwashed smell suggested a hitchhiking past. It was some time since I'd come across this particular combination, and I felt friendly. Sweat has colors. White sweat is clammy; black sweat smells of cheap cigars; yellow sweat is harsh and salty.

The old man gazed into my eyes with a friendly smile.

'Are you Japanese?'

'Yes, I am.'

'Ah. It's a pleasure to meet somebody from Japan.'

He smiled again and slowly raised his hand, as though hoisting some heavy metal tool off the floor. I rubbed my hand on my trousers before shaking his. Earnestly, he asked me about the war situation. I told him what I had heard from Yamada over dinner, though the information had gone stale overnight. The old man cocked and nodded his large head, with its coconut shell of hard, thick skull, and, after keeping it lowered for a few moments in silence, he spoke.

'I'm a Quaker, and I feel ashamed. I volunteered to serve as a civilian at the military hospital in Quang Ngai. I saw atrocities there every day, absolutely abominable cruelty. Do you know what I mean?'

'Yes. Not in Quang Ngai, but in a lot of other places. I've seen a fair bit of it.'

'What do you think?'

'It's the same everywhere.'

The man glanced at me, then looked away, grimacing. Bushy brown eyebrows scowled, and I could see obscure emotions struggling in the light blue eyes half-hidden underneath.

He spoke again. 'I've heard it said that the victims of a guerrilla war are outcasts in terms of international law. That there's nothing the authorities can do when nameless women and children die. That our laws are miles behind events and scholars don't know what to do. . . . You know, that's the sort of thing I heard when I was in the States. I read a lot about this war and listened hard, but I didn't know it could be this cruel. It's just hypocritical to talk about international law in the face of the cruelty we've seen. Our guys are doing shameful things; but they don't see it like that. That's what I'm most ashamed of. We're Christians, but we've forgotten what it means to be Christian. That's cause for shame. People back home just get on with their daily lives; taxes go up, the cost of living rises. And they're only serious when they get a draft card. Nothing worries them that doesn't concern them directly. It's the times; it's a vicious age.'

The old man slouched in distress, head bent, skin tremulous, arms hanging limp like a caveman. His voice was low and bitter.

'It's simple arithmetic,' he continued. 'Everybody knows the Americans should withdraw. The phony government here would collapse in a week. And the war would end. It wouldn't even take a week, maybe three or four days, that's all. Whatever the Communists do after that, I can't imagine it could be worse than this. Quang Ngai is an inferno. It's hell on earth.'

He managed to keep his voice under control, but the words quivered and broke like thin glass in the quiet shop. His body seemed to fill the place, overshadowing the bookshelves like a primeval tree, and his passionate gloom lurched towards the books, the ceiling. The old man's convictions would never rust, never cloud over. They were as simple, old and ponderous as a mountain.

Krishnan, contemplating, cheeks resting in cupped hands behind a tower of paperbacks on a wire rack, suddenly raised his head and looked at me solemnly with his deep, dark, Indian eyes. He was glowering at me.

I whispered in the old man's hairy ear. 'Let's go outside, it's safer there.' I clasped his elbow and pushed the glass door open. The deep, cool shade of a tamarind tree fell across my forehead. We walked toward the riverbank. The street was solid, taut, and not yet fetid with hot decay. The old man was a resident of New York City. He had attended meetings and lectures, had devoured newspapers and books, and watched television documentaries. Finally, unable to endure it any longer, he had volunteered his services. He had arrived in Saigon a day ago to get medical supplies, and was flying back to Quang Ngai on the following morning. A mound of moving flesh covered with coarse brown body hair, slightly humpbacked, swinging loose arms slowly by his sides, he looked exactly like a strolling caveman without a club; and he gazed around him, praising or disapproving all the time. He had praise for the young girls in their *ao dai*, praise for a girl noodle-seller, but he disapproved of the boys pestering GIs for money, and a man selling pornographic pictures from Japan.

On the quay, only a couple of barefoot children were fishing in the yellow water, glinting muddily in the morning sun. The old man and I sat on the bank and talked, dangling our legs over the water. I had expected questions and was ready to supply information, and I sifted through the long chronology of my memory and dug out the names of people and places, flushed assorted statistics from the mounds of rubbish in my mind. But the old man cut through it all with one simple statement.

'In 1945,' he said quietly, 'Ho Chi Minh declared independence and established a provisional government immediately after the defeat of the Japanese Army. Bao Dai became an ordinary citizen and served the government as an advisor. And it was France that was guilty of splitting the government in two. Look, it's simple arithmetic. Take out France and there would've been no first Indochina War, no Dien Bien Phu, no Geneva Accords. America came in and took over from the French. Take out America. No government in South Vietnam, no war. It's as simple as that.'

He gave me a slightly malicious smile and, swinging his legs, glanced at a small boat gliding gently downriver, loaded with earthen jars. The old man's homely, furrowed face was thoughtful and determined. Blinking sadly under the brown tufts, he said:

'A report from the CIA says that seventy-five percent of the people here would vote for Ho Chi Minh if they had a free election. The CIA says that!'

'Ike said eighty.'

'When?'

'Immediately after the Geneva Accords.'

The old man pulled a memo pad out of his pocket and, licking a stubby pencil, scribbled the figure in it.

'The more things change, the more they're the same, right? After ten years of war and lousy dictatorship, only five percent down. I know that kind of figure can be taken in various ways. But it sure is number ten!'

'Listen,' I said, 'there's a military attaché at the Korean embassy who I go to quite often for information. He's a touch anti-Communist, but according to him, thirty percent of the total population is Viet Cong, forty percent is sympathetic to the VC in varying degrees, and the rest are against them. In other words, in all Vietnam, seventy percent is VC. I don't think the CIA and Ike can be far off, either. According to the attaché, Ho could slip into Saigon today if he wanted to, in broad daylight.'

'My God!' he exclaimed softly and wrote again in his memo pad.

I remembered one particular afternoon with Colonel Kim. We were having our usual conversation, and he was standing in front of an enormous strategic map; and suddenly he pulled a pen from my breast pocket and, without saying a word, wrote down the Japanese characters for 'the will of Heaven'. But when units of the Korean Army were sent to Vietnam, he drew back into his shell and wanted only to talk about wine and fruit.

'It's simple arithmetic,' the old man persisted. 'Ho is indestructible. Take out Bao Dai, Ho stays. Take out Diem, Ho stays. Take out Madame Nhu, Ho stays. Take out General de Lattre de Tassigny, Ho stays. This is Ho's country. We're being punished for our ignorance and hypocrisy. We were overconfident, deluding ourselves, pursuing an ideal but blind to the truth. We're murdering women and children in a country where the wheel has just been invented and we're killing ourselves in the process. It's a question of ethics. This war is fatal to America's moral fiber. Everyone says it can't be won, yet we say we can't afford to lose it. We haven't the courage it would take to lose. It takes tremendous guts to throw your guns down, to admit defeat. The Romans killed Christ, and Christianity survived their civilization.'

He was a tireless scourge, pressing his points in a low but urgent voice. Under his bushy eyebrows, the pale blue eyes cringed like a trapped animal's. He reminded me of an ascetic flogging himself, driving nails into his own flesh. Watching his quivering lips searching for words, there were times when I was afraid he would burst into tears, though the underlying strength never wavered. It was totally foreign to see such self-torment and remorse. A mournful figure, hunched over the yellow water, he embodied conflict: conflict between innocence and desolation, between the unprotected and the armored, between torn flesh and brute strength. I thought of Wain, of the way he smelled when he said things like, 'Make those Commies bleed!' Wain was like a flood that swept everything before it, hiding all trace of the futile labor and stupidity it had overrun. Yet, spiritually, they were brothers. Their goals lay in opposite directions – one said, smash them; the other, withdraw – but the spirit that moved them was the same. Whether the foe was a 'Commie' or the crime of war itself, they both responded to the same impulse.

Ahab wandered the oceans in search of a white whale. 'The Boss' backtracked for thirteen centuries to appear at King Arthur's court; Henderson the Rain King progressed through Africa saying, 'I want, I want'; Wain flew ten thousand miles to fight; and this old man had journeyed just as far to do penance. They were all descendants of Captain Ahab, a strange, obsessive species, driven to fill their tormented souls with purpose and action. If Ahab had never found a whale, he would have borne one of his own and continued his pursuit, and if he'd lacked an ocean, he'd have invented one.

'Asians are quiet people,' the old man said. 'They're shy and sensitive. The pundits said so in the States, and I've found it to be true. But we talk loud, we howl with laughter, we want to paw each other's bodies right away, we get carried away by things we like, and turned off by the things we don't. We kill indiscriminately, so they hate us. We throw chewing gum around, so they hate us. We prop up their government, and the people here ignore it; it might just as well not exist. In Quang Ngai I realized that in their eyes we're rowdy kids dropping napalm almost for the fun of it – or tiger hunters hunting people from roving gunships. And for anyone down there in the rice fields, that's what it must really look like. We risk our necks "protecting" them, but our reward is just indifference and hate, not cheers, so we get nasty. On top of that, our friends are killed, which starts us thinking of revenge; and that's when the rot really sets in. Revenge isn't conquering; there's no future in it. All armies degenerate in a foreign country – inevitably – history is the proof. Battalions of our guys are being decimated and demoralized, and the Viet Cong feed on weakness. But we deserve it – for our arrogance and ignorance, and our contempt and fear and atheism.'

'You know,' I said, 'I think it was all a matter of giving the peasants land. All Asian uprisings start with landlords being murdered, and the first stage here was true to form. Your "advisors" knew this and warned Diem accordingly, but they couldn't force the government's hand because that would've been direct interference with internal policy. So Diem just freed the peasants on paper. And that left only one practical solution – anti-revolutionaries would have to adopt revolutionary methods.

'Japan is supposed to be almost unique in having emancipated its peasantry without bloodshed; but we could never have achieved it without the defeat of World War II and several million deaths and two atomic bombs. Our land reform drew blood, all right – oceans of it.

'If only Diem had bought up land from the land-owners early on and distributed it among the poorer peasants. . . . I can almost see their cadres sitting around with nothing better to do than drink tea and discuss the atom bomb.'

'I take it you're saying that land reform is the first step toward winning the peasants over, but that the landowners would never give in, so reform is impossible without bloodshed.'

'Yes, and a revolutionary war results. But what happens after the revolution? We can expect to see more peasants killed in outbreaks against the North Vietnamese Army – you know about that atrocity committed some years ago in the North, I suppose? Well, a lot of people are afraid the same sort of thing will happen again. I say a lot, of course, but compared to the number of peasants who prefer not to know, the figure is minute. There's government propaganda – yes, but the government itself is phony and the peasants just don't believe it. The more talk they hear, the more suspicious they get. This government is paper thin – you know it, everybody knows it. And America is wrong – that, too, everyone knows. One can see it all for oneself, but . . .'

He interrupted. 'I know they expect the Communists to kill off innocent people after the revolution. Unfortunately, politics is a process of trial and error, and with each new error people get hurt. If we withdraw from Vietnam, the Communists may just walk in, and they may start killing people. But whatever they do, we've no right to interfere. And besides, while interracial slaughter can be relentless, there are limits when only one race is involved. It's a law of nature, as true now as it ever was. With opposing ideologies and religions, they say a civil war can be as brutal as a war between different nations; even so, there are restraints. What we're doing here amounts to genocide.'

'I disagree. There's no way you could ever wipe them out. Guerrilla warfare is a war of maximum effect at minimum expense. If the National Liberation Front had fought any other type of engagement, they would have sacrificed a great many more people for the same stretch of land. A guerrilla war is a cheap war, as General Giap and his troops know very well. Count heads, and you realize just how small this one is. In Cuba and Algeria, too, if it had been any other kind of war, I'm quite sure they would have been annihilated before they could achieve any sort of goal. In terms of casualties, guerrilla warfare is horrible but almost humane. Yet it's a mistake to count, I feel. The point is, it's brothers that are killing each other. That's the crime of it.'

'We're in the same stew, we and the Communists.'

He glanced at me and turned away, slumped forward

like someone trying to sleep. That he bruised so easily I found slightly odd, but his simplicity cut me down to size. It was like seeing some fresh resource, buried under layers of leaf mold, soil and mud, suddenly well up in the sun.

A ferry, worked by hand, struggled downriver under a heavy load of passengers and basket cargo. The old man followed it with his eyes; and after a little while he straightened his heavy torso and spoke. His voice was feeble.

'One way or the other, as long as we're here, women and children go on being killed. It's as simple as that. We've no choice but to withdraw. There should be free elections monitored by the United Nations. We've no right to interfere. We should go home.'

'But will you?'

'We must.'

'When?'

'Today.'

He seemed to squeeze the word out from the core of his great body, then wiped his face with the palm of his hand.

'You smoke too much,' he added. 'You'll ruin your lungs. Switch to a pipe. Cancer's a painful disease.'

'Thanks.'

He shook my hand and thanked me politely for the conversation, then gave my hand a pat and left the quay. Head cocked slightly to the right, swinging his powerful arms, the humpbacked caveman trudged away along the promenade. If a bicyclist had shot him in the back of the head, he would have fallen on the road like a stone tower, eyes staring emptily. I lit another cigarette and watched the papaya rinds, rubber slippers and water hyacinths float down with the yellow water; watched without despair or hope, just as I had done on the banks of the Vistula, the River Jordan and the Danube.

Moments before waking at dawn, I was drifting, slipping. And as I lay there next to To-nga under the hot blanket, I felt myself drop through into violent loneliness. A dark, bleak sea welled up around my heart and closed over me. My arms and legs were nailed to the bed, I couldn't even wriggle; my innards sank. And once the fall started, there was no stopping it. Riding the vast downwave, the garage, its walls and darkness, flew away. The sea of loneliness invaded my eyes and ears and mouth and all my pores and filled me, choking, with foul water. All the faces, the eyes, the radiant evenings and yellow rivers, all the people and things past which my life had pilgrimaged, and all the thoughts that I had impregnated and aborted, everything vanished without a sound. And I woke up, submerged in dirty water. I've done my share of waking up in foreign countries, but the loneliness here was shabbier than anywhere I'd been and ate into one's bones like acid. The dawn was as sharp as a new blade and uncontaminated, but I felt cold and rotten and empty. The hoarse voice of an old man who talked of simple arithmetic and beat his breast still rang in my ears. How I envied him the purity that pervaded his large, strong body, the passion that he squandered in these fields and mountains. The outer form alone would have been enough. . . . But I was adrift in murk, lying there like a feeble pachyderm, forlorn, fat animal too heavy for its legs to shift its weight. I was a slob, immovable. Not a hyena. Not a voyeur. Not even a traveler drifting between heaven and earth. I was infinity's scum.

'*Chao-ong!*' To-nga called, with her eyes half open.

'*Chao-co!*' I replied.

Smiling, she slowly turned, and the warmth of her body spilled over and spread on the blanket, seeped into my skin like warm water. A trailing fragrance, lascivious, drifted from her round shoulders, cheeks, and hair.

'What time is it?' she asked.

'Five-thirty.'

'I've got to get up and go to church.'

'Pray what?'

'Oh, all kinds of things.'

'All kinds of things?'

'My brother . . . me . . . you. . . .'

She ticked us off on her fingers, and I folded her in my arms. She smiled in the dark like a big sister and murmured muffled protests.

Steamed gently overnight, her body was as moist and soft as moss and made a sucking noise when I slipped in. I turned my back on darkness and its menace, and let myself slide down like a ship sinking in hot honey; but she twisted aside, squashing me.

'No, no, you can't!' She bit my earlobe angrily. 'You can't do that; I'm going to church.'

She struggled briefly in the blanket, but I pinned her hips and rump, then hauled her thighs up in my arms. A ray of dim light penetrated a gap in the blocked-out casement window. To-nga's buttocks shone like pale bronze hills. Her voice was muffled in the blanket. I drifted. Dark, narrow, warm. I could have stayed blind forever and at peace, exiled in a sanctuary where time was as serene as a smoldering evening on a field in early summer; then avalanched into the shallow cave beyond.

15

I was fourteen when the last war ended, a veteran of junior high school; Tran must have been about the same age when he boarded the refugee boat at Haiphong with To-nga. The bombs had cascaded down on Osaka, had roared like cataracts, and the city, as far as you could see, had turned into a wasteland, a red desert. I used to stand on Tennoji hill, and the sky seemed larger than ever, people's shadows longer than before, and I would watch the lurid evening sun sink slowly down toward the horizon. The rain in Tokyo and Osaka fell in long, straight ropes from sky to earth, like the rain that swamped the ancient cedar forests of Mount Yoshino. Rails wriggled on the streets, walls stood blind, and the streetcars were skeletons. Scorched forms writhed and jostled, heaved and broke in a hungry tide; but grass soon grew in this inorganic land and water gushed from broken pipes in clear streams that might have come from springs; and in these streams lay shards of roof tiles, shattered, red, on which a light green moss already grew.

Makeshift huts packed close along the fringe of this expanse; black markets blossomed; and brawls broke out in broad daylight, where men and women fought with fists and feet and knives – or machine guns, as happened in one city. And plague germs came in via another port.

At night the open ground was strewn with fires where scraps of meat and rice were boiled in cauldrons, and yesterday's staunch patriots, children of the

Emperor, stood hugging soup bowls in the freezing sleet, scooping up bits of beggar's stew and sniffing back their snot. The scraps were bought from US Army camps, mixed in, they said, with cigarette ends and used condoms, but no one seemed to care. A girl with curry cooking in a halved gasoline can sold out so quickly that another can was soon stuffed with new yen notes and, laughing madly, she had to stand on them and tread them down with her rubber boots.

For men who'd wandered like nomads from the Aleutians to the Indonesian archipelago, home was a camp in this red desert where they roamed like tattered shadows and hovered on the edge of fires, drank methanol, and died in sudden agony or starved to death. One found them in some subway concourse, heads lying in dark puddles or crushed like beer cans thrown from speeding cars. Soldiers, homeward bound, would sit on freight-train roofs, and headless bodies tumbled down like sacks of rice when tunnels caught them unawares.

My younger sister, still in grade school while the war was on, had been evacuated to a mountain village and fed on acorns and potatoes, which was roughly what I'd had to eat, though I remained in the city throughout the war; but, for some reason, she came home with a fuzz of hair on her back, and looked like a baby monkey when I bathed her.

I used to take her to the Abeno bridge to watch the jeeps with me. The city crawled with convoys of pink troops, and the girders shook from the passing roar. For me, the sight of jeeps that ran on gasoline, not ersatz fuel, with ample gas to spare, was shattering. As were the bright pink cheeks of men who stood like towers in trucks parading past a throng of pale-faced tramps.

'They must be sick!' my walleyed sister would declare, and 'Do they really eat babies?' she'd ask me in a whisper.

The rumor was that it was babies' flesh that made their faces red, and that they raped anything female, whatever its age. My mother, brave daughter of Japan, announced that she would kill herself if need be, and asked the neighborhood doctor for some arsenic just in case, and was assured, in high-pitched rhetoric, that she would never die alone, that there was poison enough for all their neighbors and the cattle, too. (And so it wasn't hard, now – twenty years later – to understand the fear with which Vietnam's peasants reacted to their first sight of those same blue eyes and flaming cheeks.)

I worked until the day before V-J Day, sustained on bean lees and chickweed; and while I sweated away in a shunting yard, coupling and uncoupling freight cars from all over western Japan, I was ready to hurl myself at the belly of a tank, hugging an explosive, when the need arose. Death seemed glorious to me, easy, like something in an adventure story or a comic strip. Day after day, the sky rained bombs, and the city was flooded with refugees; one after the other, our bases in the southern and northern islands were destroyed; and not a single plane remained airworthy, so airfield runways had been turned into potato fields. And when an officer told us solemnly that alcohol would be extracted from the spuds and used as aircraft fuel, my friends and I cracked up; we couldn't help it, it *was* absurd, and yet in no way did it contradict our longing for a patriotic death. In fact, the more absurd the war became, the more we craved a hero's death. And yet not one of us had seen the 'enemy'; incendiary bombs just fell from distant skies. 'Devils' the papers screamed, but no one could tell us what sort of fiends they really were. They could have plucked an 'enemy' out of a top hat and, at a curt command, I would have charged at him, hugging my bomb, and blown us both to bits. Sacrifice seemed as easy as brushing one's teeth.

And then, one day, I was almost killed. Our yard was regularly strafed by carrier-based planes that flew so low their wingtips almost touched the cars. One afternoon, during an air raid, a classmate and I were left behind, and we dived into a nearby paddy field; and suddenly a hornet swooped. I felt an immense surge of air plummeting at tremendous speed toward the back of my head. My limbs went numb. And, grappling with my friend, I sank into the mud; and at that instant I looked up. In the glint of canting aluminum wings, against a summer sky of high heaped clouds, I saw a bulbous turret like a giant insect's eye and in it was an 'enemy' with rosy, shining cheeks. I thought I saw him smile – at least my eyes believed he did. A man could smile, and kill! And I kicked at my friend, shook off his clinging arms, and struggled to escape. And wasn't I, too, trying to kill the boy? I felt a thin shoulder go limp beneath my hand and heard him cry out, 'Mother!' as he sank away. I think I heard a 'Sorry! Sorry!' too before he fell back in the mud. And in that instant his voice became a hand that slapped my face. A stranger's hand. Not a boy content to be the butt of everybody's jokes at school, but a giant. I fell among the rice plants, and sweet mud stuffed my mouth.

'I wonder if he's sick!' my sister would ask.
'He isn't.'
'I wonder if it doesn't hurt, he's so pink!'
'Americans are all like that.'
Tugging my sister by the hand, we walked into a station and climbed aboard a crippled train with an overheated engine; and in a while the train began to move, steaming, fuming. Trapped in the crowd inside,

her shoulders and elbows between someone's body and a huge oil can, my sister stood twisted, looking up at us with wide eyes like a baby fish.

I was frightened of the bodies of people who had starved to death. I was used to death; we saw it often in the school grounds after air raids, saw it in the gutters running through bombed ruins; but starvation outlived the war, and its victims turned up all over Osaka. I'd seen railway workers find a corpse in some dark corner of a subway station and grab it by the hair and raise its face, then let it drop back in a puddle on the concrete platform with the wooden thud of a post being driven home. Starvation had taken its slow course and left the body hardened – stone or wood. And no familiarity with bodies burned or crushed to death could harden me enough, or cushion that awful sound; and I could see myself becoming that kind of corpse before too long. Our house was dark and empty as a hollow tooth, our furniture and clothes were sold, and Mother wept. We'd sit around a small basket of steamed potatoes on the dinner table, the three of us, and gape at the wretched meal, spying on each other, scowling. An empty stomach made me shake, spurt sweat, and feel that I was being gnawed by swarms of little animals. I almost fainted when the smell of broiled fish, roast meat and rice pounced out at me in the camp on the station square. And large, intelligent, muscular-looking adults, too weak to walk, just squatting on the roadside gazing upward in despair, made me panic with fear. Death had lost its glamor and simplicity and turned to brackish water.

I avoided school. Contact with classmates was torture. Boys from comfortable homes made quick recoveries, but I was slowly dying. During the lunch hour I'd sneak out and fill my belly with water, then kill time somewhere out of sight. The water in winter smelled of lead and disinfectant, and cut into one's teeth with the keenness of a knife. I was vain, determined to hide my poverty. I remember strolling back to class one day after the usual waterfest and finding a large loaf of bread wrapped in newspaper on my desk – and dashing out into the corridor again. The boy in the desk behind mine ran after me, pushed me into a corner, his face crimson with embarrassment, and blurted out something about both his parents being alive and having just about enough to eat; he'd told his mother about me and so she'd baked the bread which . . . take it . . . just a gift. . . . He left me speechless when he slunk away – and not with gratitude but despair, and unbearable shame. I felt that I'd been condemned, and that the sentence laid me almost side by side with those dead paupers. A few days later, I saw a want-ad for a baker's apprentice pasted on a telephone pole and decided to take the job on the spot.

Since then, I've been in countless workshops and come to know the gentleness of things. Useless objects, the kind that clutter vacant lots, and tools like lathes – there's no real difference, each is pure and vigorous, yet complete within itself. Stoking ovens or kneading dough, my old attacks would often reappear and lay their stifling hands on me; but standing at a lathe in a corner of some small plant where the smell of hot metal and oil hung round me like the soft sunlight from a window overhead, I found an inner peace and joy. The sight of a delicate yet powerful bit, without fuss or hesitation, cutting into the body of a metal cast was almost sexual. I could keep going all day on just a pack of cigarettes. My mind was blocked and rusty, doubting everything, but in my hand I held an absolute conviction that shaped and moved things and created value. I knew no doctrine I could kneel before, but worshiped things. And now I wonder why I ever broke the trance in which I used to work.

The desert had a fleeting life. Before we realized that it might have been a land of orange orchards, we'd lost it. In no time, man had covered it with a skin of asphalt and encrusted it with matchboxes and instant slums. Besieged, then parceled into tiny lots, the desert withdrew toward the sea and ultimately drowned. The horizon disappeared from the city, the setting sun dissolved in smog, and the sky was boxed in by toy-block walls and windows. Even the rain and wind quailed. And words glittered and turned to ash the minute they were written. The age of shadow-boxing literature had begun. And as I watched the desert being hunted down and driven out of sight, I found a hollowness in me that deepened day by day.

Nothing will ever replace the vast, harsh clarity of that expanse, the things in it that gave my solitude and aimlessness external form. I lost an outer world that corresponded to the spreading void within, the growing alienation that I felt. One sees an object and becomes the thing oneself. I am a desert. I look at myself, and when self-definition blurs, a desert appears amid some hotel's chandeliers and brandy glasses and suits of shiny cloth; and with it comes a flood of scorched-red forms, the utter dryness of an inorganic world, a premonition of starvation advancing like a tide, my mother's and my sister's tears, the hellish din that hovered over camps, the gurgling sound a woman made when she was being raped in a dark sidestreet, and a large man standing at a street corner with one ten-yen roll for sale . . . and when someone offered him five yen for it, he tore it silently in half and sold him that, and sold the rest in half a minute.

One fine day, if there's a flash in the sky, a mushroom cloud, nothing will happen to me, because I've already been there.

16

I pulled out my jungle fatigues and aired them in the
sun. The outfit was crumpled and a map of dried
sweat had spread like an acid stain; it was like reading an old postcard. Then I began to put away books
and newspapers, liquor bottles that had cluttered the
room, but noon came and I went out for lunch with
Yamada and Yasuda at the floating restaurant on Bach
Dang Quay. Yamada ordered steamed crab, Yasuda
sweet-sour pork, and I had roast pigeon. It was a calm
day; the big guns sounded muffled and remote, and the
smell of roast squid sold by girls on the riverbank trailed
over to our deck. Two or three children were laughing
brightly in the yellow water. An old fisherman floated
past, casting a net from his dinghy.

Yamada stared after the drifting boat and said: 'The
whole scene makes one hope he has an *i lu ping an*, a
safe journey.'

We got onto the subject of a rifle that had been
displayed at the USIS the previous evening. In some
Central Highlands battle, a bullet had gone straight
into the muzzle of an American corporal's gun. This
miracle had saved the soldier's life, of course, but the
steel barrel had split right up the middle, the two halves
curling back like wood shavings. The correspondents,
who'd been bored stiff during the news briefing, perked
up a bit when the rifle was shown around. Then the
information officer went on to announce that a bull-
dozer in Copenhagen had accidentally cut through an

underground cable and caused a temporary breakdown in the White House-Kremlin hotline. And no one cared a damn. Someone sitting next to me muttered, 'So what else's new, man?' And they were told again that for fifteen minutes the world had been without one means of preventing a nuclear war, and still there wasn't a flicker of interest. The officer looked down at the mutilated rifle, said, 'One big war . . . and one little war,' and left the room.

Yasuda munched some hot pickled pepper and drank his beer; and after talking about the rifle for a few more minutes, he turned to me.

'What was the worst thing for you at the front? I've never been under fire. I'm interested. I haven't seen anything you could really call "front-line action".'

'Nor have I,' I said.

'They say the belly's the worst,' he went on gloomily. 'I wouldn't mind if it was instantaneous, but God help me if I have to crawl around dragging my guts along. I couldn't take it. I can almost feel them being grabbed in there and hauled out. Think of the sort of power that can peel a barrel like a banana and imagine what it would do to your belly. I mean, you've only got a bit of lousy skin over it, for Christ's sake. It's just jelly!'

Yamada smiled calmly, picking at his crab meat. 'I saw a lot of action on the middle China front. The worst is a ricochet, a bullet hits something and bounces off. A direct shot pokes a straight hole, but a ricochet jumps in and spins around, and it makes a godawful mess. One shot can scramble your insides forever. The whole works sometimes just flops out. Your guts, you see, are packed in under pressure, so when the skin and peritonea are torn, they just spill right out.'

Yasuda winced and sipped his beer in silence. The waiter brought us a tempting-looking dish of pork on sautéed spinach, but Yasuda only looked at it blearily and left it untouched. Yamada shot a sidelong glance at him and bit off a chunk of white meat from his huge crab's claw. I lowered my eyes and poked intently at the pigeon on my plate. The information carried quite a bit of cruel weight. I had never imagined the details. It caught one right under the belt.

'Waiting isn't much fun, either,' I said after a while. 'Operations aren't scheduled every day and you have to wait for a week, ten days at a stretch. Which means all night, every night, in a trench or one of the huts. From midnight to six. I tell you, that's rough. You just wait there without knowing when they'll attack. You almost want them to attack just to break the suspense. It's like being eaten alive by ants. It all depends how much your nerves can stand. Mine got pretty frayed.'

'Isn't there some way correspondents could be marked like the Red Cross people so that nobody'd shoot at us? I mean, I know bullets are blind, but couldn't we have some kind of international press agreement?'

'OK. I'll contact the Hague Convention for you,' Yamada said, dipping plump white meat into soy sauce. 'Just let me finish this crab and I'll fire off a telegram.' Yasuda laughed uneasily. Yamada laughed, too, and I joined in halfheartedly. For a while there was silence as crab, pork and pigeon disappeared into three mouths. I bit into the bird's small head and sucked the brains, debating whether to take things any further with Yasuda. There was no escaping it. Unarmed, shot in the dark, helpless. Or punctured with a knife. Lying like a dying dog looking up at its killer's eyes until its life ran out.

'Well, you guys, what about a nap?' Yamada said after a cigar, and he stood up.

Yasuda rubbed his belly, sighed 'Aaaah . . . the good life,' and we adjourned.

I left the other two by the river, picked up a cyclo, and returned to my room and the job of straightening it out. I piled the newspapers and books in separate mounds on the tiled floor and lined up the bottles outside the door. I moved around the room like a pair of shears clipping through clinging strands of sloth that had formed around me like a moss cocoon. It was some time since I'd moved at all, for I had sprawled in bed for days on end, half naked, glued by sweat to soiled linen, drifting those long afternoons away in a cloud of sweet flatulence, reading, dozing, getting drunk. A banana peel I'd dropped onto some newspaper had lain there like a starfish, splayed, and then begun to melt, turned black, and shriveled up into a crisp black skeleton; and I had watched the thing decay from day to day, incapable of reaching out, removing it, as if the bed had teeth that held me back. No image, however vivid, survived past 10:00 A.M.; its life just flickered for a bit and wilted as soon as the sun began to rot the tropics. And I was left, amoeboid, putty-soft. Revolution, wasteland, starvation, solitude: whatever I took to bed and fumbled with collapsed immediately. To keep my mind alive, I tried to review all the deaths that I had seen when I was a boy: victims of fire, malnutrition, altruism, accident, stupidity. I tried to see the blood that spurted from the chests and temples of those two young terrorists, tried to remember the single valediction; but despite the hard focus of their deaths, the memory of them was now a haze.

And when the room was clean and tidy, I sat down on the bed and, lighting a cigarette, said 'Now, then . . .' to myself.

Yesterday, after the news briefing, I was in the

reference room flipping through some recent official reports when I noticed that someone had dropped a document on the floor; it was a casualty list. As I ran my eye idly down the long columns of names, I found a 'Dr. Robert Percy'. I stared at it for some time, but the typewritten words didn't change. I went into the office and showed it to the red-haired girl there. She was a small, fat, comfortable-looking female with mountainous breasts, but she was efficient and helpful. She disappeared immediately and came back with a card.

'It says he was killed in Dong-xoai.'

'Was he transferred there?'

'I don't know. I gather the action there was pretty heavy. It says KIA – killed in action. If he wasn't transferred, he was probably sent there to help out. It's not unusual.'

I thanked the girl, who smelled of chocolate, and got into the elevator. In the fluorescent light, the skin on my arms and hands looked like a frog's, and the cooled air suddenly felt like dirty ice.

Outside, in the smoky evening, I passed along Le Loi Boulevard until I found a Vietnamese dining hall where I knew I'd be alone. I went inside and ordered a Coke. Lizards squeaked on the damp walls and scrawny men, one knee drawn up, were drinking coffee in small cups or eating *cha-gio* rolls. I leaned against the wall and lit a cigarette, watching the crowd outside. I wondered how he could have died. It was as though my own flesh somewhere had been torn. In a distant dusk, I saw the torso of a man stoop over me and hand me some water purifiers. His lean, sharp face smiled, without a word. He used to give me malaria pills and mosquito repellent without my asking. I remembered seeing his drawn face pop up one morning in the next trench, in the pale dawn mist. I remembered his story about taking some BCG to a village and finding that the Cong had beaten him to it and warned the peasants that it stood for Birth Control Government. I wondered if it wasn't really just a joke that he'd made up sometime after a nap.

When I paid for the Coke and stood up, I was ripe with a decision.

After cleaning the room, I packed some lighter fuel, a notebook, some underwear, medicine, and a map in a field bag. As on my previous trip, I put Garnett's translation of *The Idiot* in my breast pocket as a talisman. Thanks to the long-windedness of all Russian intellectuals, the book was thick. I would wear it over my heart and sort of hide behind the gunner's flak jacket in the helicopter.

I moved off the steaming boulevard into the cold white halls of the USIS and asked the information officer there for a reservation in a helicopter. The major telephoned the airport on the spot and said that if I came by at seven on the following morning, a car would take me out there. We shook hands and I stepped out into the steam again. I followed Tu Do Street back to the quay, went into Yamada's chilly hotel, and knocked on his door. He was lying in bed, studying the ceiling. Sitting in an old-fashioned leather armchair, I briefly explained my decision, then handed him a thick bundle of letters. I asked him to burn them if I didn't get back.

'The whole lot?'

'Yes.'

'You don't want me to send your wife's letters back to her?'

'No.'

'The whole damn thing?'

'Yeah.'

Yamada got out of bed and started to say something but, deciding against it, put the letters away in a desk drawer. He poured some Cointreau into a glass and handed it to me. He also gave me one of the Manila cigars he'd been hoarding. There was a sense of *déjà vu*, of having gone through the same thing some time ago. I seemed to have been facing him then, sitting in a darkening room, a glass of liqueur in my hand, looking at a window alight with evening saffron.

Yamada spoke softly.

'I've been trying to contact the front for the last few days. I don't know when the circuit'll open . . . but would you be interested in going over to the other side?'

'I would. Very much. Let's face it, anyone can poke around with the ARVN, but it's not many who've seen things over there. There's nothing I'd like better. Frankly, it doesn't matter which lot gets me. Can you arrange to have me handed over?'

'Yes, but can't you wait?'

The Cointreau was sweet, the cigar bitter. I sipped the liqueur without answering and puffed on the brown tube. The lingering fire had faded from the window and night poured in like water. Cholon would be bright with lights and dinning gongs and women's keening voices. I couldn't wait. If I put it off, I'd slip back. That hot bed would decay me. Futility swelled like a sponge soaking up the gloom of this sticky heat. For twenty-four hours I had exposed my decision to the heat and nothing had changed so far. I must avoid my room, avoid people, conversation, beds, chairs.

I put down the glass and stood up.

'Call me up by field radio if you need to. I may come back right away. No news is good news.'

'I won't stop you.'

'Take care.'

'Watch out for ricochets.'

'I had enough of them at lunch.'

'You'll be all right.'

Yamada smiled bleakly. His swarthy coarse-skinned features seemed torn between pity and composure. I remembered the poem he gave me in a second-floor restaurant in Hong Kong and recited it:

> I stand in the wind longing for the north;
> The geese, without a word, winged forth.
> The Pearl River flows eastward to the sea
> To nurse the green paulownia tree.
> What fate, what reunion, await you and me?

I pulled the door open and Yamada's still smiling face was gone. Green paulownia. Here it was tamarinds. Paulownias shed their leaves. What about tamarinds? I imagined they only had dry and rainy seasons; no autumn. They probably never aged.

I could still have reversed my decision. The door of the opposite room was open and a black soldier was visible, reading something, his small round head resting on a white pillow. He looked like a huge child home in bed with a cold.

The Caravelle Hotel, the Hotel Continental, 'Café Jeunesse', Café Brouillard': I avoided all the places where I might run into familiar faces, and strode down Tran Hung Dạo toward Cholon, like a man with a purpose. When I got thirsty I stopped at a stall and drank some coconut milk, and then marched on until the blood drained down to my heels and my legs began to shake. As usual, people thronged the streets of Cholon; children yelled, red and blue neon lights blinked, and exhaust fumes hovered like fog. It was like creeping into the belly of a whale that had just been cut open: humid, smelly, the blood still pulsing; everything was sticky with grime, and yet the air itself seemed nourishing.

I squatted by the roadside in the gaudy heat, huddling with cyclo men and slurping from a chipped bowl of rice gruel with bits of pig intestines in it; and the fetid street smelled like an unwashed crotch. It was all so like the camps through which I'd drifted twenty years ago: raw lives wedged in together, straining in the crush. Nothing remained within itself; all merged – a heaving, tangled flux. A storyteller's droning tale blurred into the gongs of street theater; cabaret walls quivered with a trumpet's last, long, tapering breath, and drums responded to the jungle guns with heavy rolls. I stirred the soup bowl and chased a scrap of offal with my chopsticks. I'd been living in the belly of a whale for the last twenty years; and it made no difference whether it heaved itself into the air or sank toward the ocean floor, whether there were storms or days of calm, for I never moved from a wall-less cell, imprisoned, talking to myself, alone.

I went into a movie theater whose walls were green with rot. The place was full of soldiers, but their grenades stayed in their belts, so there was no explosion. The audience sat crushed together in the dark; their bodies had a salty tang that stung the eyes.

We watched an evil brute of a judge try to seduce a girl. She was poor but beautiful. Her lover was tortured for protesting. Her mother wailed and beat her fists on the ground. And the father hung his head and grieved. And just when all this suffering reached a peak, up popped a magic monkey. Its eyes were blazing. It took one giant breath and blew out bands of phantom troops, who attacked the wicked judge by shooting needles at his eyes. The villain died – he bled to death under a pagoda tree; the troops withdrew into the monkey's mouth; and the monkey sailed off into the clouds. The girl ran laughing into her lover's arms; the young man helped the mother up and stared up gratefully at the sky; and the father smiled, and from a web of wrinkles gazed out fondly on his family.

Packaged in Hong Kong, the picture was a blend of mind-boggling simplicity and unmitigated cruelty, but the audience cheered – and sweated, panted, blew their noses, and, whenever possible, spat. Drops of sweat kept forming on my chin and with a flick I'd wipe them off. And suddenly I thought I heard a whisper in Chinese. It was the same southern Chinese I'd heard at the front: harsh, guttural, dark and energetic; the same voice that airwaves had carried across the scrub and rice fields that late afternoon on patrol.

I stiffened and looked around.

When To-nga and I got home from 'Plaisir', I took off my clothes and splashed cold jar water on my chest and shoulders. My skin both flinched from the shock and reveled in it; but my body felt hard and heavy, impregnable. I couldn't believe that in a couple of days my guts might slide out onto a bed of dead leaves somewhere.

To-nga shivered and cried out softly, '*Froid, froid!*'

I felt eyes lying in ambush somewhere in the garage. They weren't the eyes of VC agents looking for recruits. They weren't living eyes at all; but powerful, vacant, and immobile, tireless, undiscriminating eyes.

'Hello.'

'Hello.'

I peered down into my odalisk's eyes – large and moist, unchanged – and I began the ritual of kissing them, but first her forehead, and then the lips and breasts, and downhill to her navel. She quietly raised her arms and with slow strokes began to rake my chest, my sides and thighs, as far as her hands could reach. The old skin was plowed in and my whole body stirred. With my mouth in her bush, I turned to gooseflesh beneath her small, quick hands, rocking on a dark tide of swelling fear. Diffidently, her face approached and fingers drew my phallus into a small, warm mouth. Teased by my tongue, bunched petals soon grew moist.

Those eyes watched me tirelessly. Beyond the mosquito net, I felt their frightful stare on the back of my head, behind my ears. To-nga's heat seeped into my chest and we grew furnace-hot; but flickering in the dark I saw a myriad faces, lights, forests and cities, entangling. To-nga began to moan, breathing hard, pushing my chest with her hands, suddenly scratching my sides with her nails, opening her thighs completely, then squeezing me, and abruptly giving way. A shining tide rose, inundating the net and walls. It was as though we lay in the middle of a wide night plain. Never before had the resonance been so clear.

'Oi. . . . Troi . . . oi!'

A wave of heat scourged my hips.

The darkness exploded and, for a second, opened its glittering core and then was gone. It was exactly like the clear, blinding void that had appeared behind my eyelids that morning of the execution. I erupted, clinging to her slippery form. A sweet nausea passed slowly over her hair, and the darkness rejoined the night, rumbling.

'All right I smoke?' I asked after a while.

'Go ahead,' she moaned softly.

The sweat ebbed and a cold tidal flat remained. My skin reverted to the dull hide it had been before; the stream dried up; and the murmur died away. Idly,

I watched the smoke curl up through the mosquito net. Languidly, her eyes calm but absent, To-nga raised her head and pulled the blanket over me, then fell back on the pillow like a tired whore. My heart gave little leaps with each tiny crepitation of my cigarette. I decided not to say anything to To-nga about going to the front. Unable to speak Vietnamese, I couldn't possibly explain it to her.

With the antennae of limited vocabulary, we'd fumbled toward each other, with words enough to fill no more than three or four pages of a dictionary. Love is possession, they say. But in reality one's claim is only that part of another person that can be influenced and changed. People possess the shadows of themselves, or the illusion of possession. The hours I spent with To-nga had an animal innocence, had depth and subtlety, with none of the staleness of custom. She was an island with fine forests and secluded shores, and I had landed there and strolled along the forest verge, but not effected any change or even wanted to. My only need had been to burrow in that soft, warm part of her that concealed passion and yet remained serene. Being mute refined me. What could be more secure and peaceful than sitting in the dark, distilling simple sounds like 'bat', 'owl', 'basket', word by word? She'd clapped her hands like a child, and cocked her head, absorbed. I was a pilgrim who'd smiled at her, and picked up shells in the sand, and would move on.

Again I felt those other eyes on me; no other feeling now remained. Would I come back in one piece? My throat tightened. Or would time always pass in woodworms' terms, and long nights ooze, and would I always wallow in soliloquy's dead water? I wanted to stand up and face something absolutely real, authentic. I hadn't fought, hadn't killed, hadn't helped or plowed or carried; I hadn't instigated or planned or taken anybody's side. I watched. And I could only expect to die like a dog, quivering, eyes glazed. If by seeing something one becomes that thing, then wasn't I already partly dead? And no one would ever peer under *my* scalp and see what went on in my mind. Why court destruction on a pointless exercise? War wasn't an adventure. Adventure was discovering a continent, opening up new land or sea routes, linking continents by air, a courier galloping from coast to coast. It was carving a highway a hundred yards wide, almost overnight, through the wild, grassy plain of the Ishikari River. And probably, to the boys in the jungle in rubber sandals, this war was that adventure. They lived in a century of adventure; they'd just discovered zero. They thought that man could beat machines, that human bombs could blow up tanks. And death was glorious for them, as once it was for me. Hate poured from their narrow shoulders and raked the fields. They acted out their dreams. And fulfillment might be flawed, they might feel doubt as soon as they began to act, but pride would cover up the cracks. And they might even lose their faith and, disillusioned, turn back toward the jungle they had started from, and find that they had lost their freedom to resist; and some would crouch down on the ground, feeling helpless, and some might rise again with only clubs to fight with and be killed. And as for me . . . I couldn't lift a finger. I watched. Yes, watching was all I'd ever do.

My legs jerked suddenly and I woke up. I flicked my Zippo lighter on and looked at my watch; it was six o'clock. I crept out of the blanket and groped my way past the mosquito net. Three steps to the northeast in the cool darkness and my fingertips touched the damp skin of the water jar. While I was washing my face, I felt that something hard and large and dark – a crystal – had formed inside me. I pulled on my trousers, tightened my belt, put on my shoes, and left an envelope stuffed with money on the windowsill.

'*Tu pars?*' asked To-nga in a muffled voice.

'Yes.'

'What time is it?'

'Six.'

'See you tonight?'

'Yes.'

To-nga giggled as she used to when I first taught her how to finger-wrestle. She turned over and reached out a hand under the mosquito net. I touched the palm, which was slightly damp, and left the garage. Crossing the dark streets where early-rising laborers stood gulping noodles at foodstalls, I returned to my own place. There, I changed into jungle fatigues, shouldered a bag, and locked the door, trying it several times before heading off.

I found a cyclo man asleep on the street and tapped him on the shoulder.

'*Di, di.* . . .' I clapped my hands lightly.

My war had begun.

17

Until the sun rose, the morning was crisp and fragrant. The air we breathed was fresh and still, though fronds and vines were tangled like the armpits of some headless, tailless thing. Advancing through them, pushing the lower foliage away, was like diving under dark waves. Branches sprung out at one from nowhere, slapping cheeks, ensnaring knees. And we tripped and staggered on a bed of slippery leaves.

By the time we entered a rubber plantation off the highway skirting it, it was six o'clock and the air was filled with the creak of frogs and ticking crickets, which formed a swaying tremolo. Twice, in the east, we heard a sound like urgent knocking on a midnight door; it carried clear across that other ceaseless, lulling noise, and I remembered early morning fishing trips when I was young, and guessed that it was clapper rails calling in the marsh reeds. My father used to say they wintered in Japan, migrating south from Siberia and Korea; but did birds from such a distant north travel this far south?

The sun rose at precisely 7:10. A damp haze drifted in the foliage, and the misty half-light overhead, through which a flash of scarlet streamed, receded like ebbing water. Wain's powerful neck and shoulders pushed slowly through the fronds, and to his right and left were silent soldiers moving forward with their rifles held in front of them. When the shimmering sun emerged, morning poured out from all the leaves, the vines and trunks in a sudden flood of heat. The vines turned sticky with their sweat, and hard, sharp leaves sighed heavily and went limp. The dew evaporated drop by steaming drop. The frogs and crickets had stopped singing long ago. The piled leaves sank beneath our boots, and what at first had been a modest, humid, compost smell was soon a stench that clung to us like spore. Thorns scratched our skin, sweat stung the wounds. The men broke off branches as they passed and stuck the foliage in their helmets and elsewhere on themselves. The captain and I followed suit. Antlered, indistinguishable, Wain moved smoothly, silently, heavily through the forest, hacking at vines to left and right. A small radioman called Miller, stooped beneath his set, followed in Wain's steps, nibbling at his fingernails. The Viets pressed on in silence. Kiem, who was in high spirits and often laughed, stopped sometimes to consult a map and summon Wain; and after each summons, Wain – subdued, accommodating – took the phone from Miller's shoulder and called in a salvo from the unit in our rear. The call signal for the day was 'Junkman'. One heard a dull explosion far behind, a shell would screech past high above our heads, and a dull crump follow from a distant target. Judging from the sound they made, they were 155s.

'Hey, Wain,' Kiem would say in his Froggy voice. 'Tell the *artilleurs* to give four or five more. Strong, strong. Tell them to *araser* strong. The same place.'

And Wain acknowledged the command, picked up the phone, and called out, 'Junkman! Junkman!'

While Wain was giving his orders, Miller stood by gnawing neatly at his nails, stopping to appraise his work with a solemn, vacant look, head tilted to one side, then nibbling them again. From time to time, quite casually, he blew out nail chips from a pouting mouth. Our operation was scheduled for three nights and four days; and at this rate, he'd have finished his fingers by the following day and would move on to his toes.

After a while, we found the makings of a trail and headed deeper into the wilderness, now in single file, treading a narrow, faint, but unmistakably man-made path that wove unerringly between the trees; a path that rubber sandals and bicycle wheels had worn in the course of thousands of trips. Obeying the trail's own enigmatic whims, we twisted left and right, drawn up a private road that wound through an immense estate toward the enemy's country seat; and we had just passed through the outer gates. Our eyes sought out an ambush, but only when the trap was sprung would we react. At our goal for that day we expected to find at least five hundred members of the crack 'Autumn' unit of the VC's 300th Battalion lying in wait. If they didn't shoot, there'd be no fight; if they did, we'd return their fire. The opening move was theirs. We were a target, advancing slowly through the forest. Some of us behaved as if we were explorers, some strolled along, and all of us were sheep. We dangled metal bowls, cabbages and chickens from our hips and shoulders; and someone even had a small white puppy in tow.

A young medic kicked at an anthill like a hard, white, clay dome and stood there looking at the tip of his boot. A radioman gazed skyward, eating a banana. A lean, intrepid-looking liaison officer strode past us with a transistor radio that he kept on lifting to his ear, and a harsh young Parisian soprano was belting out 'My Little Singing Doll'. Miller, nibbling, stared, and Wain swung his head away in disgust, muttering, 'Can't stand that French crap!'

More than once, I felt a seizure coming on. Everything seemed futile in that corroding quiet, among those glaring shafts of light. There'd be a clash, a brief frenzy, and fatuous deaths. It filled me with regret. I knew my being there was entirely my own doing, but I still couldn't believe it could turn out like this.

That morning when I left the garage and hurried across a dark Saigon, I'd felt a crystal hardness in me. A fierce vitality had spurred me on. But it was only resolution for resolution's sake. I might return alive and weave some words together that shed some light on my motives and ambitions, but the effort would be as meaningful as froth churned out behind a ship. In the hard chill of dawn, I'd thought I could take myself in hand, and felt the intense and solitary joy of the stoic. But my footsteps, the hurried sound they made, betrayed it for what it really was: an illusion. And the sad fact was that I had nothing else on which I could depend.

Since then, I'd lived for nine days in a trench or in a hut, awake all night or sleeping in bed with my shoes still on, playing horseshoes or chatting with the men, napping, drifting wherever chance took me. I used to feel that opportunity had taken fright like cattle in a storm, that I was condemned to doze forever in a red clay hole and wait. I had hungry ants for company, but otherwise was free – free from people and their beliefs, from politics. I repressed the feeling that at the heart of this new freedom was just a vague fear; I rather enjoyed wallowing in a premonition of death, a chill that pervaded the stillness of the night hours. It was fun to play with morbid notions in that mudhole, knowing I was barricaded by sandbags, minefields, barbed wire, rings of firing lines, and GIs at their posts. Of course, as long as the reality remained that one close mortar shot would finish me, just snuff me out, the sweet security was nonsense. But the desolation of the minefield, revealed in the sweep of a searchlight at the dead of night, was a mirror image of the ravaged world another war had printed on my skin; and looking at it, sitting by a wall of earth, slapping at mosquitoes and ants, I felt a kind of savage joy, a vitality, spring up in me.

My luck had finally turned a day ago, in the evening. Lying in bed after dinner, I was reading *The Idiot* when Wain came into the hut. He crouched down beside me and began to talk about an operation that he'd just worked out with Kiem. Three small companies, about five hundred troops in all, would cross the D-Zone jungle on a four-day mission. Kiem saw it as a 'search and destroy' operation and indeed that's what it might have been, but Wain considered it a demonstration. By invading an enemy sanctuary that hadn't been penetrated for several years, we would show them that we also had the will to fight. Victory wasn't the point, though winning would be fine. We'd 'waited and watched' for far too long. A war had just begun; it was something that had to be done sometimes, the captain said. His voice was calm and slow, he weighed each word; but he seemed to be making an elaborate effort to control his emotions, and a fierce, cold power escaped from his broad shoulders. His eyes at times betrayed a killer's fervor. It was he who had sent Doc Percy, Jones and Haines, along with several others, to help out in Dong-xoai, and he had lost all three of them, and more.

Even to me it was clear that the plan was reckless. Applying a rough law of guerrilla warfare, it would need a manpower-firepower advantage of about ten to one to be successful. It was like pulling the whiskers of a wounded tiger, without a gun at hand. Yet knowing this, why wasn't I scared? Was I hooked on that gloomy passion that surged up from Wain's lion-fierce soul? Or did I feel secure in his powerful calm and ruthlessness, which let him go along with doubtful orders knowing full well what their execution would entail? Or was I numb, exhausted by the nine days waiting, by the sleepless nights? My lips moved without my having time to think, and, in my longing for the out-of-doors, I stuck a hand out from the safety of my cage. And the opportunity to escape hooked its claws into my shoulders before I had a chance to touch it, look it over.

Wain asked me quietly, 'Would you like to join us?' glancing at me.

'Yes,' I answered hesitantly.

'I'll see you're OK.'

'Thanks.'

'D'you want a rifle?'

'No.'

'Tell me when you do.'

The captain stood, took his helmet and canteen off the wall and put them on my bed, then left the room in a couple of long strides. One shot could puncture the helmet. A bullet could put a hole in that canteen as if it were a plastic bag. I wouldn't know where the bullets were coming from and no one was going to stop them. I lit a cigarette, and fear and helplessness rushed in for the first time; it felt as if hot acid had been spilled in me, slowly boring holes. By now the inky night, borne on a tide of humid heat, had streamed into the hut and risen to the ceiling, burying everything.

In the morning, at four o'clock, I woke up with a jolt when Corporal Eagan touched me lightly on the shoulder. I dragged myself over to the mess and, without talking to anyone, had orange juice and bacon and eggs, along with everybody else. Jones's bacon used to be burned but at least not cold. Chewing one of several cold slices that a hefty-looking new cook with a red nose had carefully heaped onto my plate, I suddenly remembered Jones, and Percy, Haines, and missed them bitterly. Their faces, hands, their white teeth floated in and out of that distant morning light. Outside the boarded walls, engines rumbled and heavy steel machines thundered across the camp in the crisp dawn. Fear had taken the shape of a burning halo; it glowed in the fluorescent light, soured the aftertaste of orange juice. I thought I might shit myself that day, so I went back to my room and put on two pairs of new underpants. Stuffing my pockets with cigarettes in the dark, I suddenly remembered Tran saying, 'If two water buffalo collide, a mosquito dies.' The harsh peasant humor had an ax's heavy edge. I wondered which adage, this or 'between the devil and the deep blue sea', suited my circumstances better. The mosquito? Had I finally changed at last? No longer a hyena, but a mosquito without a sting, unable to suck blood because I happened to have landed on a buffalo's horn?

The company crept through some scrubland, crossed a grassy meadow, ducked through more scrub, crossed another meadow, and arrived at a wide swamp before noon. It basked in the bright sun, framing a stand of tall, dense reeds; the stillness was primeval. The vast sky had abruptly unfurled and a castle of cumulus clouds floated clear above the line of trees that dominated the opposite bank – an interminable green wall, so dark and deep it must have stood there since the beginning of time. We had reached a threshold: the garden ended here, and behind the long wall dwelled infinite patience and purpose. Mortars were set up on the bank and round after round poured in; but the wall was still, not a sound emerged. The explosions banged emptily in the blurry heat, and brave echoes died away over the great swamp.

Kiem was pleased. 'OK, OK, let's cross,' he said. 'Let's go, Capitaine Wain. They're not there. They run away. *Là-bas*. Mustn't lose chance. Ask the *artilleurs* to cover us.'

'If you say so, sir,' the captain answered in a tired voice.

The soldiers rose sluggishly and began to wade across. Even there, a narrow path of trampled reeds reached to the other bank, and though the swamp was wide and fairly shallow, there was no other trail. And, as before, the men trooped faithfully along it. To save their strength? Or was it that they also shunned the loneliness of unknown ground and thus preferred to tread where other men had passed?

'Junkman, Junkman, we're crossing the swamp. Keep throwing it in, OK? We're wide open. Looks dangerous. Keep their heads down. Just don't stop.'

The reeds were high and I was hidden up to my chest. Now and then, my boots slid off the trampled stems and muddy water rose up to my knees.

We were almost at the edge of our artillery's range. The rasping screech and the explosions were now much closer, not fireworks any more; and in no time the air was violent with unbroken noise.

Stands of ancient, giant trees and brushwood made up that jungle wall, and visibility was little more than fifteen feet. The sun was blocked out overhead and one's hands turned green. Again, a faint ribbon snaked through the dead leaves. In places, L-shaped or W-shaped trenches appeared. The gray earth was still fresh and bore the marks of shovel blades. There were thatched shelters like woodsmen's bivouacs, and black scorched patches on the ground suggested cooking fires. Punji traps were not uncommon, but they were old and the bamboo shafts had almost rotted through. We passed a crude picture done with tar on a tree trunk and a slogan scrawled beside it: 'Down with American Imperialism! Long Live Independence!'

Wain came up and whispered, 'There's a mine somewhere around here. Probably a booby trap, too. Some Special Forces guys and a clean-up platoon came through two days ago and checked things out, but be careful. Try not to trip on vines.'

He was already bathed in sweat. His strong face swiveled to left and right as he moved along, fingering the trigger of his rifle, ducking branches and stepping lightly over roots, cutting his way through walls of vines. And it dawned on me suddenly that it would no longer shock him that people in Japan condemned the war for its inequity; the days were past when he could smile in the dying light and raise a glass of 'sippin'' bourbon, or sit on a grassy bank beside a pond and joke about magic fish. His war was being transformed, and possibly the change was already complete. One felt it wasn't boy guerrillas he was fighting, but this cruel, chaotic sea of vegetation, the wilderness he hacked at with a cold ferocity that greedy, rootless water plants might have; and like them, too, he seemed untethered, released at last from a hateful, sedentary life by the force of his resentment. It made me think of men in covered wagons, those ancestors of his who rode into the great plains and drove the Indians out. Moving, plowing, praying after killing, repenting and moving on, arriving at a goal and, once established, drinking hard and sometimes ending their own lives in violent ways. Men of excess, both heaven- and hell-bent. Wasn't it their strange, restless blood that flowed in him?

Trinh, the old orderly, had given me a rice ball and a chicken wing, which I had for lunch. In fact, I only ate half the rice and, wrapping the rest in newspaper, stuck it in my bag; and I rationed myself to one mouthful of water, refusing the temptation to guzzle more. Kiem chucked what was left of his rice ball away, but Trinh pounced on it, carefully brushed off the mud and leaves, and put it in his pack, murmuring to no one in particular, 'Viet Cong eat.'

Not long before this, Eagan had appeared through the undergrowth and joined our force. Apparently the other companies were nearby, behind a screen of trees. Eagan belonged to the second group, infiltrating from the east; the third was moving from the north; and all three were due to link up soon. Eagan was carrying a carbine, but he'd slung his helmet from his belt and wore a jaunty yellow baseball cap instead, and had a scarlet scarf tied around his throat. He was Errol Flynn. A good target. Like shouting, shoot me, shoot me!

'Hey!' he called out. I was sprawled on the ground. 'You still alive?'

'And kicking.'

'That's good!'

'Haven't been shot at once.'

'You will soon.'

'I guess so.'

'Take it easy.'

'How?'

'You just take care of yourself,' he said, walking slowly away and finding somewhere to lie down. Wain, Miller, Eagan. Three Americans. Only three of them in a company of two hundred. One a radioman, and neither of the others in command. Kiem held the reins.

The remarkable Colonel Kiem, master of our fate. It was his decision whether to advance, retreat, attack, or defend. Wain drifted through the dusk, unable to either help or interfere.

The other night, while I was taking a shower after dinner, I heard Eagan singing a little song that made the others laugh. He sang it so fast I couldn't make out the words. So I asked him to write it down for me and everyone laughed again. I was back in bed, smoking, when Eagan poked his head in, dropped a piece of paper on my lap, and went out, chuckling.

> Load her up and bang away
> Load her up and bang away
> Load her up and bang away
> With my eighteen pounder.
>
> Well, up she came and down she got
> Then she showed me her you-know-what
> Asked me if I'd like a shot
> With my eighteen pounder.

The colonel came through the trees with a radioman. 'Let's cut siesta and move,' he suggested, looking cheerfully at Wain.

Wain jumped up happily, nodding his approval. 'Good! Fine!' he said. 'The choppers'll be here any time. Yeah, let's go. That's fine with me.'

The men had begun to doze off. Reluctantly, they picked themselves up and, when their scattered gear was sorted out, began to march. The foliage smoldered in the afternoon's white heat; the air was of a steamy, breathless room. We straggled, forced apart, as if the forest was a comb and trees its teeth; and specks of bright sunlight filtered through and danced on the soldiers' faces. As I brushed past, I caught a salty, acrid whiff of Asian sweat and, reeking of the same, walked on.

Gunfire suddenly crashed out of the undergrowth to our right, followed a second later by firing from the left. Behind and in front of us the roaring spread, waves moving in a ring of noise. A swift, invisible arc of violence swept through the brush. Wain and his radioman fell flat on the ground and Eagan dived into some nearby scrub. I rolled behind Wain and Miller, digging my face desperately into the dead leaves. The waves quivered and moaned, they shrieked and surged, and second and third waves roared in without a pause, scattering leaves, snapping branches; the area was now convulsed with noise, shrill cries. It's here! This is it! It's finally here, I thought – hurling its brief, dry, inorganic fury at us. And from the moment of encounter, I shook, closed up completely. I kept blinking, nose buried in the dark fertile smell of rotting vegetation. And in separate, fleeting frames, I saw ants fidgeting around my eyes, one reeling along with a dead leaf clamped in its jaws, the leaf much larger than itself.

I heard Kiem shout, then Captain Wain, both yelling at each other. Moments later, shells fell to left and right with thunderclaps I thought would leave my skull scraped flat, and mud gushed up as high as the trees and slopped back down on us. Which side would my bullet come from?

'Chopper! Chopper!' Wain bawled into the radio. Kiem let off a smoke signal. Thick, orange-juice-yellow smoke bellied up.

'Can you see the smoke? See it? It's yellow. Fire east-south-east, fifty to a hundred yards. Blow the shit out of them!'

Immediately, a squall of explosives swooped down. Rockets burst in sprays; machine guns let out their throaty, savage roar; and helicopters and an L-19 plunged straight down, brushing the trees. It felt as though a dinosaur were rumbling overhead.

Wain lay flat on the carpet of leaves with Miller's phone at his ear, calmly shouting orders to Junkman and the choppers, then listening to each burst and barrage, and shouting in the phone again. 'OK, one click to the east!' I heard him say; and 'Shit!' and 'Give 'em hell!'

Flat behind a fallen tree, Miller stuck it out, lips quivering. He wasn't chewing his nails. His pale blue eyes were clouded, unfocused, and when our eyes met, I felt I saw myself in them.

The enemy were there in strength. We pounded them with rockets, poured in bullets and howitzer shells, and nothing broke their stride. There'd be a second's masking roar, and the pattern of fire continued. They were firing machine guns and rifles. Amid the gay, incessant, rattling noise, the muffled spurts of single rifle shots hit me right in the gut. Those were the ones that would get me. I felt them scuttling just under the ground to which I clung – like rats, right under my belly. Bullets clawed at us from every side.

At one point, their fire seemed to be coming from the right, so I worked my way over the tree and rolled to the left of it. A Viet was already hiding there, his carbine on the ground, eating a banana. His young eyes were empty, and his jaws moved with slow deliberation, finishing one mouthful at a time. A bit later, when the firing shifted to the left, I rolled back to the tree and squirmed over to the other side. And when I rolled back to the left again, the boy was peeling another banana and quietly watching me. And another guy was sitting near him, butt flat on the ground, eating a bowlful of rice that he'd scooped from a basin, calmly working his bamboo chopsticks. He gave me a perfunctory glance when I rolled up at his side, then lost interest in me. When bullets began to slap the trunk and branches, spattering bark, he simply moved the basin to his left and casually shoveled more rice into his bowl.

Kiem's command post was behind an anthill. The refuge was as hard as concrete and virtually bulletproof; but he had his adjutant and radioman with him, and angrily chased off any more of his troops who tried to join them there. The rejects looked at him and moved away, then sat down, propped against tree roots; and if they were hit, they just keeled over and died.

Eagan, who hadn't said a word till then, suddenly began to shout. Even in the clamor of the attack, I could hear him clearly.

'Shoot! Shoot, fuck you! Shoot! What's wrong with you, you bastards! Goddamn it! Fire over me, you fuckers!'

Under the yellow baseball cap, his gray eyes blazed, and his cheeks were flaming red; but the men had put their guns aside and, leaning on the roots, just gawked at him, an American shouting crazily. And when bullets hit them, they . . . slowly . . . tumbled . . . over.

Their reactions as a whole were strangely sluggish and silent. Bloodstained soldiers reeled out of the undergrowth on both sides, but in the raging cross fire they dawdled, as if out for a stroll. A young medic squirmed over on his stomach, wrote something on a card, and hung it from a wounded soldier's neck, then stuck an alcohol-soaked cotton ball into a large hole in his thigh and stirred it around with his forceps. The alcohol in a jar he was carrying had already turned a strawberry color. The soldier didn't even shake, or bite his lip, though the bone was almost bare. His cheeks were taut

227

and twisted, but all he did was grip his thigh with both hands, staring blankly at the dark hole in his flesh, like a child looking at a broken toy.

Kiem suddenly stood up behind the anthill and began to run. And his radioman and adjutant followed. Without a word to anyone, leaving the medic and wounded troops behind, Kiem ran for his life. Anybody who could keep up chased after him. Wain, Miller, Eagan and I joined in. Miller dropped his radio when he stood up and tore the cord off when he stepped on it. Kiem and Wain quarreled as they ran, disputing our line of retreat. The captain said south, the colonel east.

'Wouldn't south be safer?' Wain shouted politely in that scorching, relentless barrage.

'No. *Est, est!*' Kiem barked.

'But the south's open!' the captain countered, towering over him.

And Kiem looked up and yelled imperiously. 'Run *est!* I know! They're not in the *est*. This is my country! I give commands. You don't know anything!'

And Kiem dashed frantically ahead, thrusting branches and vines aside, and Wain stayed right beside him, still shouting 'South!' and both ran eastward braying at each other, pushing and shoving through the undergrowth. And then they must have seen something, for both turned back, ashen-faced, and fled toward the south. On every side bullets flailed at us, paralyzed our eyes and tongues. And still there was no living sign of them, though they were close enough for us to hear the sound of bullets working through their guns. I tripped on a tree root and sprawled, and several shots flew just in front of me, ripping off bark three inches from my eyes. Some shots I didn't even hear go off – you hear a bang if a rifle is reasonably distant and you're still alive. My cheeks were spattered with bark. I pulled myself up and, steadying my shaky knees, began to run again; but I managed to land right in the fork of a split tree that I'd meant to avoid from the moment I saw it. And I was stuck, sandwiched, couldn't budge, and soldiers streamed past, running for their lives. Mustering the last of an ebbing strength, I struggled blindly to get out and, after God knows how long, came unstuck. My hands and cheeks were grazed; my heart had leaped into my throat; my lungs creaked; and my knees shook uncontrollably.

When next I stopped to look around, I was lying in the shade of a large tree. I don't know when, but the firing had ceased and the forest was as hushed as the bottom of a lake. Wain and the other two Yanks were under another tree. I counted only seventeen soldiers, leaning against tree roots – all that was left of a company of two hundred. One young ARVN officer was lying there covered with blood. He'd been shot through the shoulder and it had soaked the jacket of his jungle fatigues. Eagan crept over to him on his elbows, carbine in his hands, and talked in a slow voice, spacing out the words.

'You got hit pretty bad, but the choppers'll be here soon and you'll be going home. You'll be in Saigon tonight. OK? When you get there, buy me some French cognac at the PX in my name, OK? You drink a bit of it and send the rest to me. French cognac. Tell the others they'll be drinking French cognac. Tell everybody that, OK?'

The man lay white and still on the fallen leaves and listened in silence. Eagan finished his gentle whispering and crawled back to his friends. And, after a while, the officer hitched himself onto one elbow and, dribbling blood, began to drag himself away.

Eagan looked at me and said, 'Number ten!' then got up on his knees and started pissing, fiercely, like a water buffalo. Some of it splashed my face. Still lying on the ground, I pulled my own cock out. Eagan's head was pink and limp, but mine was shriveled, so I had to pull and stretch it once or twice.

'Don't move. You might get hit,' Eagan whispered when his stream ran dry, and he lay back on the cushion of brown leaves.

A ring of sounds hung around us like a shower curtain. The jungle had found its voice again. The insects chirped, the birds cried, and the monkeys squealed, leaping from branch to branch. Less than five minutes after the firing had stopped, the inhabitants of the forest were back to form. Their voices rained down from the higher branches, rose from the bed of leaves, and, filling the sea of foliage, swelled and surged and sometimes burst like jets of steam. Despite the eruption of fire and metal, despite the juddering upheaval, nature had come through unscathed. The tide of ecstatic cries had a mysterious depth to it, a resilient abundance. I took in lungfuls of the humid smell of leaves, and my empty heart was moved. My mind was all ears, torn by the monkeys, pierced by the birds, lulled in the swell of the insects' paean of joy.

'Listen to that noise!' Eagan muttered in a baffled voice.

When dusk came, soldiers, one after another, lay down and died in the liquid light. The living moved on after five hours' rest, heading for our rendezvous. We found the other two companies clustered around a honeycomb of craters. Their ranks had also been decimated. The area was cluttered with corpses and wounded men; the ground was strewn with bloodstained rags;

and blood-smeared medics moved busily around.

Some had shoulder wounds or punctured thighs, some open chests or noses hacked off, buttocks gashed, chins smashed in. The eerie lethargy I'd witnessed in the rain of fire was at work here, too. Five hours had passed, and I couldn't believe that they could still be drugged by shock. But nobody moaned, however grim his injury. No one cried or shouted or writhed in pain. Some stood leaning against trees and some lay on the ground, but each of them was sprawled and looked at me or at the sky with eyes as empty as a flattened dog. Theirs were the postures of people in repose, of sunbathers. In one torn chest I saw a lung; blood frothed on it with each slow breath, but he lay there like someone with the flu. I stood rooted to the ground, filled with an indefinable sense of guilt.

Eagan looked away and muttered, 'It's not easy to be a soldier. . . .'

And Wain hung his head, saying, 'Brave men . . . brave men. . . .' and went around collecting cigarettes and stuck them one by one between the lips of dying soldiers. He gave the lightly injured men an encouraging tap, and for the seriously wounded, he helped the medics make up pillows. His sweaty fatigues were soon smudged with blood.

Kiem strode over to him and said there were too many VC ahead to go on; we would retreat. He claimed loudly that, though we'd taken a beating, they hadn't won, and that we'd bloodied them to the extent of about a hundred dead.

'Did you take a body count?' the captain asked.

The colonel raised his voice: 'I didn't count. I couldn't. Rockets were falling. If I go counting bodies, I'll be shot. But I know. It's my hunch. At least hundred dead. I have experience. They retreated. They don't shoot any more.'

'I'm not so sure,' Wain said. 'They're quiet now, but they'll open up again. There aren't enough of us. It's better to retreat as soon as possible, Colonel.'

Kiem said suddenly: 'You're strong. You have training and discipline.'

'So?'

'*We* retreat. You're strong, so you come after. You stay here camping tonight. We return tomorrow morning with reinforcements. We'll bring lot more soldiers. OK? OK?'

'But there are only nine of us.'

'You're good. Very strong. After you guard our retreat, camp here. You'll get Silver Star. I'll recommend you. OK?'

Wain said nothing, only looked at him with large, bloodshot eyes and walked away toward the wounded troops. For the past five hours, in fact, he had barely spoken to him, though they were only yards apart. During this time, Kiem's radioman had managed to contact other units and Kiem, in Vietnamese, had fired off a string of orders on the radio. But Wain wasn't told what these orders were. Nor had he asked; he'd simply lain there, with his face turned the other way. I remembered Kiem running for it with his two attendants, without a word of warning to the rest of us.

And all this while, more soldiers died. Death hopped from body to body without any warning bell or flashing light. Something flowed out of them without a sound and they were left like plastic bags, collapsed. One saw men propped against a tree, and watched them move to stretch out on the ground, and they were dead. When I lit a cigarette with a trembling hand and turned to pass it to the soldier with an exposed lung, I found a pair of faded, congealed eyes, and flies that fidgeted on his cheeks, rubbing their front legs together. The men fell quietly, quieter than dry leaves. So silent were their deaths that I imagined they'd revive the moment they hit the ground and hurry off into the gathering dusk, without a backward glance, as if they were late for an appointment.

With vines hacked down from nearby trees, survivors wrapped the bodies up in ponchos, then slung them between two poles and carried them away; they looked like rice cakes wrapped in bamboo leaves. There was no talk; the men moved slowly, with practiced skill.

One of the bundles was borne a little farther off. A puzzled puppy – perhaps the dead man's pet – trotted up and sniffed the body and wouldn't leave. And a soldier giggled softly, as if a finger had poked him in the ribs.

I seemed to have made a terrible mistake. For some time, I'd thought these people sometimes lovable, sometimes cruel, but dummies, men of straw. But now I wondered whether they weren't people of one simple faith – belief in self-subjection. Who taught these silent men to endure great pain without a moan? Who taught them such self-control, austerity? And if they felt, deep down, that being born was a mistake, then that itself was an article of faith – a powerful one. They dreaded the draft, preferred to creep off through the fields, hide in bamboo groves, lop off fingers. Then one day the village was surrounded and they were packed into a truck; or they were caught coming out of a movie. And they all ended up in a barracks somewhere, force-fed with the idea that communism was more dangerous than malaria or unboiled water, and told to fight it if they didn't want to live like slaves. And of all the sermons that they heard, the only one they clearly understood was that they had to kill, or be killed.

The dead had been robbed blind, though they themselves had robbed. Their meager earnings had been siphoned off by officers to pay, allegedly, for coffins and gambling debts they didn't owe. But they had stolen chickens, cabbage and sugarcane themselves when they were on maneuvers – and earned the peasants' hatred and contempt. They'd scraped and schemed and sometimes put enough together to buy a cigarette, and smoked it down in little puffs, savoring it, peering at the dwindling butt. They'd stood around a basin of rice and chirped like sparrows in the evening. They'd yelped in embarrassment when GIs hung around bare-assed after a shower; and when the movie screen had shown them white women, with big boobs, being kissed, they'd yelped again. The dead had loved eating and sleeping more than anything else – there wasn't much to choose from. They'd laughed a lot, pursing their mouths, and they'd been good at keeping dogs and parrots and making crickets fight. They'd had a genius for going suddenly deaf-dumb-blind when things were more than they could take, and still could walk around with open, empty eyes. If they were captured, they were tied to trees and disemboweled or buried alive or had their heads chopped off. But if luck had somehow saved their skins and they had been reeducated (if that's the word – their 'education' was in some doubt), then they'd have turned, like pawns in Japanese chess, reborn, refreshed and redirected, and bravely fought the 'enemy', their former messmates and Americans. But death came anyway to close the ring, and all died silently, without complaint, regardless of which field their chests had burst on, North or South.

*

Red and green turned black in the jungle in the late afternoon. One wounded soldier's olive-drab fatigues had been slashed open to expose a black hole that curled back at the edges and bulged with something large and sodden, spongelike. Another's shattered head looked like a keg of offal at a fish market. Blood dried quickly in the waning light. Their comrades squatted, scratching, looking at the sky, keeping their eyes averted from the dead, waiting wearily for something, anything. Death's face was showing, a slack, wet, pasty thing with a gaping, hideous mouth; but it caught no one's eye. No one mourned the dead or prayed for them or spoke to them. The colonel took a furtive look at them; Wain kept his head down; Miller was chewing his nails again; and Eagan gazed darkly at the trees, using his carbine as a cane. It was unmistakably human, this death that lay around us, but it was Asians dying. I shivered, chilled to the bone.

Our retreat continued.

Carrying the dead and wounded, we filed back along the narrow path that we had traced that morning. The puppy followed, sniffling. And then the jungle opened fire again – a hail of fire that hounded us no matter how far we withdrew. From somewhere in that forest wall, bullets swarmed, slamming into tree trunks, cracking branches, spraying darts of wood. Not one of us fired back; we ran, stumbling, rolling, tumbling, getting wedged in trees, diving behind anthills, and ruthlessly pushing other men away.

I heard Wain, running, shout into a transmitter: 'Junkman! Junkman! One more time. OK, OK! That's it. Pour it on. Give 'em hell! Jungle's thick with them. We have casualties. Completely surrounded.'

And the big guns opened up again and shells shrieked through the dusk. The forest shuddered and leaves flew. I dived behind the cover of a tree and found Wain crouching with his rifle at the ready. He listened carefully to the blind storm of bullets and, holding me by the shoulders, hissed:

'OK! You'll be all right. They're shooting high. Run for it! Zigzag! Keep your head down and run! OK – now!'

Bulling my way through the other troops, I ran, greedy for safety. And they, too, scrambled for their lives. It was a rout. Bundled corpses and wounded men were thrown down in the mad rush to get ahead and, like a school of fish in a narrow channel, we pushed, kept pushing forward. I caught a fleeting glimpse of an abandoned soldier staring blankly as we rushed by; I saw another man shot and stagger into a bush as though going for a leak. But the thought of helping them never crossed my mind; there wasn't a smudge, a bird's shadow of concern. I just ran, panting. In the dark undergrowth on both sides, voices began to call, 'Hoooo . . . Hoooo. . . .' They were hunting us down like rabbits. And those Stone Age shouts were terrifying to our ringing ears.

When we arrived at the swamp, the long day was drawing to a close. The sun was sinking toward the treetops on the opposite bank, burning with a fire's last urgent flame. The high clouds had a fuchsia sheen and blood flowed all across the sky. To eyes accustomed to the darkness of the jungle it was painfully dazzling. Two choppers and an L-19 appeared, flying toward us. Wading through the fragrance of tall green reeds in knee-high water, the soldiers were almost hidden, with only their helmets visible, like shoals of jellyfish. The swamp was lethally exposed. In the jungle, the bullets had bounced off tree trunks, been deflected, and there were dead trees and anthills for cover. But here they tore straight through the reeds. There was nothing we could do if they shot low. A couple of machine guns would have wiped out this toy army. Was it here I was going to get my belly shot and see my guts spill out into this muddy water?

When I was about halfway across, a fierce thundering wingbeat swept down on us. I looked up and saw two helicopters gracefully swooping and wheeling overhead. Both choppers hugged rocket pods under their wings, and as they glided down toward the jungle, I could see a gunner in a domed helmet like an astronaut, fingers ready on the machine-gun trigger. An L-19 followed them. One chopper abruptly began to strafe the edge of the jungle that we had just escaped. At the same time, rockets burst from their nests with a clear, distinctive whish, and a split second later the jungle erupted. Machine guns rattled fanatically. And suddenly the treetops returned their fire. The boys were waiting in the upper branches with their own machine guns. Ten minutes before, the trees had been silent when I ran across their roots, but now they shook, and poured a plague of bullets at those helicopters. Orange flames flashed from the top foliage and long, frenzied roars crossed the great swamp. Tracers from both sides marked the evening sky, which lay like a royal city ablaze with lights. And for the first time, I saw a ghastly beauty in this war, if only for a moment.

The swamp was now alive with furious cries.

From right and left and behind us, a full-scale blitz had broken out. I flung my body into the reeds. The tepid smell of mud rose up and covered my face. Soldiers rolled in the green stems, screaming shrilly. Bullets whipped in in interlocking waves, without a pause for breath. I crept on through the mud, feeling around with my hands. When I tried to crawl over the body of a squirming soldier with his leg caught in a carbine strap, a streak of bullets grazed my hair and all the strength drained out of me. The soldier and I, immersed hip-deep, our arms and legs entangled, struggled limply. The boy's eyes were glittering, angry and exhausted. It was like trying to duck a child in water, but somehow that small, skinny body became a wall, a giant obstacle on which I climbed and fell back, climbed and fell. And choking on the sweet smell of mud that crammed my mouth, half numb with disgust at the physical contact, I suddenly felt the darkening sky fall in. I had had enough. I had had the war, as much as I could take. And I was violently lonely, wanted to give up . . . and squat in the mud . . . and cry. I wanted just to sleep, surrender. Fatigue was overwhelming and the sweet temptation of death brushed my head – the urge to stretch out on this soft rush bed and let the warm mud seep through all my pores, and sleep and soak in this thick brown cream. And rats and crabs would nibble at my flesh, and it would feel like peeling off old scabs. And I would melt, dissolve in this reedy pool, spread, turn into its soft ripples and drift.

The shooting stopped. My reflexes still worked. I rose up in the mud. The soldier clung to me with the stubborn grip of a spastic child. Somewhere, a long time ago, something similar had happened to me; in a tepid, wet summer rice field, as a child. . . . I remembered the clinging hand. Yes, that was it! And with the knowledge, my body sagged, sank further in.

The boy looked up at me and suddenly cried out. Was it 'Mother!' he said? Was it 'Sorry! Sorry!'? The little voice was like a water bird's and babbled on, stabbing at me. And I fell back, grabbing the boy's shoulder, gasping and choking in the mud. And suddenly I could climb that wall, and clambered over, rolled onto his other side. The boy kicked viciously at my shins. The pain was blinding, but I crawled off through the reeds on hands and knees, gurgling, spitting mud.

The supple reeds seemed oiled and gave no hold. I sank in every time I tried to grasp them. From water level, the stems were giant trees in some dark, ancient rain forest; the sky reeled like a broken compass; and I felt rigidly enclosed. Trembling, I crawled on like a crippled bird until I suddenly felt firm ground beneath my hands and knees: a firm, wide floor that didn't shake or shout; a forest shore. I managed to stand up, and my sodden trousers clung around me like chain mail. The remnants of our slaughtered army still writhed on through the reeds and, struggling from the swamp, ran off into the trees.

The sun was dying. The radiance had gone and the sky was stained with darkness. The swamp lay in shadow. And just as I turned around, surveying the scene, a rattling thunderclap of guns burst from the undergrowth about twenty yards to my right. My eyes squeezed shut. The enemy were here as well. The bullets lanced through the gloom, clawed at trunks like giants' limbs, and bent in ricochets all around us. Running, I heard a thud, craned around, and saw the soldier I'd been running with pitch down, diving, arms outstretched; and in the last blurred wash of ebbing light, I saw him spasm in the grass. His body had blocked my bullet. But I'd no time to dwell on this, for instantly I felt tremendous pressure on my ears, a great rushing blast that almost knocked me down; and more than once I heard no bang. And it was then I felt my last ounce of strength fly up from my heels and escape from the top of my head. My bag dragged like a ton of coal, though all it held was a paperback and a towel. I'd clung to, hugged that bag, for lack of anything else to clutch, and as I'd lain there under fire I'd only blinked and held the thing; and would have felt exposed, felt stripped of a protective shell, if I had thrown it out. For, holding it, it seemed I still retained some fragment of myself. But when that residue of strength had fled, my self-respect – most subtle of all factors controlling human behavior, instinctive guardian of the human soul – had vanished with it. And in pride's place a fleeting freedom came, and I relaxed, and soft waves warmly lapped around me, untangling nerves, like death's sweet lure that had touched me with its wing, a deep, inviting purity. I flung my bag away and, open-mouthed, ran on; and with me moved a herd of soldiers, like homing cattle without a herdsman or a dog.

On down the gauntlet we ran and, on each side, that brutal, invisible force still shrieked and moaned among the sounding trees. And I was rigid, sealed shut, and heard my heart pounding in my ears, rumbling like surf in the dark; and I was dust, had crumbled, and began to cry. Tears ran down my cheeks and off my chin. Small salty bodies bucked and shoved, a silent tide, and in it, without disgust or shame, I numbly shoved them back as we fled on into the forest. The dismal odor of moss brushed my wet cheeks. And tumbling from the hot, black belly of the whale into its bowels, I ran on, panting, gasping, through the vast, hairy, primeval night.

And the forest was quiet.